AF069754

LUCY GREENHILL

A Match for Miss Marshall

Vinci Books

vinci-books.com

Published by Vinci Books Ltd in 2026

1

Copyright © Lucy Greenhill 2024

The author has asserted their moral right to be identified as the author of this work in accordance with the Copyright, Designs and Patents Act 1988. This work is a work of fiction. Names, characters, places and incidents are the product of the author's imagination or are used fictitiously. Any resemblance to actual persons, living or dead, places and incidents is entirely coincidental.
All rights reserved. No part of this publication may be copied, reproduced, distributed, stored in any retrieval system, or transmitted in any form or by any means, including photocopying, recording, or other electronic or mechanical methods, nor used as a source for any form of machine learning including AI datasets, without the prior written permission of the publisher.
The publisher and the author have made every effort to obtain permissions for any third party material used in this book and to comply with copyright law. Any queries in this respect should be brought to the attention of the publisher and any omissions will be corrected in future editions.
A CIP catalogue record for this book is available from the British Library.
Paperback ISBN: 9781036706036
The EU GPSR authorised representative is Logos Europe, 9 rue Nicolas Poussion, 17000 La Rochelle, France
contact@logoseurope.eu

By Lucy Greenhill

The Moth Agency Romances

An Utterly Unsuitable Lady
A Match for Miss Marshall
The Diva's Daughter

More from Lucy Greenhill writing as Fran Smith

Vita Carew Mysteries

Poison at Pemberton Hall
A Thin Sharp Blade
Dr Potter's Private Practice
The Painted Penny Stamp
The Killing at Crowswood Castle

Chapter One

'I'm beginning to wonder whether Mr Murphy actually exists,' Christabel Venables remarked, over supper in the attic sitting room in Paradise Place.

The weather in Cambridge was unsteady that May of 1896; one moment high blue skies and warm sunshine, the next, a chill in the air and a downpour of rain. Both sisters were wrapped in woollen shawls that evening as banks of menacing grey cloud churned outside the skylight.

'You surely don't think Miss Peach would mislead us deliberately?' Lucia said.

Christabel raised an eyebrow. 'Is it really true that she can't climb the stairs? She seems nimble enough in other ways.' She paused to examine the food on her plate. 'Lucia, this is the thinnest slice of ham I have ever seen. You could read a letter through it.'

Her sister looked down at her own meal, which consisted, like Christabel's, of a pale sliver of ham, a small tomato and half the heel of a loaf. 'I only had sixpence left, but there are a few cherries.'

Christabel made a face. 'The last cherries from the market were soft.'

'These are better. They're still the market leftovers, but I got there earlier,' her sister said.

Christabel sighed and shook her head. 'I'm hoping several of my ladies will settle their accounts soon. There's quite a sum outstanding. Mrs Professor Perks, for example, has had three summer straws on account. Rather fine they were too, though I say so myself. Especially the navy one with the red and white ribbons.'

'You were saying about Mr Murphy,' Lucia reminded her.

'I begin to suspect Miss Peach of making him up.'

'Surely not. He is her builder.'

'Well, so she says, but we have never seen him.'

Both sisters sipped their tea and cast their minds back to the conversation they had had with their landlady when last the roof leaked. Carrying a bucket, Christabel had tackled her in the shared basement kitchen.

'Miss Peach, this bucket, that I have carried from our bedroom, is almost a quarter full of water that came through our leaking roof. Look! It dripped all night long.'

'Oh dear no, I don't think that can be so,' said Miss Peach. Their landlady was small and elderly, but sharp featured, with bright, darting eyes behind her silvery spectacles. Her large ginger cat, Blossom, was sitting on the kitchen table, which was forbidden. 'No, no, Mr Murphy assured me only last year that the roof was in perfect order.'

'Mr Murphy?' Christabel asked.

'My builder. One of Cambridge's premier builders. A craftsman through and through. Highly skilled. Absolutely reliable. Mr Murphy is very well known in the city.'

'Even so,' Christabel said, 'all this rainwater came

through our ceiling last night.' She held up the bucket before carrying it to the sink and pouring the contents away.

'I can't imagine how that could have happened,' said Miss Peach. 'Mr Murphy is very reliable, as a rule.'

'There is a hole, Miss Peach. That is the only explanation,' Lucia said.

Their landlady swatted that idea aside with a lace-gloved hand.

Blossom looked on, moving his yellow eyes from one to the other as if memorising the conversation for future reference.

'Where could the rainwater have come from, in that case?' Christabel asked.

'Well,' said Miss Peach, looking away, 'water finds its way into buckets, you know.' Both sisters looked at her in disbelief. 'I mean to say that it is easy to mistake water that one finds in a bucket for rainwater,' Miss Peach continued. 'And then to imagine that it has come in through the roof, when in fact it is ...' Lucia and Christabel looked intently at their landlady, wondering what she would say next. ' ... in fact it is merely dew, or condensation.'

The sisters were temporarily rendered speechless. Blossom jumped off the table as if he, for one, had heard quite enough about leaky roofs.

'What we fear, Miss Peach,' Lucia said, 'is that if there is another night of hard rain, the dew or condensation you mention might bring down our ceiling as well as overflowing our bucket. I'm sure you would not want that to happen.'

'I shall ask Mr Murphy to look in at his earliest convenience,' said Miss Peach, 'but he is a busy man.'

With that, she had followed the cat out of the kitchen and into her private rooms.

Three weeks and two rainstorms later, there was still no

sign of Mr Murphy. Buckets were emptied; leaking roofs were mentioned, but finding she was unable to climb the stairs to the attic bedroom to see for herself, Miss Peach still tended to favour the dew or condensation theory.

Chapter Two

The following morning was bright. New College was looking handsome with its ancient stonework bathed in sunlight and wisteria trailing a frothy haze of purple flowers along the cloisters. The young man who knocked at the door of the Master's Lodge seemed taken aback when Grace answered.

'I was hoping to see Miss Marshall,' he said.

'Yes?' She peered around the door, not opening it completely to the stranger.

'I believe it is Miss Grace Marshall that I should speak to,' he repeated, smiling.

'I am she.'

He took a step back, accidentally treading into a flower bed, and almost lost his balance. 'Excuse me, but I was expecting someone... rather different,' he said.

Grace waited. She was wearing an old apron and had a duster tied around her hair. She had been packing.

The young man regained his footing and offered his

most charming smile. 'I'm told you offer tuition. I need a little practice before I sit an examination.'

Grace blinked at him, still not opening the door. 'Examination?' she said. 'The examinations are over.'

The young man's smile faded. 'I am a special case.'

Grace scrutinised the young man standing on her doorstep. He was tall and sandy-haired, with a loose fringe falling over one eye. His academic gown fluttered around him. Beneath it, he wore a dark suit and a foppishly colourful waistcoat, giving him a Bohemian look. He was the kind of figure her father would have scorned on sight as a time-waster, someone whose attention was more likely directed at his choice of cravat than his books.

'And what kind of tuition are you seeking, exactly, Mister…?'

'Hollingdale. Daniel Hollingdale.'

They were still speaking around the edge of the door.

'What is it that you wish to study, Mr. Hollingdale?'

'Mathematics,' he said simply.

'Well, obviously mathematics, but which branch? Algebra? Trigonometry? Calculus?'

'Elementary mathematics, if you please. I can't make head or tail of it,' he smiled broadly and shrugged.

Grace looked at him in some confusion. 'But you have attended lectures and so forth?'

'Not in mathematics. I study music,' he smiled expectantly, then added, 'strictly speaking.'

James, one of the handymen, whistled a tune from the kitchen, then passed behind Grace in the hallway carrying a pot of paint.

'I am about to move house. I cannot teach anyone at present,' she said, and closed the door.

Chapter Three

'Marriage would be the obvious solution,' the Bursar remarked. He looked out of his office window towards the Master's Lodge. Miss Froment followed his gaze. Through a window they could just make out the figure of Grace Marshall bent over a desk.

The Bursar shrugged and picked up his pen. 'What about that visiting Swede? Or the mathematician who worked with her father - what was his name?'

'Dr Hillyer? He left for Switzerland.'

'Only temporarily. You have told her she must vacate soon, I trust?'

Miss Froment nodded.

'We have no obligation to house her. There is nowhere in the least suitable. We are pressed for accommodation, as you know. The new Master and his family move in at the end of the month.'

The Bursar considered the matter at an end. Miss Froment, who had worked with him for more than twenty years, was not so easily dismissed.

'Isn't there a small gardener's cottage in the grounds of Abercrombie House?' She asked this as if it were a casual enquiry.

'I don't recall one. If there is, it has not been inhabited in my time.'

'But if it could be sufficiently repaired?'

'There is no budget for rebuilding.'

'Perhaps none will be needed. If it required only cleaning and a little decoration?'

The Bursar looked unenthusiastic but did not absolutely refuse. His Head of Housekeeping pressed her advantage. 'I have your permission to inspect the cottage and use the staff to carry out minor repairs?'

'As long as she is out of the Master's Lodge by the end of the month. But it cannot be a long-term arrangement. Grace Marshall, in her own right, no longer has any role at the College. She will have to fend for herself. Or marry, as I said.'

Miss Froment slipped out of the door.

'He'd have the poor creature out on the street!' Miss Froment told her friend Miss Peach that evening over their customary Wednesday sherry.

'Shame! But you spoke up for the girl?'

'Somebody has to, Cecily. I have known her all her life. She has been her father's devoted shadow all these years. If the Bursar had his way, she would be discarded like an old shoe! New College is a venerable institution, but it takes very little notice of the ladies who quietly devote their lives to it.'

Both sighed at this mighty injustice and sipped their

sherry for a few moments in silence. They were in Miss Peach's little half basement sitting room, the evening sun illuminating the golden liquor in their glasses.

'Her father surely left her well provided for?' Miss Peach asked, eventually. 'As Master of the College, he would have been a man of means.'

Miss Froment shook her head. 'There is some doubt. The wider family is extremely humble. The lawyers are at work, but Grace cannot assume even enough to provide a living. It looks as if she will have to make her own way.'

Miss Peach offered her friend an almond biscuit to accompany the sherry. 'Well, dear, we were both in a similar situation ourselves once.'

'We were indeed.'

'But you took your position at the College, and I became a landlady. We have managed. Grace Marshall will no doubt manage too. You are fond of the girl?'

'I am. I have known her all her life. Her father's death has hit her very hard.'

'An appealing young woman, is she? In her person and her manners, and so on?' Miss Peach enquired.

'She is attractive enough, but she tends to be watchful and silent in company. Grace never was one to laugh a great deal or behave frivolously.'

'Not particularly charming, then?'

'Not obviously so. She seems to care very little for other people's opinions.'

Miss Peach looked disapproving. 'Have no college gentlemen shown an interest?'

'I suspected one—Dr Edmund Hillyer—a colleague of her father's, of having his eye on her, but he took himself off to Switzerland.'

'Her health? Her talents?'

'Her health is good enough. As to talents, I think she is only interested in mathematics.'

'Oh dear!' said Miss Peach, 'No music? No painting? No dancing?'

'She used to like a country walk but she has hardly left her desk since she lost her dear father. She has laboured night and day to finish the book he was working on. A textbook of mathematics. We have barely seen her in the college.'

'If she were interested in marriage she could visit Miss Venables here upstairs at the Matters of the Heart Agency. Miss Venables is expert at dealing with ladies and gentlemen who need to widen their circle of suitable acquaintance.'

Miss Froment looked surprised. 'I doubt poor Grace would even consider that.'

'You could approach Miss Venables on her behalf.'

'Behind Grace's back? That would not be proper, surely?'

'Why not? You would simply be a friend helping a young woman to make one or two new acquaintances.'

Miss Froment paused with her biscuit in mid-air. 'Well, when you put it like that it sounds reasonable, I must say.'

Miss Peach leaned forward and added a little more sherry to their glasses.

Chapter Four

'Lucia, would you have a word with my friend, Miss Froment?'

Miss Peach looked round Lucia's office door. Blossom did too. He was whisking his tail in a manner that usually meant trouble. Lucia did her best to ignore him. 'I have recommended your services to her.'

'Miss Froment is seeking a companion?' Lucia asked.

'Oh, bless me no! She is my age at least! We are long past such thoughts. She has a young friend in need of your wise counsel.'

Lucia's heart sank. This did not sound like paid work, and paid work was what the Moth Agency needed. The cat threw himself on her rug and rolled about on it, purring.

'Shall I send her up?' Miss Peach asked.

'Miss Peach, about the roof...'

But it was no good. Miss Peach was already on her way down the stairs. She left only Blossom, who arranged himself in a patch of sunlight and settled in for a nap.

Miss Froment, neat in a navy raincoat, sat upright in the visitor's chair. 'I hope to pick your brains on a delicate matter concerning a young friend,' she said. 'This is confidential? I have doubts about the rights and wrongs of speaking to you behind her back.'

'Perfectly confidential,' Lucia reassured her, taking out her notebook.

'I myself am a spinster, Miss Venables. I have never known what it is to have maternal care of a young person, but I have known Grace Marshall since she was a child. She lost her mother before she was five years old–a tragedy–and has been brought up in the college by her father, a very distinguished mathematician. He was a good man, and kindly towards Grace, but he himself lived a rather–shall we say, a rather cloistered existence in the college. It was his world. He lived his life through his teaching and his books.'

'You speak of him in the past tense, I notice.'

'He died six months ago.'

'So Grace is an orphan now?'

'She is. And one with very little knowledge the world, except the world of mathematics. She has never socialised widely. I do not say that she is shy or incapable of polite behaviour at a college gathering - no indeed, but she has lacked the hand of a mother to guide her.'

'Is that where you come in, Miss Froment?'

'I would never make such a claim, but I do feel that, lacking any other, somebody must step in.'

'And what can the Moth Agency do?'

'I am not certain. Grace has very limited funds. She must earn a living for herself now. Or marry. Marriage, in fact, might be the obvious next step for her, but I would not care for her to be pressured into marriage too hastily. She seems so very ill-equipped to make a sound choice of gentleman.'

'Does she have suitors at present?'

'She has one. He has not declared himself—not that I know of—a younger colleague of her father's who has shown an interest in Grace for some time.'

'He might be the perfect match, surely?'

'He is not.'

'You seem very decided about that.'

'I am. Hints of misconduct. I cannot say more.'

Miss Froment sat upright with her lips tightly pressed together. It was clear that no more information would be forthcoming on that topic.

'So, how can the Moth Agency help, exactly?'

'Perhaps some intervention could be found that would distract Grace and avoid her feeling under pressure to accept this suitor's offer too quickly.'

'It is unusual to be asked to *prevent* an engagement. As a rule, I am asked to do the opposite.' Lucia looked intrigued.

'It isn't exactly prevention that I am asking you to arrange. It is really only delay. My feeling is that if Miss Marshall can only sidestep any proposal from this gentleman for a short time, it will give her the opportunity to see a little more of the world. That alone might be enough to prevent her making a poor choice. Am I speaking nonsense? I cannot stand by and watch a young woman with her whole life ahead of her be pressed by short term necessity into the arms of someone who will not, I am certain of it, make her happy.'

'But *are* you certain? He sounds, in terms of circumstances - a colleague, a familiar friend, an academic leading the life she is used to - he sounds a perfectly good match to me.'

'I am quite convinced that he is not.'

'In that case, you will need a plan,' Lucia said. She uncapped her pen and wrote the heading *Miss Marshall: 1. Avoiding the Wrong Suitor*.

'Step one is to avoid the pair meeting at all, if possible. Miss Marshall still lives in the College?' Lucia asked.

'She does at present, but she will move out to a small cottage before the end of the month.'

'While she is in the College it should be easy. You can watch for any unwanted approach, but once she is in the cottage alone, my guess is that WS, as I shall call him, short for Wrong Suitor, will increase his persistence. Will she be alone in the cottage?'

'I hope to arrange a maid to be there to begin with. And a decorator.'

'Excellent. They are trustworthy people? You know them well?'

'Yes. College workers, both of them.'

'Good. Recruit them to the cause. Confide in them about WS and give them the task of interrupting and intervening whenever he visits.'

'Goodness!' Miss Froment said. 'How will they do that?'

'In my experience people one recruits for such a mission are extraordinarily inventive. If they are the right people for the job, they will come up with all manner of surprising methods. And the other thing, Miss Froment, is that you - I take it you are on good terms with Miss Marshall?'

'I am, yes, but only as a friend. We have never been confidantes, exactly.'

'Well, you should be particularly insistent on the proper

behaviour being required at all times in terms of chaperoning. Make it clear to all that it is unthinkable for a gentleman to visit a single lady while she is alone. I know that College life can be quite relaxed about such matters sometimes, but you should make yourself a stickler for the proprieties in this case. Mention regularly that it is disgraceful and outrageous for him to approach Miss Marshall without someone else, preferably yourself or a nominee chosen for their strictness, present at all times. And when you are present, do not fade into the background. Interrupt. Make matters as awkward as you can. Tactics such as these will drive off many an unwanted admirer.'

'But what am I to do if Dr Hillyer approaches Miss Marshall somewhere else? Whilst she is out walking, for example.'

Lucia looked out of the window for a moment, gathering her thoughts.

'I have a small group of people I can call upon in public places,' she said.

'Whatever will they do?' Miss Froment asked, in some alarm. 'No violence is involved, I hope!'

'Violence is unnecessary. They are skilled practitioners in creating different forms of diversion. Most passers-by will imagine a random event has occurred, but in fact it will be my *interrupters*, as I call them, stepping in to prevent a declaration, or even a proposal. They are very reliable, no unwanted encounter has ever succeeded in getting past them, but there is a small cost involved, I'm afraid.'

'Oh dear!' Miss Froment looked alarmed at that.

'However, in your case, as you are acting *in loco parentis*, as it were, and protecting an innocent young woman, I feel sure we can come to some arrangement.'

'What can I do?'

'You are, of course, friendly with our landlady, Miss Peach?'

'Yes, indeed. I have known her for many years.'

'Would you consider mentioning the leak we have in our roof to her? Just to remind her? Hearing it from you might spur her into action.'

'It *has* rained rather a lot lately,' Miss Froment said.

'It certainly has, and in our attic we have the puddles to prove it,' Lucia said.

'Consider it done.'

'Excellent. Then I shall instruct the interrupters to be on alert. If you spot an imminent approach, send me a note, and I will direct them to the appropriate location. The Backs are often chosen for such discussions, in my experience, but the Botanical Gardens are also popular. Above all Miss Marshall must be kept away from punts. Punting presents a dreadfully high risk of marriage proposals - it seems to be something to do with being on the river.'

Miss Froment nodded in agreement. She was impressed.

Lucia looked at her list.

'Whilst the Wrong Suitor is kept under control, the next two parts of the plan for Miss Marshall must be firstly to occupy her thoughts with new activities, and next, to encourage her to make new friends.' Lucia added these two items as points two and three on her list.'

Miss Froment put her head on one side. 'New activities?'

'She writes, you say?'

'She assisted her father in his writing.'

'And she completed his textbook on her own?'

'Well, yes. But these are not new activities.'

'Nonetheless, writing in itself is a skill she might pursue. Does she use a typewriting machine?'

'No. Not that I know of.'

'You might try introducing her to one. Learning to typewrite would give her an occupation. It is a useful skill, and she sounds like the sort of diligent young woman who would apply herself.'

'The Bursar certainly has a great many papers that need to be typewritten,' Miss Froment said.

'Excellent. After that, you can apply your thoughts to new friends for Miss Marshall. Some genial young people are needed. Some bright sparks who will lure her out of her solitude for a while. We can discuss your thoughts on that later. I leave you to ponder.'

Miss Froment left soon afterwards, determined to direct Miss Peach's immediate attention to the leaky roof. She was, however, so absorbed by her new plans for Grace Marshall that she forgot to do so.

Chapter Five

'Any success?' his sister's voice called from above as Daniel came in and hung his gown in the hall. He ran up the narrow stairs to her room.

His sister was propped up in a bed scattered with books and discarded needlework projects.

'She turned me away at the door,' he said, plonking himself down on the side of the bed.

'Is there anyone else?'

'Nobody. I have reached the end of the list. None of them wants anything to do with me.' He sighed theatrically. 'I am a lost cause! I shall be thrown out! I shall be forced to wander the streets with my violin, busking for pennies!'

'Not on my watch, brother dear,' Edith said. 'I am sworn to keep you on the straight path, and I shall, even if I have to do it from my bed.'

'What did Dr Sallett say?' Daniel asked, remembering.

'He thinks I am making good progress. I am permitted to sit in a chair tomorrow. By Friday, if all goes well, I shall be out in the fresh air for a short walk. By next week I shall be cycling.'

'Did he say that?'

Biddy wrinkled her nose. 'Not the cycling, that was my addition, but he does allow me to get up, at last.'

'Excellent news, but Biddy remember you must not be in too much of a hurry. He prescribes rest above all for lung conditions like yours.'

There was a pause. They could hear the sound of carriages passing on Castle Hill.

'Miss Marshall was not at all what I expected,' Daniel said. He stood and looked out of the window.

'What was so surprising?'

'She was half the age I had imagined for one thing.'

'Have you not met her before, or seen her, at least, around the College? She would have been in chapel, surely?'

'I suppose so, but I had never noticed her before. I am always playing or singing in chapel. I tend to notice the music more than the congregation.'

His sister gave him a quizzical look. 'She seems to have made an impression.'

'Oh not really. It was just that I was expecting…'

'You were expecting a mathematical crone!'

'…not exactly a crone. But certainly a very scholarly, severe type of older lady.'

'And she was not?'

'She was definitely not!'

'Well, let us hope she is agreeable in her character too, because since everyone else has refused, you will have to go an ask her again. You cannot take no for an answer, Daniel. She is your last hope.'

Chapter Six

Thursday was guest night at New College High Table: the Fellows more than usually convivial; the food and wines at their finest, and the gossip plentiful and delicious. Professor Toft always dined in college on a Thursday. That evening the pickings were particularly rich.

'*Stole her?*' He heard someone say.

'Carried her off from the landing on the first floor. She's stood there ever since anyone can remember.'

The professor joined the conversation late, turning to the Bursar. 'Who or what was stolen?'

'The little marble statue of Venus that stood on the landing outside the Waverley Room. Nobody noticed for several days,' said the Bursar, adding to their port glasses. 'An end of term jape.'

'Good to see the old traditions upheld. I recall some magnificent end of term shenanigans in my day,' Professor Toft remarked. 'Remember the chamber pot on the top pinnacle of the steeple? It stayed there for a week before someone thought to shoot it down.'

'Anyway, she turned up in the chapel. On one of the plinths. A naked Venus standing there among the saints. The congregation enjoyed the joke, but the Dean did not. He was outraged. He has demanded the culprit be sent down before graduation.'

'It would be absurdly harsh to expel anyone just before graduation,' Toft said, reaching for the walnuts. 'The Dean always did lack a sense of a humour.'

'The statue was a gift from the Queen. Everyone assumed it was a reproduction. One sees such marble Venuses everywhere. But as it turns out it is an early and rare example, excavated from a temple in Rome. Unique and extremely valuable, even if it had stood in a dark corner behind a door for a very long time.'

'And the culprit?' asked Toft.

The Bursar rolled his eyes. 'Nobody knows. There are several suspects among the undergraduates. The youngest Hollingdale boy has been mentioned. The organ scholar.'

'One of the mathematical Hollingdales?'

'The youngest, but he is musical and not mathematical. A tear-away. In trouble several times before.'

'And will they send him down?'

'The Dean wants to make an example of him. The Acting Master has already involved the police, apparently.'

'The police? Ridiculous! He clearly does not know how we handle matters here at New College. The police indeed! It would be harsh even to send the boy away without graduating, but involving the police is positively vindictive. Isn't he rather talented? Besides, student pranks are a fine tradition.'

'Not if they upset Her Majesty.'

'The Queen is upset?'

'She might be, if she knew about it.'

'Did it all end well? The Venus is in one piece, and restored to the landing?'

'That is the odd thing. She is restored in more ways than one. She had lost a finger and had been cracked around the knees for decades, apparently, but now the cracks are repaired and her finger has been expertly replaced.'

Professor Toft was not the only one to make a diversion after dinner to inspect the statue of Venus. Nobody had paid her much attention before, indeed she had often been used as a hatstand and draped with coats, but now, cleaned and restored, her pure white marble beauty attracted universal admiration.

The typewriting machine arrived in the burly arms of a college porter. Grace answered a knock at the Master's Lodge door and found him standing there along with Miss Froment who was herself carrying a large box overflowing with papers.

'I have come to throw myself on your mercy,' she declared, stepping straight inside and urging the porter to do so too. 'There is a crisis in administration. Two clerks are absent due to illness and one is on leave. There is nobody to take over. We are falling seriously behind!'

A regular enough visitor to know her way to the dining room, Miss Froment passed her hostess on the threshold, led the way there, and saw to it that the typewriting machine was set on the dining table, and the porter sent away. The cover was lifted aside and both ladies stood back and looked at the large black machine.

Grace had seen typewriting machines often enough, but never close up. This one was impressively solid. Its bulky body was black, ornamented with gold lettering. The round keys had brass rims and the jointed bars which jumped up and pounded a letter onto the paper seemed to lie, fanned out, waiting.

'You expressed an interest in learning to use a typewriting machine. Do you remember? You said it might be useful to type your father's notebooks. Well, Miss Marshall, what I was hoping. *Very much* hoping. Was that, if I lent you a machine, I might prevail upon you to learn to use it by typing some of the notes from this box.'

Grace opened her mouth to utter a protest, but before she could, her visitor produced a large volume from under her arm. 'I have brought a very ingenious instruction book. Just look! It shows, you see, which fingers to use on which key. There are practice exercises. It is nothing difficult.'

'Is it really possible to teach oneself,' Grace asked, 'without instruction other than a book?'

'Oh, perfectly possible. I did so myself, and so did several of the staff. Everything one needs is in here. It is merely a mechanical skill. One picks it up readily, if one has the aptitude.'

'I may *not* have the aptitude.'

'I'm sure you will. The speed takes a little time to develop. At first one concentrates on accuracy and using the correct fingers on the correct keys. Once that is conquered, it becomes possible to increase the pace. People can learn to type at a rate of four dozen words a minute, or even more, without error.'

Grace frowned, trying to estimate how fast four dozen words per minute might be. It sounded extraordinarily fast.

'That will take time, of course. To begin with, one simply works one's way through the book of instructions. It is really perfectly simple.'

'And you would like this pile to be turned into typewritten script?' Grace looked doubtfully at the untidy box of assorted papers Miss Froment had set on the table. 'What papers are they?'

'Well, that is a tale in itself, I regret to say. Our Bursar is on a great many charitable committees and at some point he decided that it lent more authority to his committee work if the minutes of the meetings were typewritten, and carbon copies distributed to the members. But, as I explained, there has been nobody to type them, so they have accumulated, and now there is to be an inspection.'

'An inspection of these papers?'

'Of these papers and everything else to do with the workhouse they came from. They all concern the St Benet's Union workhouse. Questions have been raised about its management, I'm afraid. It may have to be closed down. Anyway, the inspectors will need to read all these papers, and as you can see, they are hardly presentable as they are.'

The nest of papers, even from a distance, was clearly not presentable to anyone. Miss Marshall looked through them briefly and found all manner of bills, account books, transcripts of official hearings, and what appeared to be hastily jotted letters as well as the scrawled minutes of meetings. The documents were carelessly piled, and in some cases ripped, creased and grimy. One whole bundle appeared to be smeared with soot, as though it had been rescued from a fireplace.

'There have been certain difficulties at the workhouse lately,' Miss Froment said, avoiding Grace's eye.

'When would you need this work to be completed? There seems a great deal to be done.'

'Oh, not until the beginning of next term,' said Miss Froment. 'The inquiry will not begin until then. You have several weeks. I was hoping you might be able to spare a little time. Typewriting is such a useful skill to acquire. It is modern accomplishment, useful in many walks of life. There is even the possibility of being paid for such work, although not in this case, sadly.'

Miss Froment smiled at Grace, briefly, then added, 'A certain amount of discretion is needed. There are sensitive matters here. You are the perfect person to help, Miss Marshall. A safe pair of hands, reliable and discreet. I wonder I hadn't thought to ask you before.'

Neither Grace Marshall nor anyone else had ever managed to withstand Miss Froment at full tilt, so the typewriter stayed.

Chapter Seven

Packing was well under way, and the Master's Lodge was full of boxes. The decorators had been working around Grace for several weeks already. She took a deep breath, inhaling the now familiar smell of paint, sat in front of the typewriter, and opened *Typewriting for the Novice*. Spacing and alignment she found very difficult, but the actual use of the keys, the correct placing of the fingers and so on, came easily enough, and in a short time she was working her way through the exercises. She began to know the machine's quirks. Its 'e' key often stuck, and the space bar could be stiff, but in general she and the Imperial Sovereign, as it was self-importantly named, were off to a good start.

The first document she pulled from the box was headed *Notes of the Extraordinary Meeting concerning the arrival of three orphaned children at St Benet's Workhouse on 23-24th March 1896. Hearing held at the White Horse, Chittering Lane, in the presence of St Benet's Board Chairman, Dr H.B. Winfrith and witnesses*. The spidery handwriting was that of a the Union Board shorthand writer who identified himself as T. Sedge. Grace typed what he had written very slowly, struggling to line things up.

Chairman: You are Albert Higgs? Mr Higgs, where were you at about midnight on the night of March 23rd?

Witness 1: In the High Street, sir.

Chairman: You were walking home?

Witness 1: I was taking a short rest, sir.

Chairman: A rest? In the street?

Witness 1: I was the worse for wear, sir.

Chairman: The worse for drink, you mean?

Witness 1: Yes, sir.

Chairman: I see. But you saw something?

Witness 1: I saw a cart come along slow. The nag was old. It stopped by the workhouse.

Chairman: Did you know the cart or the driver?

Witness 1: It was too dark to say, sir.

Chairman: And what then?

Witness 1: I never saw the rest. I was taking a nap, I expect.

Chairman: You are no sort of a witness, Mr Higgs. Stand down. Whose idea was it to call this man? Are there no other witnesses?

Constable: There is one, Your Honour. A Frenchman. Arnauld Valle.

Chairman: He knows English?

Constable: He knows enough to tell what he saw.

Chairman: Call the Frenchman. You are Arnauld Valle?

Witness 2: Yes.

Chairman: You were near the St Benet's Union House on the night of March 23rd?

Witness 2: I was.

Chairman: What did you see that night in the High Street?

Witness 2: I saw a cart stop outside the gate of the big house there. They tell me that is the workhouse.

Chairman: And what then?

Witness 2: I was not near. I saw only some things put out of the cart.

Chairman: Things?

Witness 2: Bags. Or sacks.

Chairman: Did you observe the driver of the cart?

Witness 2: I saw two people. I was far off. I could not see their faces. One was a woman, I think.

Chairman: Did you see what the bags contained?

Witness 2: No, sir. I thought coals or potatoes.

Chairman: Did you inspect them?

Witness 2: Inspect?

Chairman: Did you go over and look at them?

Witness 2: I did not. I was going to Cambridge. I was hurrying.

Chairman: What was your business in Cambridge after midnight?

Witness 2: I have a lady friend there, Monsieur.

Chairman: I shall clear the room if there is another disturbance! Call Mrs Lemman, if you please. You are Mrs Iris Lemman, of the St Benet Union workhouse? You are the Matron at the workhouse?

Witness 3: I am, sir.

Magistrate: Tell us what you saw on the morning of March 24th 1896, Mrs Lemman.

Witness 3: I thought it was three bags outside the door, when I opened it in the morning. Bags of rags, I thought. People leave us rags like that. But when I looked closer it weren't rags.

A Match for Miss Marshall

Chairman: What was it?

Witness 3: Three little children, sir. Wrapped in old blankets.

Chairman: What did you do then?

Witness 3: I called for someone to help, Sir. Jane came, she works in the house. She helped me take them inside. We carried them to the sick bay. They were three young girls, half dead they were with cold and hunger. One was a baby. All pale and skinny and thin. They was in rags and needed a good wash.

Chairman: They were sick?

Witness 3: They were sickly but they had no fever or disease I knew of. What I thought was strange was that they was quiet. None of them made a peep, not even the baby. I put them to bed in the sick bay.

Chairman: Did you know these children?

Witness 3: Nobody knew them.

Chairman: And was there any means of identifying them?

Witness 3: There was a sort of a note with them, but no name on it.

Chairman: Do things like this happen often at the workhouse, Mrs Lemman?

Witness 3: Not nowadays, sir. There might be an old man or a tramp outside in the morning from time to time, but I never seen children left at the door before. Not in my time. It happened in the old days, but not now, thank the Lord. I thought them days was gone for good.

Grace searched through the papers in the box and found a fragment roughly torn from a paper sack. Someone had written on it in scrawled pencil: *Please someone be kind to my little darlings. Their names are Violet four yrs Rose two yrs Ivy 9 mths. I tried my best but cannot go on. I must work. I beg you with all my heart to keep my darling girls together.*

The paper was wrinkled and blotched in patches, as if tears had fallen on it.

Grace had wept very little since her father died, but the story of the three little sisters' sudden arrival at the workhouse brought tears to her eyes as she typed. When she looked up from the typewriter, she realised darkness had fallen in the college gardens outside. She had missed dinner, the painters had long since left, and the Master's Lodge was cold and silent, its shadows pressing in around her. She looked out at the pools of soft light shed by the moonlight in the wide college courtyard, and wondered what had become of poor Violet and her sisters.

Chapter Eight

Grace had lain in bed in the Master's Lodge that morning and watched the sunlight find its way into her bedroom for the last time. Even her clothes were in trunks now. The removal men were due.

She looked out of the window, across the perfect lawn and delicately tended flowerbeds of the Lodge gardens to the ancient buildings of the college beyond. The Lodge, without its furnishings, emptied of books, no longer felt like the home she had known. It hadn't been home since her father had died. She knew—had known for some time—that she needed to plan a future life, but each time she tried to imagine it, she could picture nothing at all. Her imagination simply stalled. If only her papa could tell her what to do. If only he had left her a note or letter—anything to give her any sort of guidance, but there was nothing. She had, the day before, made some rough calculations about her financial situation. The picture was grim. She had only the remains of the small personal allowance her father had given her. There would, in future, be the possibility of royalties from the new book, but not until it was published, and that could be a year or more ahead. Royalties from her father's other books were paid into an account she could not access. She would need to ask about that. Meanwhile, she must add to her income in any way she could. Her list, under the heading *Possible Sources of Income* read:

1. Undergraduate Tuition
2. Writing?

Grace chewed her pencil, and then her finger nail - both habits her father had heartily disliked - and wished, as she so often did, that he was still there to talk to.

Later that morning, while she was at the typewriter, a porter delivered Grace a note from a certain Christabel Venables at Maison Ladoré. Neither name was familiar.

Dear Miss Marshall,

I am seeking a lady with an interest in fashion and hats in particular to write articles about my latest styles. You have been recommended to me in this capacity by a customer, Miss Froment of New College. If you are interested, please call in to see me at your earliest convenience.

Christabel Venables

Proprietress, Maison Ladoré, Paradise Place

'You have mentioned me to this Miss Venables as someone who writes about *hats*?' Grace asked Miss Froment, when the head of housekeeping called later to oversee the removals.

'It struck me as something you might be good at.'

'Did it? Why?'

'Well, you can write. And you wear hats.' Miss Froment was clearly grasping at straws. She busied herself directing the removal men to avoid any further questions.

'I know nothing at all of fashion or hats!' Grace followed her into the sitting room. Miss Froment picked up a large potted plant and nodded to Grace to carry another, leading the way out to the handcart outside the back door.

'You are good at researching,' said Miss Froment, loading the plant onto the cart. 'Think of all the work you have done for your father's book.'

'How does one research *hats*?'

'By looking at ladies in the street, I imagine. Or reading fashion magazines.'

Grace had not thought of either of those methods. She had imagined searching the college library for learned volumes on millinery - and finding none. She followed Miss Froment back into the emptying house.

'But why me?'

'I am simply looking for any opportunity that might lead to interesting paid work for you, Grace.'

'Will this Miss Venables pay me?'

'Not directly, no.'

'So how will this amount to any sort of opportunity?'

'She wants someone to write articles about her hats for the newspapers. The newspapers will pay for the articles.'

'Are you sure?'

'Well, no. I'm not sure, but I imagine that's how it's done.'

'I'm sorry, Miss Froment. You have my best interests at heart. I thank you for that, it is kind, but I don't see how this idea of writing about millinery will work at all.'

'You may change your mind if you just go and talk to Miss Venables,' Miss Froment said. 'Besides, it will make a pleasant enough outing, and the fresh air will do you good, if you don't mind me saying.'

She made an excuse and hurried off before Grace had time to react.

'Gentleman outside looking for you, Miss Marshall,' one of the removal men said, over the crate he was carrying.

Daniel Hollingdale was in the hall. A different, but still bright waistcoat was on display this time, she noted.

'This is not a convenient time, I can see that,' he said. 'I shall be brief. I was wondering, Miss Marshall, whether you might be open to persuasion about the tuition? Miss Froment ...'

'What has Miss Froment to do with tuition in mathematics?' Grace spoke over her shoulder. She was bending over a small trunk over-filled with loosely bound manuscripts, attempting to press them down so that the lid could be closed.

'Only that she...'

'She is the head of housekeeping!' Grace said, managing with a distinct effort to shut the trunk, only for the lid to spring up again. She pulled a length of rope from her pocket and wrapped it round the trunk, but then could not form a knot.

Daniel reached over and held the rope. 'Miss Froment knows everything about the college and when I asked if you might change your mind...'

'...she said?'

He looked a little sheepish before replying, 'Well, to be quite honest, she said your bark was worse than your bite, and told me to try again.'

Grace narrowed her eyes at him, before pulling on the rope and tying it successfully. 'I am in the process of moving house, Mr Hollingdale. Now is not the time to put that to the test.'

'May I call at your new home? Miss Froment has given me the address.'

Grace bent to lift the box, but Daniel got there first, carrying it straight out to the handcart and stowing it among the others. Someone had chalked *G.M. Novels* on the side.

'Come the day after tomorrow at seven,' she said.

'In the evening?'

'In the morning. And Mr Hollingdale, I make no promises.'

'Would that be a new pupil, Miss?' Alice, the Master's Lodge maid, asked, passing a few minutes later with her duster.

'Possibly.'

'He looked a cheery sort. Not like some of them.'

'Alice!'

'Sorry, Miss, but most mathematics students are not very jolly. I mean they don't smile much or have a lot of charm about them, on the whole.'

'Alice, when did you start passing remarks on visitors? It is most irregular.'

'I was wondering, Miss, Have you visited the cottage? Do you know where you want things to go?'

'No. I should have, I suppose, but since I have no choice but to live there whatever it's like, I didn't think it worthwhile. Do you know it?'

'No, but Miss Froment asked if I would carry on working for you over the summer.'

'At the cottage?'

'Yes, she said you'd need some help. I said I was willing. It's an easy journey from my house, and I don't mind a change of scene for a few weeks.'

'That's very kind of you, Alice.'

'James is coming too.'

'James?'

'The handyman. The younger one who's been painting the sitting room here. The tall one with the nice way about him.'

Grace had only barely noticed James among the half dozen men working around the Master's Lodge.

'The good-looking one with the really nice laugh. Dark haired.'

'Yes, thank you, Alice, I know the young man you mean.'

'We shall be working at the cottage together, so he and I will probably see quite a lot of one another,' Alice said, running her duster distractedly over a mantelshelf.

It was clear that the prospect of working with James appealed very much to Alice. Grace also realised that she had so dreaded this move that she had barely given a moment's thought to Abercombie Cottage, or anything else in the future.

Chapter Nine

Professor Toft struggled to his feet and, tapping with his walking stick, moved slowly over to the window to peer out over his reading glasses. His rooms, on the third floor of Abercrombie House offered an excellent view of the garden.

'Harkins. Who is that?' he demanded.

'I believe that is the new tenant,' his visitor said, standing to join him. 'I did mention it last week.'

'I'm sure you did not. Nobody informed me there was a new tenant. Who is it? What does the Bursar mean by putting in a new tenant without my knowledge?'

'She is the late Master's daughter.'

'Professor Marshall's daughter?' The old man leaned forward and screwed up his eyes to scrutinise the distant figure more intently. 'I thought his daughter was a child, still.'

'In her twenties, I believe. Left high and dry by his sudden passing. The will is unsettled. There is no other family. Obviously, she had to leave the Master's Lodge in time for the new Master and his family. The Bursar took pity on her and offered her the cottage as a temporary home. He could hardly allow the late Master's daughter to be put out onto the street. What would people think?'

'Marshall did not provide for her himself?'

'He planned to, I imagine, but there are legal problems.'

'That is a very poor show. The cottage hasn't been lived in for years. Damp and leaky, one imagines.'

'I believe there were a few repairs under way,' the visitor said. 'Ah, here is Mrs Mills with your tea. I shall take my leave until next week.' He picked up the books they had been discussing, bowed and left.

'Did you know anything about this new tenant in the cottage, Mrs Mills?'

The housekeeper put her tray onto the table and poured the professor a cup of tea. 'They told me last week, Professor. I did mention it.'

'My memory is not what it was.'

'A slice of walnut cake with your tea?'

'Have you spoken to this young woman? I must have known her as a child. At least by sight.'

'Once or twice.'

'Is she agreeable?'

'The hens were a surprise to her.'

'In what way?' asked the professor, chewing. 'Excellent cake, as always.'

'She hadn't had the care of hens before.'

'Oh?'

'I told her the hens went with the cottage, and she was expected to care for them. The tenant always cares for your hens. She was surprised.'

'Grew up in the college. Not familiar with hens, I suppose. Not familiar with anything but mathematics, or calculus or algebra or whatever her father was working on. Mathematics is not the best preparation for independent life. Or for caring for hens. Still, she is an appealing enough young woman to look at.'

The professor sounded stern, but his whole manner was softened by his first mouthful of cake. 'Invite her for tea on Wednesday. I should like to get a closer look at her.'

Mrs Mills nodded, tucked the tray under her arm, and left for the kitchen.

Chapter Ten

'Alice, do you know about hens?'

'Know what about them, Miss?' Alice, was waving a broom above her head in an attempt to remove ancient cobwebs from corners of the cottage. Generations of spiders had lived there happily undisturbed for many years.

'How one cares for them.'

Alice lowered her broom and wiped her forehead with the back of her hand. She had a scarf over her head, but still suspected spiders of landing on her hair. 'You feed them twice a day and you collect the eggs, as far as I know, Miss. Nothing difficult.'

'How much does one feed them? There is grain in a bin, but I have no idea how much they want. They seem hungry. They look at me fiercely.'

Alice laughed. 'Don't take any notice of them, Miss. Chickens always look like that. My Ma keeps a few. They're always hungry. Give them each a little handful of grain each morning and evening. That'll be enough. They can find the rest they need by pecking round the garden.' She lifted the broom to the next corner.

'How will I get them into their house at night?'

'They go in by themselves, Miss.'

'Really?'

'Yes. They go to roost when it gets dark. Then you shut them in, so the fox doesn't get them.'

'Right. I understand. Food and water twice a day and shut them in at night. I think I can manage that.'

'You might need to clean their house too.'

'Ah. Every day?'

'Just once in a while. Enough for it to be healthy, Miss.'

'Thank you, Alice. Chicken keeping is new to me. I must say, if I have known it was a task that came with the cottage, I would have looked it up in the library in advance.'

The idea of studying chicken keeping in a library book made the maid smile, but she turned so that Grace would not see, in case Grace thought she was being mocked.

The fowl population of the garden of Abercrombie House - six hens and a handsome cockerel - were a surprise to Grace when she arrived that morning with her boxes and bundles. It was even more of a surprise when the housekeeper of the big house curtly informed her that she, Grace, as tenant of the gardener's cottage, was responsible for their care. It was a condition of the tenancy, apparently.

Since that day had already seen Grace removed from the only home she had ever known and displaced to a tiny house that had not been occupied or cleaned for a decade, she accepted the news with the stoic calm of one already completely overwhelmed.

Once the cobwebs were mostly gone, the floors swept and a few found bits of furniture dusted and put into place, the gardener's lodge began to look at least a little habitable.

Sun showed the dirt and cobwebs on the windows, but it also warmed the little sitting room. The removers had piled book boxes against every wall, leaving only a few feet of space by the fireplace for a chair. The other room downstairs was the brick floored kitchen, where Alice had already cleaned and lit a fire in the range. There was just room in there for a table that might seat two. A tiny scullery led off the kitchen, and a distinctly chilly bathroom was beyond that. Its bath, which must have been salvaged from a far bigger house, was extremely large, a wooden step was needed to climb into it. Alice calculated it would take all day to heat enough water to fill it, and each bucket full would be cold by the time the next had warmed up on the miniature range in the kitchen.

'You'll need some supplies, Miss,' Alice said, once she had cleaned the bare kitchen. 'Will I go to the shop and fetch some groceries?'

'Yes. Of course,' Grace said, having thought about chicken food, but not about her own dinner.

'If you let me have a couple of shillings, I'll go to the shop in Hill's Road. It won't take long,' Alice called from the scullery.

Grace took the coins from her purse, conscious that there were very few coins left now.

The cottage's only bedroom was up a winding staircase hidden in a cupboard beside the sitting room fireplace. It occupied the whole attic space, and was long and low. It was only possible to stand upright in the middle. There was a brick chimney breast at either end. The head of the bed had to go against one and the little wardrobe and night stand went against the other. A small window, let into the thatch, looked into the garden on one side.

When Alice and James had gone on that first long day,

Grace sat in her new bedroom under the eaves and looked out. The sounds of the city around were distant, muffled by the trees. The cottage was central, near roads and the railway, but somehow it felt as if it was in the countryside. Omnibuses crowded with workers travelling home from work were queuing in the street a few hundred yards away, but here, set back in the garden of the big house, the loudest sound was a thrush singing. Listening to it there on the creaky iron bedstead, Grace took a deep breath. The move was over. The smells around her were of dust and furniture polish, of dried straw in the thatch and clean bed linen. As the repeating phrases of the bird's song rang out across the lawn, she took a deep breath and was surprised to find herself flooded with feelings of comfort and peace. The cottage seemed to tuck itself in around her. She pulled out the list headed *Possible Sources of Income*. It now read:

1. Tuition - Daniel Hollingdale(?) Others?
2. Writing - Hat column for the Chronicle (?)
3. Papa's royalties?- investigate.

She then remembered the chickens and ran downstairs and out into the darkening garden to shut them in.

Chapter Eleven

Daniel Hollingdale arrived for his lesson punctually on Monday morning. It was Grace who, after a long night of typing, found herself in a flurry when she heard his knock at the door of the cottage. She was still fastening her hair with one hand as she let him in.

'Good morning! I am a little early, perhaps, Miss Marshall?' He was all smiles on the doorstep.

'No,' she said. 'You are punctual. Come in and sit down, Mr Hollingdale.'

He entered the cottage, but found only a single chair, so did not sit. Grace went to the kitchen to find a stool. Crates of books were piled around every wall.

'So why is it that are you taking a mathematics examination?' she asked, once they were both seated at the smallest table Daniel had ever seen. 'And which examination is it to be?'

His smile faded a little. 'In all honesty, it is a punishment,' he said.

Grace had heard of this. A punitive course: a serious

punishment reserved for the worst kind of wrong-doing undergraduate. It was generally an exercise in humiliation and a way of ridding the university of them. 'Ah,' she said. 'I see.'

He squirmed and pulled at his shirt collar.

'Perhaps you should tell me the whole story.'

Hollingdale sighed. 'I stole something, you see. Only for a short time. It was a dare. A prank. I was always going to take it back. But they didn't see the funny side and they had already called the police.'

'So the college is punishing you with compulsory mathematics?'

'In a nutshell, yes.'

'Why did they chose mathematics? A punitive course can be in any subject.'

Hollingdale put a hand on each knee and directed his remarks at the floor. 'My father and grandfather both distinguished themselves in the subject of Mathematics. They won prizes, medals and so forth. There is, in fact, a Hollingdale prize, named after my grandfather who achieved the highest mark ever in his Finals. Naturally, they expected me to follow in their footsteps.'

Grace had heard of the prize, and knew the reputation of the earlier Hollingdales. 'But you do not share their gift?'

'Alas, no,' he smiled, shaking his head. 'I enjoy a great many things about life here at Cambridge, but mathematics is not one of them.'

'And yet it is the whole purpose for coming to me,' Grace said. He was the same age as she was, but seemed much younger, she thought. His face wore an expression of rueful regret which did not suit it. It was a cheerful and agreeable face by nature, she thought, though it had rather too much of the naughty schoolboy in its expression at that moment.

'I must pass this examination. I shall not be allowed to graduate unless I do,' he said.

'And that would grieve your family?'

'It would grieve them to the point of rejecting me. Cutting me off without a penny. There is a postgraduate teaching position here which I stand a good chance of winning, but only if I graduate. Such posts are extremely rare. It could be the start of a promising musical career.'

'I see. Why, then, do you come to me, in particular, if I may ask?'

'I believe I am considered, by certain tutors, that is, I am thought to be, to be...'

'*Unteachable?*' Grace offered a word of dreadful condemnation she had heard her father use on only rare occasions.

He nodded, looking rueful. 'Mathematical principles do not take root easily in my brain. It was generally held that you might be open to the work.'

'That I might not be in a position to turn anyone away, you mean?'

'Perhaps. Most tutors, especially at this time of year, are more interested in preparing the coming term's work than in assisting a dull-witted chap like me.'

'*Are* you dull-witted, Mr Hollingdale? Is that true?'

'Not in music. In music I can hold my own. But I have no natural disposition toward the mathematical way of seeing things. Real mathematicians thrive on it. I've seen it in my brothers. It is meat and drink to them. My father too! And even my sister. They talk mathematical formulae over dinner, with the kind of relish others discuss cricket or politics. It fills them with energy and enthusiasm. I imagine mathematics does that to you.'

'But you yourself do not feel fuelled by mathematical energy?'

'I do not. Despite the family tradition.' He was perching awkwardly on the edge of the stool. 'You think me shallow, no doubt,' he said.

Grace said nothing because he was correct about this. He was looking at her slightly out of the corner of his eye, which made her uncomfortable.

Alice, arriving for her day's work, let herself in at the door, observing Grace's visitor with obvious curiosity as she passed on her way to the kitchen.

He continued, 'I have always loved music. All my life. Being in the choir school as a boy was marvellous. But the Hollingdales are mathematicians. They win prizes and put their skills to work running the finances of famous enterprises. Banks, railway companies, great corporations of various kinds.'

'There are no musicians among them?'

'Not one. So far.' He had been cheered by the mention of music, but now he looked solemn again. 'Frankly, Miss Marshall, I have spoken to half a dozen tutors, but none will work with me. You tutored one or two of your father's more troublesome pupils in the past, I believe.'

This was true. Students who had exhausted everyone else's patience, were occasionally sent to Grace's father, and he had passed some of them on to Grace.

'I merely guided them through the exercises in my father's undergraduate textbook. I helped him in the compilation of the text, and indeed I set some of the practice problems myself. Under his guidance, of course.'

'Ah, so you know the answers! But can you explain the principles clearly? Help a slow horse like me to grasp them? I despair of working it all out alone. I simply cannot do it. I stare and stare at the page, but nothing makes sense. My father thinks me an absolute buffoon. Perhaps you do too.'

Grace sidestepped the issue of his buffoonery by saying, 'I can take you through the exercises my father and I designed, but it is you who will have to make the effort.'

'Of course,' he said. At this indication of hope, the look of misery passed quickly from his face. It was like a thundercloud dispersing. He was suddenly struck by a thought and reached inside his jacket to produce an envelope, which he placed on the table. 'Oh, by the way, I brought the fee, as Miss Froment instructed. She told me three guineas in advance and the rest at each lesson until the examination.'

'And who will set the examination?' Grace asked.

'Professor Dewhurst in collaboration with yourself, I believe. There is, naturally, a fee for the setting the paper as well.'

Grace was already suppressing delight at the generous fee mentioned for the lessons. The bonus of an examination fee made her turn away and reach into one of the boxes of books. It would be most unseemly to show delight at this payment.

He looked around the room with bright eyes and new curiosity. 'You have a great many books to unpack. It might be difficult to find room for them all.'

'They represent my father's life's work,' she said, and he saw the sadness overtake her at the thought. 'I could not bear to part with any.' She then started up suddenly, saying, 'Oh! I have forgotten the chickens!' and made for the door, 'Please excuse me. They must be fed and released. I shall be gone only a minute.' She handed him a copy of her father's textbook as she ran out into the garden.

Daniel watched Grace pick her skirt up to keep the hem out of the dew that lay heavy on the grass. She ran the long length of the garden with her hair flying out of its pins and disappeared into a shrubbery at the end. There followed a brief interlude during which a few squawks and other chickeny protests or greetings could be heard, and then she reappeared, followed by a flurry of half a dozen hens. They looked indignant, as if she had kept them waiting, and encircled her, pecking hungrily as she scattered their grain on the grass.

They made a pretty composition, he thought, the variously coloured hens dappled by the sunlight through the trees, and the lovely young woman bending to tend to them, her hair falling loose.

The study of mathematics suddenly seemed a great deal more promising.

Chapter Twelve

Visiting a hat shop, as she did the next day, made Grace self-consciously aware of her own headgear. She had only two hats in her wardrobe; one for summer, one for winter. As it was a chilly day, and rainy weather, the winter one was the only choice. She laid it on the table and looked it over from all angles. It was a dark green trilby with a black band and a small feather. She didn't remember buying it. Perhaps it had been left at the Master's Lodge by a visitor. It was certainly several years old and a little out of shape on one side. *In the matter of hats*, she thought, *I am an ignorant novice.*

Christabel Venables, on the other hand, took one look at the same hat and identified it as coming from Routledge's millinery department in Newmarket, probably five years ago. It was of German manufacture, she guessed, well-constructed and durable, made of silk lined blocked felt intended to withstand may years of outdoor wear in Bavaria, and had been an expensive item, but had recently been neglected, badly stored, left unbrushed and pushed into too small a space. Hat neglect; Christabel saw it every day.

Such a hat, entering her shop on the head of a customer, was, however, a promising sign. It meant the wearer, without taking much interest in the details, had a sense that her old hat was approaching retirement, and a new one was definitely needed. And, as someone who had once spent a decent sum on the old hat, she was potentially in the market for a reasonably expensive replacement. Christabel stood and reached to the central shelf, so that she just happened to be straightening one of her finer hats on its stand as Grace approached.

Once it was clear that a sale was not likely, and that this was the Miss Marshall who might write about hats, Christabel set the hat back on its stand and handed Grace an old copy of Harper's Bazaar open to display an illustrated article on winter fashions. 'What I need, you see, is something like this.'

Three ladies were illustrated in graceful poses, each wearing the latest style of coat and hat. They were sketched standing on a footbridge over a frozen river. People were skating in the background. *Winter Gowns and Hats*, said the headline. It was the kind of article that Grace would normally have crossed the road to avoid reading. She thought, if she were being honest, that the ladies looked foolish and exaggerated. Their waists, hands and feet were smaller than any normal human woman's, for one thing. Their expressions, to Grace's eyes, were vain and vacant.

'Notice the hats,' Christabel said.

The hats were what her late father would have called 'traffic stoppers', designed, presumably, to impress and startle. Whilst not particularly large, they featured fulsome and extravagant decoration. One appeared to have a whole bird sitting with its wings outstretched on the brim, like the figurehead on the prow of a warship. Another displayed a prominent fan-shape standing fully twelve inches high, but only on one side. The third was covered in ruffled ribbon, asymmetrically arranged so that it sat high on one side but low, frothing out below the brim on the other.

Grace blinked at the image, perplexed. To her eyes the hats seemed overstated and absurd. She was relieved when Christabel said, 'Of course, none of my customers would wear such a hat. Cambridge fashions are quite different. Ladies here prefer a more understated style, as a rule. A single decorative item is generally enough, but they do want to be fashionable, and they are highly influenced by the Paris fashions as they are reflected in a magazine like this one. What ordinary ladies want, in my experience,' Christabel continued, 'is to read and look at high fashion designs like these, but to buy and wear a far more modest version. In other words, if these hats represent the finest champagne, my ladies want to buy the reliable house white, but perhaps with a small hint of a sparkle.'

Christabel was warming to her subject. 'Cambridge ladies, you see, are aware that Cambridge gentlemen, particularly the academic ones, are blind to most fashion and really only interested in books. Their wives can therefore either choose to ignore fashion entirely - if you look about you in the streets you will see many ladies who have clearly made this choice. Most of my customers, however, know that they are free to wear anything they please because their husbands will almost certainly fail to notice. A little extravagance here and there is even open to them, particularly if their husband progresses through the ranks at his college.'

Grace nodded, agreeing with these generalisations,

although she had never thought about any of this before. 'There are some academics of a different sort, though,' she pointed out. 'Some are so trained in critical thought, and so instinctively analytical that they cannot avoid applying their highly-developed powers of criticism to everything. Hats included. They will deliver a thoughtful, well-expressed and trenchant view whether it is welcome or not.'

'That is very true,' Christabel said, smiling. 'But on the whole the wives and sweethearts of those particular gentlemen know better than to bring them hat shopping. Nobody wants a thorough, objective analysis of a lovely new hat. Hats are art. The methods of science do not apply!'

'Except that the laws of physics would make some of these impossible to wear,' Grace said, examining the image again. 'The bird would surely pull that one down at the front. The unfortunate lady wearing it would not be able to see to walk.'

'Oh no, it would be counterbalanced, probably with a coin stitched into the back,' Christabel said, peering at the image in question. 'Milliners are experts in the physics of hats, Miss Marshall, you should never underestimate us! When did you last read of a lady suddenly blinded by her hat?'

This was a fair point, and by now both were smiling at the stylish ladies in Harper's Bazaar. Christabel gestured at the array of hats ranged on their stands around the shop. 'My shop is a newcomer, Miss Marshall. I pour my heart and soul into my designs, but I am not on a main thoroughfare here. I am, as you can see, a little tucked away in Paradise Place. Customers must seek me out. Once they do, they usually remain loyal, but I need some means of drawing more ladies here in the first place. What I should like is for someone to write a regular series of articles like this one, but drawing attention to this shop. I picture Cambridge ladies sitting by their fireside at home reading such pieces and being so fascinated that the name of Maison Ladoré stays long enough in their memory and they make a point of finding me. What do you say? Could you do it?'

'May I borrow this magazine?' Grace asked.

Christabel reached under the counter and produced a pile of such magazines. 'You may have these to keep.'

Grace took them, but said, 'You should be aware that I, at present, know rather little of hats or of fashion in general, Miss Venables.'

'What subject *do* you know about?' Christabel asked.

'Only mathematics, really.'

'Mathematics! Well, then I imagine you are quick to learn something new. I feel sure you can express your thoughts clearly in writing. That should suffice.'

'I would need to know the focus of the article I am to write. Should it be winter hats like this one?'

'Well, generally, millinery fashion pieces are about the season ahead, if you'll excuse the pun!' Christabel said. 'An article published in May would be about autumn styles. My customers tend to think in terms of the academic year. At this time of year they would want a hat for the summer vacation or the coming Michaelmas term. One that would make an impression on new members of the faculty, and their wives, as well as older members returning after the long summer vacation.'

'Something forward-looking and optimistic?' Grace suggested.

'Quite.'

'Something bold enough to make a statement about

one's position in the college, and one's intentions for the coming year, but subtle enough to do so without seeming too presumptuous.'

'I see you have the idea very well,' Christabel was smiling.

'I'll bring the first article tomorrow, then,' Grace said.

'I thought you would need at least a week.'

'I shall bring something this time tomorrow.' Grace made for the door. 'Oh, and thank you, Miss Venables.'

'Call me Christabel, please.'

'And I am Grace.'

Chapter Thirteen

'I rather took to Grace Marshall,' Christabel later told her sister. 'She was quick on the uptake when we discussed her writing about my styles.'

'Miss Froment thinks she is too trusting. She fears for Grace and wants me to protect her from a circling admirer.'

'How intriguing! Is he a villain who poses a threat to Miss Marshall's virtue?'

Christabel sounded rather too thrilled at this prospect for Lucia's liking.

'Miss Froment wouldn't say. He is an academic gentleman and she clearly dislikes him herself. She is worried that Grace might be pressured by circumstances into a hasty marriage with this man.'

'Oh dear. She would not be the first lady to settle for the nearest port in a storm, so to speak.'

'No indeed. We are hoping that the hat articles will keep her busy for a time, and bring her a little independence. Enough to keep the Unwanted One at bay for a while, anyway.'

'It truly is remarkable what hats can achieve!'

'Sadly there was no fee chargeable by the Moth Agency for my advice to Miss Froment.'

'But there may be an indirect reward, if Grace writes well enough to attract more customers to Maison Ladoré,' said Christabel. 'I have high hopes of a crowd of new customers. And if all of them want something in dove grey felt, it will be all the better because I may have over-ordered again.'

On the way back to New College through town, Grace found herself paying close attention to every hat she saw. They turned out to be remarkably interesting and varied. Grace wondered how it was that she had never had any interest in millinery until now. In the middle of Green Street it suddenly occurred to her that there were probably all sorts of other fascinating worlds that she had so far neglected. It was a thought that brought her to such a sudden stop that a man pushing a butcher's handcart had to swerve to avoid her.

It took three attempts to draft something that read like one of the magazine articles Christabel had supplied. The trick, Grace decided, was to mention fabrics and colours and then generalise in a breezy sort of way about the general effect of the styles.

By the time she had finished her first article at midnight, she was satisfied. It began: '*A slashed and upturned brim of chenille-edged felt lends this deep marine blue late summer style from Maison Ladoré a hint of luxury. Clusters of short black ostrich tips trim the sides, with a bird-of-paradise aigrette added on the left and the lively contrast of a white silk poppy between them on the front.*'

The following morning, Grace hurried her article along to Maison Ladoré, but found Christabel deep in conversation with a particularly exacting lady customer. Christabel saw Grace and gestured for her to join their conversation.

'Ah, Miss Marshall, please join us. This is Mrs Professor Lockwood. She is tempted by shape of this broad brimmed felt with the ostrich feathers, but fears it might be too emphatic. Would you mind fetching me the French navy with the roses from the window, if you please? The one with the dark grey ribbon?'

Grace, slipping into her surprising new role of hat shop assistant, lifted the French navy with the roses out of the window and carried it over, vaguely noticing a gentleman abruptly stop walking to look into the window from outside.

Mrs Professor Lockwood, a lady well into her sixties, allowed the French navy hat to be placed on her head. She turned and studied her reflection from out of the corner of one eye for several moments before turning back to the front. 'I don't think so,' she said.

'Perhaps the teal?' Christabel suggested, with a smile. 'Teal is a very becoming colour.'

'No. Not the teal,' said her customer.

'The dove grey?'

'Perhaps,' the lady said, without enthusiasm.

Grace returned the French Navy to its stand. The same gentleman was standing on the pavement studying the window display. Grace realised with a start that it was Daniel Hollingdale. He caught her eye and waved cheerily as she attempted to lift the dove grey hat from its stand, no easy task as the hat's many trembling ostrich feathers were in danger of invading both her nose and her eyes.

'Ah,' Mrs Lockwood said, as Christabel placed it on her head, 'Mmmm.'

This seemed quite a promising response at first, but after a few more moments inspecting her reflection in the mirror, Mrs Lockwood added, 'No. Dove grey is draining to my complexion. I had forgotten.'

The dove grey was returned to Grace. Turning back to the window, she saw that Daniel was still outside. He was smiling broadly, his arms crossed and his head on one side, showing no sign of moving away. She did her best to ignore him.

'It is a full brim that you favour, I think?' Christabel asked.

'Oh yes. One always prefers a full brim,' said the customer, 'so much more becoming.'

'Indeed.' Christabel nodded.

Grace waited for her next instruction. She had not realised before how much patience was needed in the running of a hat shop. Personally, she would have been tempted to tell Mrs Lockwood to hurry up and make up her mind, but plainly that was not going to happen in Maison Ladoré. Christabel behaved as if there was nothing in the world she would rather do than wait for her customer to take her slow time and try on every hat the shop had to offer.

'I wonder if the purple...' Mrs Lockwood gestured languidly in the direction of one of Christabel's more startling creations. Scarlet and black feathers adorned the brim, some narrow and angled upwards, others curling round in a wavy froth. Christabel nodded, confirming the wisdom of this choice, and raised a finger to Grace who lifted it from its stand.

Daniel Hollingdale, following this with interest from the

street, widened his eyes in surprise as if this was not the choice he would have expected. Grace, feeling she had enough to do without offering free entertainment to passers-by, did her best to avoid his eye.

The hat, once on Mrs Lockwood's head, was duly inspected in its turn. This time the faintest hint of a smile - it was really only the aura of a possible smile - could be seen. She turned her head both ways for a side view, lifted her chin for a tilted front perspective and even tried glancing up coquettishly from under the brim.

'Now *that* is more like it,' she said. 'Unfortunately, I have an appointment in ten minutes. I must suspend our transaction for the time being.'

Her smile unfaltering, Christabel removed the hat and handed it back to Grace. While Mrs Lockwood made her way out, Grace returned the hat to its stand in the window. Daniel nodded his head, as if he had long ago predicted the purple hat was not the one for that particular customer. Grace refused to acknowledge him, hoping he would now go away.

'Was that a particularly difficult customer?' she asked Christabel, once the door had closed behind the departing lady.

'Difficult? Mrs Lockwood? No, not particularly difficult. But it always takes three visits before a purchase. She has, in the past, bought both dove grey and French navy hats, incidentally.'

'She seemed taken by the purple this time,' Grace said, carefully.

'Yes. Mrs Lockwood has no fashion sense whatever, and wouldn't know a becoming hat if it bit her on the nose!' Christabel remarked. 'She simply chooses the most expensive hat in the shop and asks me to change the feathers. She does this three times a year. I am happy with the arrangement and so is she. And there you see the foremost trick of the millinery business revealed: smile and smile and never disagree with a client. I hope you will not put that information into your articles, however, it is a trade secret.'

Chapter Fourteen

The door opened, ringing its little bell, and Daniel stepped in. He was an imposing figure in his long black gown. He removed his hat, revealing his tousled sandy hair and smiled amiably at Christabel. Grace's reaction was to avoid him by hurrying into the back room.

Gentlemen visitors were not entirely unknown in Maison Ladoré. They collected their wives' ordered hats occasionally. On rare occasions a gentleman actually chose and purchased a hat for a lady. Academic gentlemen, in Christabel's experience often had none of the shyness when it came to hat shopping that other gentlemen might feel. They were unaware of social niceties in general, so they treated the purchase of a hat in exactly the same way as they might treat the purchase of, for example, a pork chop, or a bicycle pump.

The gentleman before her today, however, seemed a little different. He was tall and broad. The rugby-playing sort, she imagined, and he occupied a lot of space in the small shop. He looked about him, frowning a little, examining the hats from a wary distance, as if he feared they might spring off their stands and pick a fight with him.

Christabel generally allowed customers to meander about the shop for a few minutes, taking in the range, familiarising themselves with the atmosphere, and the general sense of what Maison Ladoré had to offer. But on this occasion the gentleman looked as if he needed rescue, so she spoke up, making him jump.

'May I be of any assistance?'

'I'm looking for something for a young lady. As a birthday gift,' he said.

'Did you have anything particular in mind? A formal, decorative hat, for example?' she gestured towards the row of elaborate styles in the middle, 'or perhaps she might care for something a little more everyday. A beret or one of these neat little toques.'

The gentleman furrowed his brows even further. '*Toques?*' he repeated.

'Smaller hats like these, more upright, with no brim.' Christabel pointed to a row on a lower shelf. 'They have a fresh look. Younger ladies often favour them.'

'She dresses quite simply, as a rule,' he said, looking about him.

'And as to colours? Does she favour any particular shades that you know of?'

'Her coat is a dark grey tweed.' He said this with certainty, relieved to be on solid ground.

The door opened and a delivery boy backed into the shop with his arms full of two large boxes. 'Delivery for Miss Venables?' the boy called over the jangling of the bell on the door.

'Oh, excuse me, I shall have to see to this delivery,'

Christabel told her customer. 'Grace?' she called, 'Perhaps you could help this gentleman, if you wouldn't mind?'

Grace, surprised, stepped from the storeroom and not knowing what else to do, played her part as shop assistant and smiled encouragingly at Hollingdale. He was too engrossed in studying a row of hats to notice, scrutinising them from a distance with his hand on his chin.

The delivery boy dropped the boxes onto the counter, where they took up all the space.

'No, no! In the store room, if you please!' Christabel told him, but he was half way out of the door. 'Two more on the cart,' he called over his shoulder. The bell jangled violently again as he left. Christabel tutted and began moving the boxes into her storeroom herself.

Daniel had moved further into the shop. He was peering at a small toque. 'I really don't know where to begin,' he said, addressing Christabel. 'It is a birthday gift for my sister.'

'Well, if she dresses in simpler styles as a rule, it would probably be best to choose something straightforward. She might not care for large plumes, or a great many ruffles, for example,' Grace suggested, improvising.

He turned, surprised, and looked, for several moments, at Grace, wondering whether to greet her, but something about her expression discouraged it, so he turned his attention back to the hats. 'Something like this—he indicted an exceptionally grand hat, with a cluster of long ostrich feathers and several silk flowers—is certainly…eye-catching.'

Hollingdale turned on his heel and looked at Grace again. He was already beginning to smile, and catching her eye, he smiled more. The sleeves of his long academic gown swirled around him as he turned, flying dangerously close to a row of hatstands.

They both looked again at the oversized ostrich-feathered hat. 'My sister's accommodation is on the small side,' he remarked. 'I fear a hat like this one would expect a room of its own.'

Grace was confused for moment. Was he serious?

'And perhaps its own maid,' he added. 'There is also the problem of whether it would fit through the front door.'

They contemplated the oversized hat together for a few moments. 'Well, such a style would not be to every lady's tastes,' Grace said, eventually. 'There are several others here that will easily fit through most front doors. The berets, for example, will even fit into a pocket.'

The door slammed open and the same delivery boy came in with two more large boxes. He carried them into the back room, where Christabel was already checking the first delivery against a list.

'The age of the lady in question might influence your choice,' Grace added.

'She is twenty-one. This hat is to be a birthday gift.'

'A lovely thought.'

'She has been unwell,' he added. His smile had faded.

'Something that will raise the spirits, then?' Grace suggested.

He smiled again at this, but it was a tight smile. Grace concluded that his sister's illness had been severe.

'There is something optimistic about these little upright styles,' she said. She was conscious that Christabel would be listening from the stockroom and made an effort to sound knowledgeable, using some of the phrases she had learnt from Harper's Bazaar. 'They need very little decoration, just a little flower or a feather or two lends them an elegant finish without being too formal.'

'I must say, I like them too. The moss green is particularly charming,' he agreed. He turned again, but this time the flowing sleeve of his gown flew out and made contact with one of the taller hat stands. It wobbled and then tipped to one side, hitting the one next to it, throwing the hat onto a row of three below, which cascaded onto the four below that. A colourful avalanche of hats and wooden hat stands was then unpreventable. They flipped and tossed themselves from the shelves as if they had been waiting eagerly for the chance to fly, spinning through the air before piling themselves in a colourful wave around their ankles on the floor.

Hollingdale and Grace both stood in wide-eyed dismay at first, Grace pressing her hands to her mouth in alarm. He started to laugh, but then saw the gravity of the situation and immediately stooped to collect hats from around his feet. They both looked anxiously towards the store room door, but Christabel had closed it to prevent the delivery boy running off before his order had been checked.

There ensued several frantic minutes of silent struggle as Daniel and Grace attempted to straighten a dozen wooden hat stands and return a hat to each in the tightly confined space of the shop. They had only just managed the task when the door flew open and the delivery boy strode out.

'That is the third time in a row that they have sent me the wrong buckram. I shall be sending a note to your manager!' Christabel called after him. As the doorbell rang behind him, she turned and suddenly caught sight of the two guilty-looking parties standing among the hats. Her eye ran around the randomly placed and dishevelled display, noting every tousled feather and dented brim. Her face froze, but, far too professional a saleswoman to react violently, she only raised a single eyebrow. 'My goodness, you have been busy!' was all she said.

Ten minutes later Daniel had ordered a jaunty moss green toque and asked for a cluster of peacock feather tips to be added before it was delivered. He gave an address on Castle Hill, and left.

Christabel said nothing more about the incident, turning instead to Grace's article, which she read swiftly as she stood beside the cash register. Her expression was stern to begin with but softened as she reached the end and looked up. 'You have it, Grace. This is exactly what I wanted. If you could write such an article once a week, I feel sure that it would introduce my shop very nicely to the readers of the Chronicle.'

'But first the editor has to agree to publish them,' Grace said.

'Why should he not? His lady readers would certainly enjoy reading such articles.'

'When will you ask him?'

'I? I shall not be asking him. It is for you, the journalist, to approach him, surely?'

Chapter Fifteen

After the next day's early morning lesson had been accomplished, and Daniel sent off with a chapter to read and a set of questions to answer, Grace set the typewriter on her little kitchen table and went on with the workhouse papers. The pile included notes and transcripts of meetings, and excerpts from accounts, but the bulk were letters that formed a prolonged and irritable correspondence between the St Benet's Workhouse Board and Mrs Lemman, the workhouse Matron.

Mrs Lemman's letters were a litany of complaint. She needed more funds for this repair, for that expense, to cover the rise in the price of food, fuel, clothing, soap, laundry services. The coalman wanted sixpence more, the baker wanted another penny a loaf. Hardly a day went by without some new expense to be met in the upkeep of the workhouse residents, who, according to the register were 23 men between the ages of fifteen and seventy-four and nineteen women between the ages of sixteen and sixty-three.

The replies to Mrs Lemman from Dr P.B. Price,

Chairman of the Board of Trustees, were short. They almost always refused the request for more funds on the grounds that a) the expense was unjustified, and b) the Board had insufficient funds to add to the budget already agreed. The usual reason given for the additional expense being refused was that - and this phrase recurred in letter after letter - 'local and national policy is for workhouse provision to be intentionally of a lower quality than the poorest family might provide for itself'.

After several of these drearily routine letters, the new expense of caring for the abandoned children appeared in Mrs Lemman's letters.

Dear Mr Price,

I mentioned last week that the three children we have in the women's wing need to be moved on. They have no suitable quarters here, only one of the women's sick bay rooms. There is only Annie and myself on the women's side and with seven elderly women in residence, we have not the time to spend caring for infants. I have written to the National Children's Home in Haverhill, but have not yet received a reply. I have been approached by a Mrs Henry from Corringsea, who is willing to foster one of them, but only if it is a healthy child, and she expects payment for it.

I am applying for an extra shilling a day for each of the children's upkeep and for the two shillings and sixpence I have had to pay Dr Williams for the treatment of the youngest of the three girls, a weak child with a poor appetite who keeps running a fever.

Dr Williams has prescribed cow's milk, and he insists they have an attendant with them at all times, so I have had to pay Agnes Cornhill a daily rate to sit by them. In my opinion this is unnecessary as they do not move very often or play at all. They were perfectly safe if I locked them in alone. The middle one, Rose, shows signs of a bad behaviour, and the baby is sick and so stays quiet. The older girl,

Violet, does not speak. Dr Williams suspects she is not normal, probably an imbecile, and perhaps deaf also. If she is, she will have to go to the home for sick children in March. The Haverhill home will not accept an imbecile child.
I remain your humble servant,
Iris Lemman (Mrs)

Grace typed several letters in the same vein. Mrs Lemman found the three little girls a nuisance and a severe drain on her budget. The doctor urged extra food and extra care for them. This she bitterly resented providing.

'Excuse me, Miss.'

Grace jumped, she was so engrossed in the papers that she had lost all sense of time.

'I just wanted to remind you that the neighbours invited you to tea?'

'Oh yes. Thank you, Alice.' Grace began to collect the papers up and return them to their box. 'Alice, do you know anything of St Benet's Workhouse?'

'I walk past it sometimes,' Alice said. 'It's not a nice place. I hope I never have the bad luck to see it from the inside.' She shuddered at the thought.

'Its reputation is not good?'

'Mrs Lemman who runs it, is a terrible woman. None of the tradespeople nearby will have dealings with her.'

'What of the inmates?'

'Most are sick or old.' Alice said. 'We see a few in church sometimes on a Sunday. They don't mix. They all dress the same. Nobody sits too close.'

'Why not?'

'They're not clean, Miss. They scratch and they cough

so. It's not their fault, but you don't want to be downwind, if you know what I mean.'

'Are there children among them?'

'Not that I've seen. They're expecting you next door at four o'clock, Miss. Mrs Mills said you should go straight up to the top floor. That's where the professor lives.'

Chapter Sixteen

Abercrombie House was a grand red brick mansion which boasted a mock-medieval turret and several stained glass windows as well as a front door that looked as if it belonged on the Tower of London. It was open. Grace ventured in and found a small board in that hall which indicated by means of a sliding panel that Professor Toft was IN. The other named resident, H. Von Robst, on the other hand, was OUT.

'I'm delighted to meet you, Miss Marshall', the professor said, when Grace arrived on the top floor. 'We always make a point of welcoming new tenants, don't we, Robst?'

'Indeed yes. Delighted to welcome such a charming young lady to the premises.' The other gentleman, who spoke with a definite accent, stepped forward and took Grace's hand with meticulous German politeness, bowing over it, clicking his heels together.

Grace, slightly overpowered, took the seat they gestured to.

'This is Count Heinrich Von Robst, a visiting scholar

from Germany, and I am Professor Henry Toft, retired Director of Studies in Law,' the professor said. 'How do you find the cottage? Not damp, I hope?'

'No, perfectly dry, as far as I can tell.'

'It is a humble enough home for someone moving from the Master's Lodge, no doubt, Miss Marshall,' said the professor.

'I am glad of it. Humble or not,' Grace said.

Mrs Mills poured the tea and handed round the cups.

'You are not concerned about our reputation, I hope?' said the professor.

'I know nothing of your reputation. Is there something I should fear?' Grace asked.

'No, no!' the German gentleman put in. 'This is only a light-hearted remark from the Professor. You have nothing to fear, I assure you of that!'

Cake was distributed by Mrs Mills, who, judging by her expression, disapproved of the conversation so far.

'The tenants of Abercrombie House are, by tradition, the eccentrics who cannot reside in the college itself. We are generally thought too odd, so they house us here at a safe remove,' said Professor Toft.

'The professor exaggerates, Miss Marshall,' Von Robst said. 'I, for one, am not odd or eccentric in any way.'

'You are a German Count with a duelling scar who is the foremost expert in the world on marshland botany. I think that qualifies you as eccentric, Heinrich.'

The Count bowed graciously, accepting the truth of all this.

Grace could only smile in return. 'And you, Professor?'

'I am merely a curmudgeonly old law professor who keeps odd hours.'

'Also you keep chickens,' added Von Robst.

'Oh, the chickens are yours?' Grace asked.

'They are.'

'But their upkeep falls to the tenant of the cottage?'

'That was always the arrangement, when there was a tenant before,' said the professor. 'Mrs Mills had to step in while the cottage was empty. I trust you feel able to accept the responsibility now?'

Mrs Mills handed out slices of cake, keeping her head down and saying nothing.

There was a pause in the conversation. Everyone seemed to await Grace's reply.

'I have quite taken to the chickens. I am happy to care for them,' Grace said. Relief spread through the professor's sitting room. If the chickens were a test, Grace had passed it.

'They thrive already under your care. I can see them from this window. The cockerel can be a little fierce, I'm told, Miss Marshall. Feel free to keep as many of the eggs as you need. Mrs Mills will take the rest. She makes fine cakes with them.'

'Are there other tenants in the house?' Grace asked, 'Or only you two gentlemen?'

'The other apartments are used for visitors to the college. They come and go. You never know who you might meet on the stairs at Abercombie House. It is one of the pleasures of living here, is it not, Count?'

'Indeed, yes. There was that Russian pianist last year.'

'Such playing!'

'He did not care for our piano,' Mrs Mills remarked. 'Said it was out of tune.'

'And Dr Hirohito,' added the German.

'Lovely gentleman. Very neat,' said Mrs Mills.

Grace was not used to a housekeeper who expressed her

opinions quite so freely, but the gentlemen accepted it as normal.

'Now, Grace, tell us about yourself,' said the professor, 'I knew your father very well.'

After tea was over, the two gentlemen watched from the window as Grace crossed the garden back to the cottage.

'It strikes me that we must keep a watchful eye on that young woman, Heinrich.'

'You are concerned for her? Why so?'

'She is an innocent and alone. There are those who might wish to take advantage of her good nature.'

'Surely not!'

'Oh yes. The dreadful Hillyer is one of them, I gather.'

'Hillyer? Do I know of this name?'

'Second-rate mathematician. Tarnished reputation. Nasty little social climber.'

'How do you know this?'

'You should know by now, Heinrich, that I invite all the best college gossips and ply them with Mrs Mills' cake in return for their little overhearings and observations. Nothing at New College happens without my knowledge. Grace is also tutoring the Hollingdale boy. The one who stole the statue of Venus. I knew his father too, of course. World class mathematician and world class bully, if you ask me. Chess today or backgammon?'

'Chess,' said the Count. 'I want my revenge after last week.'

Chapter Seventeen

Edmund Hillyer hovered in the doorway of Miss Froment's office as she completed her accounts for the week. He had the determined look, she thought, of a gentleman with a plan.

'Dr Hillyer. May I be of assistance?' she asked.

'A brief inquiry only,' he said.

He stepped into the room and turned thoughtful immediately, studying the rug with his hands clasped behind his back. 'Yes?'

'About Miss Marshall,' he continued.

She waited again. Dr Hillyer was never one to be hurried.

'She is a great deal alone?'

'She is. She has been working to complete a project of her father's.'

'That would be her father's *Introduction to Undergraduate Mathematics*. I knew she was editing, proof checking, and so on.' He nodded. 'She does not go about very much? She is still keeping to herself?'

'For the main part, yes. As far as I know.' Miss Froment was not sure that it was proper of a gentleman to ask searching questions about a lady in this way, when he might easily speak to her himself.

'The Bursar tells me she has vacated the Master's Lodge.'

'Yes. There is a small cottage.'

'A *small cottage*? Difficult, surely, to adapt to that, after the splendour of the Master's Lodge?'

Miss Froment felt it would be wrong to comment.

'Has she mentioned plans for her future?' he asked.

'She is teaching herself typewriting.'

'Typewriting? The use of a typewriting machine? Whatever for?'

'It is a useful skill,' Miss Froment said.

Hillyer chuckled. 'For certain young women ambitious to be employed in offices, it might be, but Grace Marshall can set her aim a great deal higher than that! I plan to call on her with an alternative suggestion. A far better one.'

He now looked distinctly pleased with himself, Miss Froment noticed, but the thought was interrupted by a knock on the open door. It was Daniel Hollingdale bearing a cardboard box.

'Oh! Excuse me,' he said, when he saw Dr Hillyer was already in the office. 'I was only delivering these.' He opened the box and took a pair of china teapots out, setting them on Miss Froment's desk.

Miss Froment examined the teapots one at a time. 'Marvellous!' she said, 'I really don't know how you do it, Mr Hollingdale. The smaller one was in several pieces. I thought it was fit for nothing but the rubbish heap.'

Hollingdale looked pleased. 'A little glue was all it took,' he said.

'*Hollingdale?*' Hillyer said, repeating the name. 'Aren't you an undergraduate?'

'I am, sir, yes.'

'You are one of the mathematical Hollingdales? I was taught by your father,' Hillyer said. He stepped forward and shook Daniel by the hand. 'Edmund Hillyer. Please remember me to your father when you see him next.'

'I shall, sir.'

'And why are you delivering teapots to Miss Froment, may I ask?' The question was asked in a teasing way, but it was clear that Hillyer was puzzled by what he had seen.

'I mend them, Sir. Repairing china and marble objects is a pastime of mine.'

Hillyer was so astonished by this that he could only repeat it in phrases, 'A pastime? Repairing china and marble?'

Hollingdale just smiled, and picked up his box. 'I have seen Miss Marshall, and the classes are under way now. I thought you would like to know,' he told Miss Froment. He left with a nod to Hillyer.

'Why is that young man seeing Miss Marshall?' Hillyer demanded.

Miss Froment did not care for his tone of voice. Her office was really only a cupboard under the stairs, but it was her domain and she did not care to be cross examined in it. 'Daniel is taking tuition from Miss Marshall,' she said, reluctantly.

'Is he indeed?' Hillyer said. 'We'll soon see about that. Does Miss Marshall visit the College regularly? When might I intercept her?'

'She follows no routine that I know of.'

'No afternoon turn along the river? No regular shopping trip?'

'She visits the library regularly, but apart from that she has hardly stepped out of doors since the loss of her dear father.'

'But that was months ago. She will ruin her constitution. Grace is clearly in need of good advice and proper companionship.'

Dr Hillyer had lost a little hair since she had last seen him, Miss Froment thought, as he left. Or perhaps it was just the Swiss barber. His waistcoat seemed a little tight too. They ate well in Zurich, evidently.

Chapter Eighteen

Grace generally used the back entrance to the library, slipping up the spiral stone steps that led to a hidden doorway. The librarian, a long-time ally, turned a blind eye, as she no longer had any official right to use the books. She was hurrying along the cloister with a heavy armful of mathematical reference books when Dr Hillyer stepped so suddenly out from behind a pillar that she dropped three of them, one landing heavily on his foot.

'Oh! Dr Hillyer! You startled me,' she said, struggling to retrieve the fallen volumes. 'I hope Rice's *Developments in the Theories of Algebra* did not injure your foot.'

'Only a little,' he said, wincing.

Grace bent to collect the dropped volumes. He looked down at her stooping but did not move or offer to help.

'I do apologise,' she said, straightening up. 'You must be visiting from Switzerland?'

'I am considering returning to Cambridge, as it happens. I was hoping to speak to you, Grace. I'm glad we met. Would you care for a turn along the Backs?'

Grace looked at him over the pile of books that almost reached her chin. 'Perhaps after I return these?'

'Of course. Take your time. I shall wait for you by the river gate.' He turned and headed that way before she could speak.

Grace climbed the stairs and returned the books, wondering all the while why Dr Hillyer wished to speak to her. Perhaps it was to give her his condolences over the loss of her father in person. He had already done so by letter. But she wasn't convinced that was all. He had a different look about him. It gave her an odd, uneasy feeling. Perhaps he was going to ask her to proofread his next book. He knew she helped her father with his manuscripts. It might even be an offer of paid work.

She pressed her back to the curved stonework and caught her breath for a moment, then stepped down the rest of the well-worn stone stairs and followed the path towards the river. The weather was unseasonably chilly that day, with an overcast sky and a hint of rain. Very few punts could be seen on the river.

Doctor Hillyer was standing on the hump-backed bridge over the Cam looking oddly unrelaxed. He looked, Grace thought, as if he had been told by a photographer to pose as a gentleman enjoying the view, but was not quite succeeding.

'Shall we take a turn along the Backs?' he suggested, when she approached.

They strolled in that direction. A young woman cyclist flew past, standing on her pedals to build a run-up of momentum and carry her machine over the hump of the bridge.

'Really!' Dr Hillyer remarked, stepping aside on the path. 'I fail entirely to see the necessity for high speed cycling, especially for young women. I find it ungainly. Why should they be in such a hurry?'

'An appointment, perhaps?' Grace suggested.

'What sort of appointment could a lady have to necessitate an undignified rush? A hairdresser? A dressmaker? You never see such things in Switzerland. A more civilised approach to life avoids the need for hasty cyclists to threaten pedestrians and risk their own life and limbs. Don't you agree?'

Grace turned and looked at the stream to avoid answering. She was not a cyclist herself, but something about Dr Hillyer's statement suddenly made her feel that she might like to hire a cycle and try it.

Dr Hillyer strode on for several yards before discovering she was not beside him and looking back, puzzled. He had pictured this stroll among the lovely scenes of Cambridge several times on his long journey from Switzerland, but so far it was not going as he had imagined. Grace was, as he looked back at her, thinner and perhaps even taller than he had remembered. She was certainly appealing enough in her looks, for a dark-haired lady, although her grooming lacked the elegant formality he so admired in the Swiss. Did she always favour such drab colours? But these were all matters that could change, he told himself. Once she adapted.

'It has been a difficult few months, I imagine, Grace, alone in the Master's Lodge.' Hillyer said, continuing along the path.

Grace followed. 'I miss my father, of course,' she said. 'It was a comfort to continue with his work. He left a book unfinished, and since we had planned so much of it together, I was able to complete it as he intended.'

'Editing, and so on?'

'Editing, and indeed writing some of the chapters he left unstarted.'

'You originated material yourself?'

'From his outline, yes. I knew what he intended.'

Dr Hillyer paused and looked sternly at Grace. 'You have spoken to the publisher about this?'

'You think there might be a difficulty?'

'Well, it is not the book they commissioned. Presumably they agreed to publish a textbook written by one of the foremost mathematicians of his day, not by his daughter.'

Grace noted the flourish with which this remark was delivered. Hillyer's face was naturally inclined to haughtiness, she thought. It might be something to do with the high brows and forty-five degree angle of his nose.

'Anyway, it gave me an occupation and I took comfort in the work, but it is finished now.'

'Indeed. And what plans have you next? I believe you have moved out of College now.'

'Yes. To a cottage in the grounds of Abercrombie House.'

'Abercrombie House? In Station Road?'

'Yes.'

'But that is notoriously the last refuge of the college's elderly dons. That dreadful old gossip Toft used to live there. In my day it was a laughing stock, occupied by eccentric old Fellows with no family to look after them as they approached senility.' Dr Hillyer chuckled at the memory.

'Well, I have joined them, it seems.'

'I have always taken a close interest in your welfare, as you know. Before I accepted the post in Zurich, I had a number of discussions with your father on the matter of your future, as it happens.'

'I did not know that.'

'I put it to him that, with your agreement of course, that we, you and I, might possibly have a future *together*.' He turned and fixed her with a meaningful look.

Grace walked on, ignoring the look. 'That we might collaborate professionally?' she asked. 'That I might do some proofreading for you?'

'Well, yes, that you might assist me in my work. Your familiarity with your father's scholarship would certainly mean that you brought excellent skills in editing and proof correction.'

'I would enjoy another publishing project, I must say.' Grace said.

'But I also thought…'

'The only thing is that now that I am in a less secure situation financially - I hope you won't mind me mentioning this, Dr Hillyer?' She stopped and turned towards him.

'Not at all. Consider me a friend and ally you can always confide in.'

'Thank you. It is just that I must now earn a living of my own, you see. So work that once I performed in a spirit of helpfulness for my father, I must now turn into professional and fee-paying employment. I need to adopt a more business-like attitude, if you see what I mean.'

'*Business-like?*' Hillyer seemed to dislike that term.

'What I mean is that frankly, if I am to proofread or edit a textbook on someone's behalf, I should be obliged, now, to ask that they pay a fee.'

Hillyer smiled at Grace, saying, with a small chuckle, 'I don't think that is quite the footing I meant to convey.'

'I have missed your point?'

'Yes. I was, you see, intending to suggest that a partnership of a rather different kind might be open to us, Grace.'

They had turned, now, onto the path along the Backs.

The famous view of King's College chapel was on their left beyond a river meadow. They paused, he to admire the prospect; she to take in the implication of his words. Dr Hillyer took a deep breath, hoping to seize the moment. On his journey from Switzerland this had been precisely the location where he pictured himself declaring his intentions; perhaps the moment they would look back on in years to come.

'In many ways, Grace, I think of you as my fiancée already,' he continued, turning to face her. 'Your father and I spoke of your future so often. We were in agreement, you see, that you and I are so alike—our interest in mathematics so closely aligned—that it seems only natural for us to make a life together. I feel I know you so very well, Grace. We are such old friends. I see our future so clearly.'

Unfortunately, Dr Hillyer's vision was not shared by the pair of black spaniels that suddenly hurtled along the path towards them, barking and chasing and covered in mud.

'Rolly! Jake!' cried the owner, running behind, waving their leashes, 'Here, dogs! Come back here!'

The pair, joyfully free and deaf to his calls, threw themselves into a playful fight, rolling and snorting for joy, scattering mud and leafy debris all around, their long ears flying this way and that.

Grace smiled at their wholehearted dog joy, but Dr Hillyer, when she looked around, was suddenly out of sight. Puzzled, she looked up the path, and saw his face peering from around the trunk of a horse chestnut tree. The dogs ran on, pursued by their owner, and as they approached the tree, Dr Hillyer worked his way round it, keeping the trunk between himself and the spaniels. Only when they were well past, did he step back onto the path and return to Grace. His coat now had green smears on it from the mosses on the tree. Clumps of mud clung to his shoes.

'Dogs!' he said, by way of explanation. 'One really does not care for them. They should be kept under control. It is irresponsible to allow them to range around in a wild and uncontrolled manner.'

Hillyer looked back at the handsome profile of King's Chapel, but the moment had gone. Grace was no longer looking so approachable. She might even look, if he interpreted her expression correctly, the tiniest bit amused.

Ah well, he thought, *another time would have to do. And somewhere without the risk of marauding dogs.*

Chapter Nineteen

Grace spent Saturday morning researching hats whilst shopping at the market. New to housekeeping for herself, she was surprised at how many domestic items she suddenly needed to remember: lamp oil, butter, bread, flour, the list was long, but at least she had the tuition fees to pay with. There was satisfaction to be had in choosing for herself and adding the items one by one to her basket. Meanwhile, the ladies of Cambridge were displaying an interesting array of Saturday hats. These, Grace noted, tended to be jauntier and more practical than Sunday hats. Sunday hats were 'best' hats, Sunday hats said *admire me, if you please*. Saturday hats were incidental hats that said *I may have a striking feather or a fetching flower, but other things are probably more important today*.

At a fabric stall, Grace found herself wondering whether a new dress might be in order. Perhaps in a colour she hadn't tried before? She watched a pair of young women in deep discussion over a light blue cotton with a delicate floral print and couldn't resist touching the material herself. Naturally, she had worn mourning black for several months, but even the rest of her wardrobe tended towards the brown and grey. Was it the dressmaker who had urged these shadowy colours upon her? She had never given it much thought before. Daniel Hollingdale's colourful waistcoats came to mind. To her own surprise, she found she was thinking of them rather fondly.

'Is that Grace Marshall?' A voice interrupted her thoughts. 'It is! I'm glad I have seen you. You have taken the Hollingdale boy on, I believe?'

Grace turned and recognised Professor Dewhurst, a senior colleague of her late father's. He was a short round, beady-eyed figure in black. A shopping basket over one arm gave him the look of a solemn beetle running errands. Dewhurst's famously abrupt intensity caused undergraduates to quake in his presence, but Grace knew him well enough to make allowances. She turned and smiled at the old curmudgeon.

'Professor! You are well, I hope,' she said.

'Quite well, quite well, but bothered, frankly, by this Hollingdale scallywag's misadventures.'

'The punitive course in mathematics? It is under way.'

'Is it? You are a brave soul to tackle that lad. Nobody else had the stomach for it. It is waste of time, of course. It was all his father's idea, you know. He insisted the lad to have a taste of real study for once.'

'Real musical study does not count?'

'Not in that family. They are influential in the college, as you know.'

'I am to set a final examination, I think?'

'Yes. I'm sure you'll do your best to teach him, but we expect him to fail horribly. He sings rather well in chapel, but he clearly has no mathematical abilities whatever.'

'But for form's sake, he must sit an examination?'

'Yes. His father insists. An abbreviated form of one of the entrance examination papers would do. They are simple enough. There are copies in the library. I leave it to you to adapt one. I shall need the result by the end of next week.'

Grace looked at the professor aghast. Entrance examinations were designed to weed out all but the most promising candidates. Daniel would hardly know where to begin.

They had moved during the conversation and were now standing beside a confectionery stall selling colourful sweets in rows of glass jars.

'Ah!' said Dewhurst, ending their conversation by turning away. 'Peppermint creams. My favourite!'

Grace called in at New College library and borrowed a selection of entrance examination papers on her way home. The slightest glance confirmed that her pupil had not even the remotest chance of passing. Diverting, on the way out, to seek out the little statue of Venus that was the cause of all this trouble, Grace found her on the landing where she always lived. Larger than Grace remembered, perhaps half life-sized, she still stood in her dim corner, but her pure white marble seemed now to glow. She was depicted naked and shyly holding her hands as if to hide her naked body from the onlooker. Her head was turned modestly aside, as if she wanted to hide. Each lock of her hair and each joint of her fingers was so exquisitely carved that she almost appeared to move and breathe.

She was flawless, beautiful, touchingly vulnerable. And nobody had paid her any attention until Daniel carried her away.

Back at the cottage, Grace took a housewifely pleasure in unpacking her shopping, but then found herself drawn to the typewriter. The pointless examination paper could wait. She wanted to know what was happening at St Benet's workhouse.

It was slow work, but it was absorbing. Mrs Lemman's self-righteous letters continued, but the doctor was clearly beginning to resist her iron will. He demanded better conditions for the children; she protested at the expense. He insisted on a more varied diet; she asked for more funds to pay for 'extras' such as vegetables. He asked for warmer clothing to be provided; she responded by having the girls' heads shaved 'it is the normal practice, for reasons of cleanliness, which a doctor should know well enough.'

And so it went on. There was a report by the regional inspectorate, but it was several years out of date, and lukewarm at best in its assessment of the workhouse . Mr and Mrs Lemman, it said, were 'in general, fit and suitable for their roles', even though their record-keeping was 'below the recommended standard'.

Grace took breaks to feed the chickens and shut them in for the night. She stopped for a bread and cheese supper, but apart from that, she typed long into the dark. Her neck stiff, she was about to give up for the night, when she heard a knock at the cottage door. It was after eleven. For a moment she was afraid, but then she heard the voice of Daniel Hollingdale calling.

'Are you quite well, Miss Marshall? It's Daniel Hollingdale. Your pupil. I was passing on the way from the station and saw your light burning. I wondered if you were quite well.'

'I am perfectly well, thank you,' Grace said through the door.

'Oh good. I caught the last train. Normally I would pass too quickly to notice a light on, but I have a puncture and needed to push my bicycle. I saw your light through the trees.'

'Can you not mend your puncture?' Grace asked.

'No. I need water and it is too dark out here.'

Grace opened the door. 'I can supply light and water, if it helps.'

'Marvellous! I will not be disturbing your night, I hope.'

'You will not take long?'

'Not at all.' He wheeled his bicycle into the cottage and turned it upside down, balancing it on its saddle and handlebars before producing a small tool kit from a saddle bag, removing his coat, and bending to loosen the spindle of the rear wheel.

He was wearing full evening dress, she noticed. Many men looked awkward in a tailcoat, but Daniel, probably because he wore one regularly for a performance, looked easy—handsome even—in his.

'Why is water needed to mend a puncture?' Grace asked.

'To find the hole in the inner tube,' he said, working the tube out from inside the tyre. 'One looks for the bubbles.'

Grace could only watch as he found and patched the hole before returning the inner tube and re-inflating the tyre. It was swiftly done.

'There!' he declared, straightening up. 'Done! Many thanks.'

'I visited your Venus in college today,' Grace said.

He looked surprised. 'How did you find her?'

'She is very beautiful.'

'She had lost a finger when I took her. Some hooligan

had broken it off. There were several bad cracks as well, around her knees and at the plinth by her feet.'

'She has no such cracks now. And she has perfect hands and fingers.'

'I mended her,' he said.

'But why steal her in the first place?'

'That was a foolish dare, I must admit. But I found her missing finger, it was tucked in under the plinth. Once I had that, I knew I could mend her. So I did.'

'Well, she is lovely now. I really think the college should be grateful to you.'

'I probably should not have put her in the chapel, if I wanted them to be grateful. A naked and unchristian lady on display among the saints did not go down well with the Dean.'

They both smiled.

'You are very formally attired tonight,' Grace said.

'Oh, it was an operatic recital. Part of the entertainment at a great ball. A lot of dancing and dining. You know the sort of thing.' He said this casually, as he shrugged his tail-coat back on. 'I play in a small dance quartet with friends. We play dance tunes and popular classics. Polkas, Viennese waltzes and so forth. Do you dance often yourself, Miss Marshall?' he asked.

'*Dance?*'

'You have never heard of dancing? It is the common human practice of moving rhythmically to music. It is a group activity, but also often carried out in pairs.' He was laughing at her, as he finished replacing the back wheel of the bicycle and flipped it over.

'Thank you for that definition. I had heard of dancing.'

'And have you ever participated?'

'Well, no. Not as such.'

'You have never danced? *Not once?*'

'No. Well, as a child I may have capered about in my room, but I have never danced as such.'

'You never attended a college ball?'

'Yes. Several times, with my father. But I did not dance.'

He looked at her curiously. 'Nobody ever invited you?'

'You will be wanting to leave now, I expect,' she said. 'But for the record, I was invited on several occasions. I did not accept the invitation because I did not know the steps of any dance. I worried that someone would ask me, and I would humiliate myself–and them–in public.'

'But dancing is the easiest thing in the world!'

'If you know how to do it, it may be, but I do not. I never had a lesson. Nobody ever thought to teach me, I suppose.'

'I could teach you to dance in ten minutes.' It was playfully said. He was smiling down at her, wiping oil from his hands on his handkerchief. 'The waltz, for example. You simply step forward, and then to the side.'

'No, no,' Grace said. 'I can't...not now!'

'Come!' he said. 'Stand here beside me. Right foot forward, left foot steps to the side, then right foot joins it.' He took the steps himself, humming a waltz tune under his breath as he did so. 'Then the same, but backwards. You're stepping in a square, you see.'

Grace stood beside and copied the pattern of his steps, frowning in concentration at first, but then, as her confidence grew and the pattern became easier, her movements lost their stiff anxiety. Daniel's singing became louder and she began to smile.

'But one does not simply dance in a square over and again.'

'No. The gentleman holds the lady and guides her around.'

'How does she know which way to turn? I've often wondered.'

'The pressure of the arms, I suppose. It is difficult to describe, but it feels like second nature. I could show you.' He turned to face her, standing close because the room was small and the bicycle was still taking up a good proportion of the floor space.

Grace stopped dancing immediately. 'No. Your puncture is mended, Mr Hollingdale, you had better go home now.'

'Of course,' he said, reaching for his jacket. 'Thank you for allowing me to mend the tyre.'

'Not at all.'

'I shall be back tomorrow for my lesson at seven prompt.'

Grace could hear him humming the Viennese waltz as he pedalled away.

That night she dreamed she was waltzing with effortless skill and elegance round and round a vast but empty ballroom. Her dancing partner seemed familiar, but she couldn't quite see his face. A pair of spaniels was running in circles in the background.

Chapter Twenty

Miss Froment looked critically around the cottage when she visited the following Monday afternoon. She had brought a strong porter and several more pieces of furniture with her. A pleasant stick-backed armchair now took its place by the fire in the sitting room, along with a small side table. A chest of drawers was squeezed up into the bedroom - the porter lifting it easily, but struggling because the stairs were so twisted and narrow.

The porter was sent to the kitchen at Abercrombie House for his reward in the form of a cup of tea and some cake, but Miss Froment remained. 'It is a pleasant afternoon, Grace. Shall we take a turn around the garden?' she asked.

They walked across the lawn.

'The staff all miss seeing you around the college, Grace,' Miss Froment said.

'I miss them too, but the cottage is much more welcoming than I had expected. I have taken to it already.'

'And have you thought how you will manage?'

'I have made a reckoning of my finances. They are certainly limited, at present.'

'Your father's books will provide for you, surely?'

'I have no way of knowing. I plan to earn my own living as far as I am able. Thank you for sending Daniel Hollingdale, by the way.'

'Ah, Hollingdale. He is in all sorts of trouble at present, but I have always liked the boy. He sang like an angel when he was a boy. He still sings well, but people visit from all sorts of places to hear him play the chapel organ now. His pieces are famous. He mends my broken china, you know.'

It was Grace's turn to look surprised.

'It's a talent he has. Undergraduates are forever breaking plates and cups and teapots. I keep the pieces and give them to Daniel and he puts them back together. He does it very well. It saves the housekeeping budget a considerable sum.'

'How very strange,' Grace said.

'He came and offered when he was a lad in the choir school. I suppose he was about twelve. He's done it ever since. I gather this course in mathematics is his last chance to graduate. It's hard on the young man, if you ask me. I know you have had your successes with difficult students in the past.'

Miss Froment walked a little further before sitting on a bench under one of the Scots pines. 'It is perhaps not my business, Grace, but we are old friends. I hope you will allow me to speak my mind.'

'Of course. I am very grateful to you. I imagine my tenancy of this cottage was your initiative, rather than the Bursar's.'

'He did need a little prompting, I admit.'

'You have done me a great favour. What was it that you wanted to say?'

'I wanted to urge you to widen your circle of acquaintance. Accept invitations. Take up new interests. Look about you. Do not bury yourself day in day out in solitary study.'

'I see,' said Grace. 'Well, all that sounds easy enough.'

'You might also consider speaking to someone I know.'

'Oh? Who?'

'Her name is Miss Lucia Venables. The sister of Miss Christabel who runs the hat shop. Lucia runs an introduction agency, the Matters of the Heart Agency - very discreet, very proper in every way. Miss Venables introduces ladies and gentlemen seeking companionship. She selects the candidates most carefully. She really only plays the role that a careful and kindly parent might play.'

Grace laughed. 'I'm sure she does, but if I am seeking anything, it is further gainful employment. I have already written a number of hat articles, thanks to your introduction to Christabel. I make good progress with typing up the workhouse papers.'

'Several people have told me it was wrong to burden you with them.'

'Burden me? I have learnt to use the typewriter, and I have discovered a great deal about workhouses that I did not know before.'

'I was told it might distress you. Was it distressing?'

'More enlightening than distressing, although the three little girls still prey on my mind.'

'Which three little girls?'

'They are called Violet, Rose and Ivy. Mrs Lemman has kept them in the workhouse. She complains a great deal of the additional expense of it in her letters.'

'Oh dear.' Miss Froment looked off across the garden.

'The Bursar will not want to be burdened with committee problems.'

'Even so, I shall have to speak to him about it. I have no plans, however, to speak to Miss Venables about matters of my heart, but thank you for the idea. Have you asked her to act on your own behalf?'

Miss Froment looked astonished. 'Mine! Oh no! Not at all. I work all my days with gentlemen at the college. Frankly, my dear, I am glad to be without them in my own little home. Gentlemen are such tiresome creatures!'

Chapter Twenty-One

Grace presented herself at the front office of the Cambridge Chronicle the following day. She had written half a dozen more articles about hats, finding it surprisingly easy to invent themes: *Which Hats are Best for a Windy Country Walk? The Stylish Hat to Complete a Formal Outfit. Hats to Stand Out in a Summer Crowd.* Clutching them in an envelope she approached the office, carefully rehearsing the persuasive arguments she had prepared. She had not expected the loud crowd she found pressing into the tiny space between the newspaper's reception desk and the door. It seemed that half the population of Cambridge had business at the Chronicle that morning. The three young ladies behind the counter were at full stretch. Grace joined the queue behind a lady in black. The gentleman at the far counter was arguing fiercely with the clerk.

'It is a misprint!' he said, waving a folded copy of the paper. 'The name is Higginson, Archibald Higginson. Not *Hickson*. It's disgrace!'

The clerk nearest rolled her eyes slightly and gestured the lady in black forward. 'Obituary notice, is it?'

'Yes, dear. For Harold Crickett.'

'How do you spell that?' The clerk asked.

'What?'

'Crickett? Does it have two ts or one?'

The old lady looked blank. 'I couldn't tell you, dear,' she said. 'I never seen it written, and I never wrote it down myself neither. Never had call to. He was my cousin. He lived up Barnwell.'

'I need the right spelling for the death notice.'

'Well, what looks right to you?'

'They both look right, Madam. It's important to get the spelling right. It's an official notice. It's how people will remember him. You need to ask someone who knows him. And what's his middle name?'

'Middle name? I don't think he had one.'

'Most people do,' said the clerk.

'It might have been Arthur. Yes. Arthur. Or was it George?'

'You need to ask someone that too. Otherwise the whole notice might be misunderstood. There might be another man of the same name. It would cause confusion.'

The angry man at the other counter stomped away after a final threat never to buy another copy of the paper if they couldn't get the spelling of people's names right. The clerk wearily gestured to Grace to come forward.

'May I see the Editor, please?'

'He's at a meeting,' the clerk said. 'What's it concerning?'

'Hats,' said Grace.

'Are you placing an advertisement for hats?'

'No, I have written some articles about hats, and fashions. I should like them to be published in the Chronicle.'

The girl looked at Grace blankly. 'And does the editor know you? Did he commission these articles?'

'No, not yet. I was hoping he would read them and put them into the paper.'

'You can leave them with me. I'll see that he gets them.'

Grace felt suddenly protective of her envelope. 'They will definitely find him?'

'I'll see that he gets them. Is your name and address inside?'

'It is, yes.'

'Then leave it here. He'll be in touch. Next please.'

'Perhaps I will come back later,' Grace said, unable to part with her envelope. Not knowing what else to do, she turned to leave, but at the door she stumbled into Daniel Hollingdale, who was hurrying in. It had started to rain. His hat and the shoulders of his coat were dripping wet.

'Hello!' he said. 'Not in the hat shop today?'

The lady in black now wanted to leave. They had to step outside onto the pavement to let her pass, then stand against the shopfront in an attempt to keep out of the rain. Grace ignored his question.

'I had hoped to see the editor, but he is not there.'

'Ah. That is a shame. I had hoped to see him too.'

They both looked out at the rain which was hammering so hard out of a granite grey sky that the raindrops were bouncing on the cobblestones and washing in streams along the gutters. Neither had an umbrella, and water was already beginning to soak through Grace's boots.

'There is a teashop just here. I wonder, would you care to step inside? It seems unwise to stay out here and be soaked,' he said.

Chapter Twenty-Two

The teashop was crowded with others hiding from the rain, but a corner table was secured and they ordered their tea.

'What brings you to the Chronicle offices, Miss Marshall?'

'I have written some articles. I hoped the editor would consider them for publication.'

'Well, that is a coincidence. My mission was exactly the same.'

'You write?'

'Oh,' he said, 'not really. Just reviews of concerts and theatrical performances. Eddie Parks is keen on the arts, he publishes them now and then.'

'Is Mr Parks the editor?'

'You haven't met him?'

'No. I am new to all this.'

'I see. Well, he is a decent sort, but the budget is tight at the Chronicle. He's pressed constantly by the owners to increase the circulation and bring in more revenue from advertising. He can't always be as generous to freelancers as he might be. He pays me now and then, but I generally write reviews in return for free tickets.'

'My pieces are about the latest hat fashions,' Grace said.

Hollingdale nodded seriously, as if there were nothing odd about his mathematics tutor writing such articles. 'Have you been writing for long?'

'The articles I just handed in are my first attempts. In all honesty, I know very little about millinery, or fashion in general. I was trying something new.'

'But you are employed in the trade in the little hat shop?'

'I was really only visiting.'

'You sold me a hat, nonetheless!'

'Did the lady like it?'

'She shall have it tomorrow, on her birthday. I'm certain she will be delighted with it. Maison Ladoré seems to have a very fine selection. Have you known the proprietress for long?'

It was still raining cats and dogs outside. The windows of the café were steamed up, but they could see people hurrying past, hunched into their collars and clutching umbrellas.

'Not long. She asked me to write something about her designs. Until now I have only helped my late father in editing his textbooks. It was something I grew up doing.'

'Your father was well-known and respected among the mathematicians in my family.'

'Thank you. I miss him a great deal.'

'It was a sudden loss, I understand.'

'It was.'

'Your family?' he asked, after a moment.

'I have only a great aunt in Scotland, but I would rather stay here.

'Perhaps the college will send you more of their difficult undergraduates.'

'Perhaps.'

'It is honest work, Miss Marshall, teaching people like me, but not easy, I imagine.'

'I am enjoying it far more than I expected,' Grace said, in an unguarded moment.

He looked across the table at her to see how serious she was, but found it hard to tell. Grace looked out at the rain. 'I am on my way to New College to see the Bursar. I have been typewriting committee papers. Do you know anything about workhouses, Mr Hollingdale?'

'Workhouses? Nothing, I'm afraid. Except that they are best avoided. Places of misery and suffering, generally speaking. Why do you ask?'

'There were more than twenty of them in Cambridge at one time.'

'Twenty? That seems a lot.'

'There are fewer now, but still more than you might imagine. It is a world that exists in parallel to ours. I have only just discovered it. I feel shocked by how little I know.'

'About the world outside the college walls, you mean?'

'Yes. The world in general. The world of fashion, the world of poverty, orphans, workhouses, the world of newspapers, your world of music. Everything seems so much more complicated now.'

Her face, as he studied it across the table, was serious, but her eyes—such eyes!—dark brown at first sight, but on closer inspection the pupils were flecked with hazel and gold—were shining.

'You find yourself at a crossroads, I suppose,' he said.

'Yes. I hardly know where to begin!'

'That is exactly the way mathematical problems make me feel.'

Grace laughed. 'Oh but, mathematical problems are simple by comparison. There is a method; one follows the method, beginning with the obvious first step.'

'What if that doesn't work?'

'You retrace your steps until you find a point of certainty and then try something different. It always works, eventually.'

He smiled back, leaning now across the table. 'A point of certainty? Is that guaranteed?'

'Of course.'

'What if there is no certainty?'

Grace put her head on one side, looking at him steadily across the table. He had an odd sensation in his chest, as if someone had tightened an internal string. 'There always is,' she said. 'You just have to find it. The difficult part is abandoning what you were doing and setting off in a different direction.'

They both heard a bell chime the hour in the distance. Daniel started. 'My apologies, I must get to the chapel. I must not be late. Please excuse my hurried exit, Miss Marshall. I'll settle the bill on the way out. I shall see you for my lesson tomorrow morning.'

Chapter Twenty-Three

It was still raining, but less vigorously, when Grace arrived at New College. 'I should like to see the Bursar, please, George,' Grace told the Head Porter, after they had exchanged greetings.

'I believe he is in his office. Shall I send a messenger to tell him you're here, Miss Marshall?'

'No thank you. I'll just go up. I won't keep him long.'

Grace strode around the familiar courtyard and up the winding stone stairs to the Bursar's office. He was at his desk.

'Miss Marshall. Everything is comfortable at your new residence, I trust?' he said. His words were friendly enough but his expression was less than welcoming.

'Everything is comfortable, thank you. I wanted to raise another matter. I am typewriting papers from one of your committees.'

'Are you? Why would that be?'

'The office was looking for someone to help with the task. I accepted the commission.'

'I see.'

'They are the papers about St Benet's workhouse, wanted by the inspector.

I wondered how familiar you were with the contents?'

'General correspondence about the running of the place, I imagine,' he said, showing very little interest.

'They reveal some details which I believe need your attention.'

'I shall be the judge of that, I think.'

'They seem important.'

'Your commission was to typewrite these documents. Not to analyse them. Leave them with Miss Froment if the contents are not to your liking.' He looked down at the papers on his desk, dismissively.

Grace continued, 'Most of the records are new, but some date back much further. They show that children occasionally pass through the workhouse. Small children and infants. They are documented as arriving and then they leave. Where they go is not clearly recorded.'

'I can't occupy myself with the minutiae. I sit on many committees, Miss Marshall.'

'But there are three children there now, according to these papers, and they appear to be sick and poorly cared for.'

'You can tell all this from the minutes of meetings?'

'In this latest case—the three little girls—there are also letters, and notes from the doctor. Mrs Lemman petitions constantly for more funds to pay for their needs. She plans to send them to the National Home.'

'I'm not sure why this concerns myself, or the college.'

'They are not being well cared-for.'

'Mrs Lemman is perfectly competent. The workhouse is

inspected regularly and found to be meeting the standard required.'

'The standard must be a very low one, if it leaves three little girls shut up for an indefinite period in a sick room,' Grace said.

His expression did not change, but a different light came into his eye.

'Have you taken up social campaigning in the few days since you left the Master's Lodge, Miss Marshall? How very admirable.'

'I thought you would want to know, and to take action. My father, when he was Master, would certainly not have wanted the college to be connected in any way with an establishment that treated helpless children cruelly.'

'Your father's demise was a great loss to the college, Miss Marshall, but there is a new Master now. When he is installed, this sort of matter will fall under his remit. Until then, I am holding the fort, so to speak, and I can only tell you that I have dealt with that Union Board, and with Mrs Lemman for at least a decade, and that during that time there have been many inspections that found both Mrs Lemman and the general running of the workhouse perfectly adequate. Thank you for your concern. I think it would be better if you returned the papers as soon as possible to Miss Froment's charge. They clearly contain matters you find distressing.'

'So no action is to be taken?'

'I shall bear what you have said in mind, and I shall certainly read through the papers myself, but Miss Marshall, I sit on at least a dozen charitable committees of one sort or another. I cannot be expected to follow every last detail. I assure you, if action is required, I shall make the necessary arrangements, but the new Master would need to approve any changes. The next inspection is due shortly, if I remember rightly.'

'These children are sick already. They need help sooner than that.'

'A doctor is paid a regular fee to see all patients at the workhouse. Mrs Lemman calls upon his services as necessary. These papers will already be out of date. She has in all likelihood moved these unfortunate infants away already, and seen to it that they received the treatment they needed. Now, Miss Marshall, if you will excuse me, I have a great deal of college business to complete before the arrival of the new Master. I shall send a porter to collect the papers. Frankly, I wonder what Miss Froment was thinking, allowing them to leave college premises. You need trouble yourself with them no further.'

What made Grace divert from her homeward path and slip into the back of the chapel was uncertain. She was seething with irritation at the Bursar's dismissal of her worries about the workhouse; perhaps it was that. Perhaps she was simply drawn to a calm place where she could gather her thoughts. Whatever the reason, she approached, slipped through the half open doors at the back of New College's familiar wood-vaulted chapel, and slid into one of the carved wooden pews that lined the walls. A small rehearsal organ was playing, and a number of singers were standing near it among the choir stalls along with the Director of Music, a short man in a billowing black gown. They were talking among themselves, at first, but then the music changed and they began to sing.

Grace knew very little about music. Just how little was driven home to her that afternoon as the final rays of the sun sloped their way through the high stained glass windows and illuminated the young men singing. She guessed that what she heard was the music of Bach, but it might have been Handel or someone completely different. Anyway, their interweaving harmonies seemed to Grace to follow one another in long ribbons, spooling out as effortlessly as if the choristers simply breathed them. The sounds filled the lofty chapel, seeming to lift the air and come to Grace from every side at once. The lyrics, perhaps they were in German, were absorbed and borne along by the music. Now and again the singers reached a conclusion, or an interval, but they only paused for the briefest moment before continuing. It was an experience of being bathed, submerged, washed away in music, such as Grace had never known before.

Then, just as easily as they had begun, the singers completed their final chord and the rehearsal was over.

'Very good. Until tomorrow. Don't forget the music for the G Minor Mass.'

The choristers, their work done, began to disperse. It was only then that Grace recognised Daniel Hollingdale among them. He remained, in conversation with the musical director. They seemed to disagree about a certain line of music.

'No, you hold the note there,' the Director of Music said. He hummed a note or two, picking out a melody on the keyboard before pointing to the score they were both studying.

Daniel, reading from his score, sang the note and the few notes beyond it.

'Yes. I have it.'

Both nodded, closed their scores, satisfied, and turned to leave. Not wanting them to pass and see her, Grace slipped out of her seat and left the chapel, crossed to the main gate and started for home.

It was late afternoon. People were leaving offices and shops in town for home. Grace walked towards Station Road with the sounds of the choir and organ still playing in her ears. Listening to the music there in the chapel, was exactly as she imagined heaven. What must it be like to live your daily life among such music? Hearing it, singing it, knowing it so well? It certainly hadn't changed Daniel into an angelic being. It was all very strange.

Chapter Twenty-Four

'Workhouses?' Eddie Parks leaned back in his chair. The rest of the Chronicle's untidy offices were empty. It was nearly seven in the evening and everyone else had left for home. 'Why are you asking about workhouses?'

Grace was sitting in a well-worn visitor's chair, 'I heard something,' she said.

Thursday was publication day for the Chronicle, so by Wednesday evening the paper was being printed, and apart from the editor, the staff had left to catch their breath before the weekly routine began again. Grace had spotted the lights in the office as she passed. She still had the articles she had written in her bag. The door of the office was open, so she ventured inside, and finding the front office empty, went through another door into a large open office. The editor's office was off to one side, signed and lit, so she knocked on the door. Afterwards she decided this sudden onrush of courage must have been due to the music of Bach. There was no other explanation.

Eddie Parks turned out to be a man in his late forties

who was drinking a glass of brandy and sitting with his feet on the desk. He made no attempt to move or put down his glass when he called 'come in'.

'Mr Parks?' Grace had asked.

'Yes?' He had said it with a sigh. He had been enjoying the Wednesday evening peace.

'I have written some articles about hats. I hoped you might publish them,' Grace said.

'Did you indeed?' He looked Grace over for a moment, then stretched a hand out and took the envelope she was holding. Pulling her articles out of the envelope, he ran a professional eye over them, before dropping them on the desk. 'Alright,' he said, 'they'll probably do for the Ladies of Cambridge column, but you'll have to write about other shops and not just this Maison Whatever-it-is.'

'Ladoré,' Grace said.

'They seem the right sort of thing, but they all mention a single shop. That won't do. I need as many shops as possible to be named, so that they all pay for advertising. With a bit of luck they will get into competition with one another for advertising space, and I can sell more.'

'Is there a payment for such articles?' Grace asked.

'Lineage,' he said.

'What is lineage?'

'You are paid by the line, Miss …'

'Marshall,' she told him.

He tutted and rolled his eyes, as if the name in itself were mildly annoying.

Grace had never been spoken to as rudely before. He still had his feet on the desk. A gentleman would have stood up. A gentleman would have introduced himself. It was infuriating, but at least she felt no obligation to be polite back.

'Farthing a line,' he said. 'Or thruppence a column inch.'

'So each of these would earn me …?'

He glanced over at the typewritten pile of papers containing her articles. 'About one and six.'

'And you would use one a week?'

'Probably,' he said. 'The first two or three would have to be a trial. In case the readers didn't take to you and your hats.' For some reason this thought amused Parks, making him chuckle wheezily to himself.

'One and six a week is not a great deal,' Grace remarked.

'It is the going rate. Have you written for many other newspapers, Miss Marshall?'

'No. None.'

'This is your first attempt?' he nodded towards the articles.

'Yes.'

'Well, they're not bad, from what I've seen. But one and six is all you'll get from the Chronicle.'

'I accept. If there is any other work—any other writing—available, I would be glad to hear about it.'

'I'll bear you in mind.' Parks said, in dismissal. 'Close the door on your way out.'

It was then that Grace asked about workhouses. The question caused a different manner in Parks. He registered something approaching interest.

'They're closing them down. High time too. Fearful places,' the editor said. 'I ran a story or two last year. Irregularities in accounts. And someone died suspiciously at one of the smaller workhouses out towards Ely.'

'They still serve a purpose, though, surely?'

'They were built with good enough intentions, but that

was years ago. In practice the system has never been anything but harsh. And the parishes penny-pinch. Terrible food, poor buildings and so on. What makes you concern yourself with workhouses, Miss Marshall?'

'There might be a workhouse taking in children, I heard.'

'Children should go to the big orphanage at Haverhill, not the workhouses. Or there are foster homes.'

'Would you publish it, if I could find enough for a piece about bad practice at one of the workhouses?'

Parks sipped his brandy. He looked only slightly interested. 'If the police brought charges, I would. I can't run with anything unsubstantiated. You'd need a good set of evidence. And it would have to be something big. A few pounds missing in the accounts of a run-down workhouse doesn't amount to much of a story.'

'There might be something underhand going on. It involves these children, I think.'

'Your proof would need to be very good indeed before I could run a story like that.'

'But if it were good?'

'A scandal involving local children would sell a lot of papers. Especially if there were illustrations. The reading public loves an illustration of a poor orphan.'

'That is certainly an unsentimental view of the welfare of children, Mr Parks.'

Parks shrugged, finished his brandy and shook the empty glass. 'It's been a long week. I may be a little less harsh after another of these. Come back with the article when you've written it. I'll have a look.'

Chapter Twenty-Five

Edith Hollingdale was so taken with her birthday hat that she declared the day a holiday and proposed an outing and luncheon in a restaurant. She was still pale from her recent illness, but her brother agreed the fresh air would do her good.

They strolled along the Backs, where bluebells were flowering under the trees in the garden of St John's College. He told his sister about the near disaster in the hat shop, and about meeting the salesgirl who surprisingly turned out also to be his mathematics tutor. By the time they reached the mill pond, he had told her about their meeting at the newspaper office as well. The mathematical hat lady had, Edith calculated, already occupied twenty-five minutes of her brother's conversation.

'I think you might have a bee in your bonnet about this girl, Daniel,' his sister remarked.

'What? Oh no, I was only... it was just fresh in my mind,' he said, startled.

Edith smiled. 'Is she a presentable young lady?'

'Oh stop!'

'Why should I not ask? I might like to meet her myself.'

'I hardly know her.'

'There would be no harm in it, you know.'

'No harm in what?'

'In furthering your acquaintance with a pleasant young woman. You seem to have set your face against such things, lately.'

He fell silent. They had reached Silver Street bridge and paused to look over it along the pretty view of the river running beneath Queen's College walls, and the mathematical bridge.

'Let's find some lunch,' his sister said. 'I suggest the Copper Kettle.'

'That seems a modest choice for a birthday luncheon.'

'We have a modest budget, besides, they do very fine mushrooms on toast, which is exactly what I hanker for.'

'Are you sure? I could truly run to something grander. The Chronicle bought two of my reviews lately.'

'That is kind, but I choose the mushrooms at the Copper Kettle.'

'Speaking of having bees in bonnets,' Daniel said, once they had taken a table in the window of the Copper Kettle. 'How is young Doctor Sallett?'

'Very well, I believe.' his sister replied, looking down at her knife and fork.

'You have seen him since last week?'

'Perhaps.'

'Now Biddy, you cannot withhold that sort of information from me, I am your favourite brother, and I can read you like a book.'

His sister made a face. 'We have met, yes. He comes from a family of eleven children, he told me.'

'Eleven!'

'Four of the sons are doctors. Medicine is the family business.'

'In Dorset, was it?'

'Yes. Bridport. His mother breeds champion racehorses, apparently.'

'Good heavens! The Salletts sound a force to be reckoned with.'

'It's an army, isn't it? That many brothers and sisters and all their husbands and wives and children. A sort of tidal wave of Salletts. I'm not sure I could face it.'

'Might you need to face it? I mean will you take things further with the good doctor?'

'He is good company,' she said, but sounding sad.

'Then why not?'

'I am so ill. I am no fun. I can offer very little.'

'Biddy! That is untrue.'

She looked down her mushrooms and shook her head.

'Besides, Sallett knows all about your health. As a doctor, he knows your situation.'

She looked back at him, the sadness of her expression touching his own heart. 'I fear he might be motivated mainly by pity.'

'No! Surely not. Don't underestimate him.'

She turned away and looked out of the window. The view was of the ornate front gate of King's College across the road. A porter in a top hat stood in the entrance.

'We are both of us hesitant, aren't we?' she said.

'Hesitant about making new friends?'

'Yes. For different reasons, perhaps. I am afraid that my illness will only make someone else unhappy, if they become too fond of me. You seem to hesitate because—well, I'm not sure. Why do you hold back, Daniel?'

Her brother looked over at King's College himself. The sky above it was pale and streaked with grey cloud. 'My future is so uncertain. I may soon be thrown out of college in disgrace. I had hoped to make a life in music, but that offers very little security at the best of times. Without my degree, I shall be lucky to find work in an orchestra pit. A hand to mouth existence stretches ahead, not to mention a possible court appearance.'

'Father would not see you starve, Daniel. He would find you work.'

'As a clerk, perhaps. It would kill me to work in one of his offices, Biddy.'

'You are extremely talented! Your music is going well. Your compositions are admired. The mathematical hat lady…'

'…Her name is Grace Marshall…'

'Well, someone like Grace Marshall would listen to your point of view. I'm sure she would.'

'She is brilliantly clever.'

'And lovely?' His sister was teasing.

'Yes! She is intelligent and beautiful. Why should she have anything to do with me—a troublemaker and a duffer about to appear in court and be sent down from college in disgrace?'

She nodded. 'What a gloomy pair we are, hiding from life in our different ways! These mushrooms are good, though.'

'They are. And your hat, my dear sister, is the handsomest I have seen in Cambridge today.'

'I honestly think it might be,' she agreed, touching it and smiling back at him.

Chapter Twenty-Six

Dr Hillyer visited Abercrombie Cottage that Friday. It was a fine afternoon and Grace had propped the cottage door open. Several chickens, now identifying Grace as their friend and source of food, had wandered over to visit and were pecking and scratching in the sunny grass just outside. Grace was at the table, sorting the papers from the workhouse box. In particular she was trying to dust and straighten one package of papers that was sooty and blackened. These seemed to be accounts stretching back over several years.

Hillyer picked his way between the chickens, shooing them away with his feet. He was carrying a small bunch of anemones.

'Ah, Grace. Hard at work, I see. You are alone?'

In answer to this question Alice appeared from the kitchen, wiping her hands on her apron, but retreated when she saw the guest.

'So, this is your new abode?' Hillyer said. He stepped in and looked around, his expression uncertain. 'Well, it is altogether different from the Master's Lodge! Quite an adjustment. Not too distressing for you, I hope.' Hillyer stood in the middle of the small room and glanced around him with a look Grace could only interpret as fastidious disapproval.

'Distressing? Why should it be distressing?'

'You are very pastoral here. I imagine this was a gardener's cottage. It hardly compares to the Master's Lodge at New College. You had a cook and a butler there, didn't you? Here you have nothing but chickens for company.'

'The cook and butler were long gone by the time I moved,' Grace said. 'They were only ever for special occasions.'

'Even so, this place is very small. It would be perfectly understandable if you felt a certain loss of—well, of status. In a way, it is this that brings me here today. I wish to speak to you, Grace, on a serious matter.'

'Perhaps you had better sit down, Dr Hillyer,' Grace said. She led him to the only two chairs - rustic stick-back affairs Hillyer had only ever imagined in a servant's kitchen. He placed the flowers, still wrapped in their paper, on the table between them, having forgotten to present them.

'May I offer some tea?'

'I should prefer to pursue my topic without delay.'

'I see.'

'Grace, you are aware, of course, that I took up a post in Zurich last year. It is a teaching post. The institution is of the highest reputation.'

'So I believe,' Grace said.

'I have made a good impression there, though I say it myself. My teaching attracts a wide range of the most promising students.'

'I'm sure it does.'

A loud clatter of iron pans on a stone floor was heard all of a sudden from the kitchen. Both looked that way in alarm, but no other noise followed.

Hillyer continued. 'My salary is—well, I shall only say that it is commensurate with the responsibilities I hold in that worthy institution. I shall shortly be publishing my work on the German and Austrian developments in the study of algebra. I'm told it is widely anticipated.'

'How interesting.' Grace was, indeed, curious about this topic, and would have discussed it with pleasure, if the gentleman opposite had been looking at her. Instead, he was frowning and looking intently at the surface of the table.

'I am, in addition, possessed of an independent allowance from my family. They are in farming and land, in the West Country, mostly.'

'I see,' Grace said.

Had Dr Hillyer looked up, he might have noticed that she did not appear particularly enthusiastic about any of this. He did not look up. He ploughed on. 'Miss Marshall, I know that the death of your father is still very recent, but I …'

Another tremendous crash shook the rafters of the little cottage. It sounded as if Alice had hurled every pot and pan in the kitchen simultaneously onto the flagstone floor. Grace rose and hurried out of the room.

Hillyer shook his head and sighed.

A pair of chickens wandered into the room and began pecking at the rug.

'Shoo!' he told them, flapping a hand. The sooner Grace could be given a proper home—a city home, well away from invading poultry and furniture that looked as if a farmer had knocked it together, the better.

Grace returned. 'Nothing to worry about. A shelf just fell off the wall,' she said.

'It truly grieves my heart to see you here in such surroundings.'

'Oh, does it?' she asked. 'It is a peaceful enough place, usually. Alice wasn't to know that the shelf was badly fixed to the wall. The college has lent me a handyman. He will repair it by the end of the day, if I know James.'

'You face your change in circumstances with admirable stoicism. I do so admire it in you.'

Hillyer felt this was a promising theme and was about to expound further on his admiration, having memorised one or two sentiments he thought would set the right tone, when he was interrupted by the sudden arrival of a third chicken, who on examination turned out to be the cockerel.

The bird strode across the room and squared up to Dr Hillyer, craning its neck and raising its wings as if challenging him. He seemed to suspect Dr Hillyer of stealing the two youngest chickens in his flock.

'Oh! I say! I think this bird is…going to attack!' Hillyer said. He grabbed the flowers from the table and held them in front of his face. 'Miss Marshall! He wants to fight me! Get behind! He may go for you too!'

Grace stood and walked to the door. All three birds immediately fell in behind her and followed, squawking, up the garden. She returned alone after only a few moments, having shut them into their run.

Hillyer was looking annoyed. 'It is not safe for that bird to be wandering uncaged. Evil-looking creatures. They often attack human beings, you know,' he said.

'I apologise, Dr Hillyer. I have the care of the chickens, so they know me, and it has led them to assume they can wander into the house whenever they please.'

'Why do you have to care for them? Surely the maid should do that? Or a groundsman?'

'They come with the cottage, I was told. I am happy to do it.'

'Good heavens! They expect you to act as a poultry farmer? Do they not know who you are? It seems a disgraceful insult to the daughter of a late Master of a college.'

'It really is no hardship. I have quite taken to them. They are agreeable enough in their own way. I never cared for an animal before.'

'Nor should you have to now! Allow me, please, to speak to someone at the college in the strongest possible terms.'

'I would rather you did not.'

'You are afraid they will take it badly, and that you will risk your tenancy? I would not permit it!'

Chapter Twenty-Seven

'Please Dr Hillyer, let's leave the subject of the chickens now. Tell me more about mathematics at Zurich, I am keen to know how they approach things there. I believe there are a fair number of women students at the university. Do any study mathematics with you?'

'Two, I think. One Swiss, one French.'

'How marvellous! And they study exactly as the gentlemen study? And are permitted to graduate and earn their degrees?'

'As far as I know, yes. But I am not aware of the details of these young women's arrangements.'

'You do not approve of women students?'

'I can't say that I do. It appears to me, frankly, to be rather a waste of my teaching time. The female brain—there are scientific studies to demonstrate that this is true—the female brain is not structured for the retention of scientific or mathematical learning. Not beyond a certain level, at least. An intelligent young woman, such as your good self, can retain the fundamentals of the subject in such a way as to provide valuable assistance, but one does not look to the ladies for advanced or original work of any sort. I have read this in several learned sources, and from my own experience I would definitely say it is true. Wouldn't you agree?' He inclined his head toward her, smiling.

'I would *not* agree,' Grace said.

This was not the reply Dr Hillyer was expecting. He blinked and shook his head a little. 'But you must admit that none of history's great theorists has been a woman. Can you name a single great mathematical thinker of the female persuasion? I don't believe you can. No. The ladies have their own role—an essential one—that of procreation! Where would we be if young women in large numbers gave themselves over to abstract thought instead of bearing children and raising the next generation, as nature intended?' Dr Hillyer chuckled merrily at this ridiculous idea and seemed surprised when Grace did not laugh at it too.

Grace looked away for a moment. Her eye alighted on the box of papers from the workhouse and she was struck by a thought. 'What do you know of workhouses?' she asked.

Hillyer was jolted by this sudden change of subject. 'Workhouses?'

'Yes. Institutions for the poor. To house them, and so on. There are many in Cambridge.'

'Perhaps there are, but why should I know of them?'

'I just wondered whether you had any sense of how they were run. You might have been on a committee while you were here. Or been caught up in some charitable work. Many university men are.'

'I tended to confine my charitable work to the university's own committees,' Hillyer said. 'I was active in supporting the Light Opera Society, for one.'

Grace did not seem to hear that. 'The university does not have a workhouse committee, then?' she asked.

'The university occupies itself with the welfare of the more deserving poor. The Poor Law Unions look after the workhouses, as far as I know. They are quite separate. But why do you ask?'

'I need to ask someone about workhouses. I don't know where to start.'

'If I may say so, Grace, I see no good reason for you to occupy yourself with such unwholesome matters.'

'You do not believe I should occupy myself with mathematics or take an interest in conditions in workhouses,' Grace said. 'I imagine you do not approve of my writing about hats for the newspaper either. Dr Hillyer, you disapprove of everything I do. Even looking after the chickens. I am surprised that you trouble yourself to visit me at all.'

Hillyer was brought to a halt by that, but only for a moment. 'I do so because I wish to offer you another future, Grace. A different, far better future.'

Hillyer leaned towards Grace across the table, his elbows pressing forward in a sudden, urgent movement, but before he could say more, the table top flipped, hurling the flowers in one direction and a small jug in the other. The jug smashed on the floor so violently that pieces flew, bouncing and spinning to all four corners of the room, and the water it had held arced through the air and splashed onto Dr Hillyer's trousers. Hillyer leapt to his feet, shaking his leg, attempting to brush the water away.

Both Alice and James ran into the room. Alice began collecting the pieces of the broken jug. James picked up the table top and examined it.

'I'll fetch a cloth for your trousers, sir,' Alice said.

'Don't trouble yourself. I am leaving,' said Hillyer. He stood, looking extremely annoyed, and took a step towards the door, but then stopped, bent to pick up the flowers he had brought, still in their wrapper, and carried them off with him as he left.

Chapter Twenty-Eight

'Alice reports an attempted proposal,' Lucia remarked. She was in Maison Ladoré, sitting in front of one of the mirrors modelling a striking blue hat. Her sister placed a scarlet silk poppy on the brim and stood back to examine the effect.

'Alice? Who is Alice?'

'One of Miss Froment's domestics from New College. She is helping Miss Marshall to settle in her new house. Miss Froment recruited her to the cause, at my suggestion.'

'You and Miss Froment have *spies* working in Miss Marshall's house?'

'I wouldn't call them spies, exactly, but yes, Alice, the maid, and James, one of the college handymen. He is carrying out repairs. The cottage is old. Miss Froment confided in them, and they agreed to report it, if any gentleman were to approach Miss Marshall.'

'But the Wrong Suitor went so far as to attempt a proposal, all the same?' Christabel removed the red poppy, and replaced it with a gold silk chrysanthemum, standing back again to check the difference.

'They are a resourceful pair, Alice and James. It's fair to say that they have thrown themselves into the work. I don't know what the gentleman has done to offend them, but they are utterly determined to prevent him approaching Miss Marshall. Alice caused a ruckus by throwing pots and pans in the kitchen while he was attempting, but the big success went to James, who loosened the table top so that anyone who leant on it would tip it over.'

'Well done, James!'

'And wait until you hear this. The Unwanted Admirer had brought flowers - nothing much, a few anemones - but when he left in a temper, he actually took them with him!'

'Reclaimed his flowers? That is a very poor reflection of character. Who is this hopeful?'

'An academic, don't you remember?'

'Ah yes, and Miss Froment dislikes him, but would not say why, exactly.'

'It sounds as if her instincts are sound. James and Alice certainly agree. It was rather a brilliant idea I came up with. Engagement prevention turns out to be quite an enjoyable commission.'

'As long as he only approaches Miss Marshall when she is at home. What if this unwanted admirer strikes in another place, or writes her a letter?'

'The Moth Agency has contacts all over the city,' Lucia said, 'I have put them on alert. I have already used Victor and his spaniels. That worked very well.'

Christabel looked impressed, but then turned her attention back to the decoration of the hat. 'The red or the gold?'

Lucia turned her head to see the flower in the mirror. 'The gold, definitely.'

'Agreed.'

Chapter Twenty-Nine

'Hello!'

Grace was making notes for Daniel Hollingdale's next lesson, when a voice called from the front door and a young woman peered in.

'You are Miss Marshall?'

'Yes?' Grace said. She couldn't help staring. Her attention was held by the girl's short hair. The visitor wore no hat, and her curly brown hair was no more than three inches long all over, something Grace had never seen on a young woman before.

'You are tutoring my brother, I believe. I wonder if I might have a word?'

'Your brother is Daniel Hollingdale?'

'Yes. I am Edith Hollingdale, but people call me Biddy. How do you do?'

Edith stepped forward and held out her hand, which surprised Grace, but she shook it nonetheless. 'I have come to ask a favour, Miss Marshall. It may surprise you, but I shall ask it all the same, if I may.'

'You may ask, certainly.' There was something lively and energetic about this short-haired young woman in brown tweed. It was hard to resist her energy.

'My brother is no good at maths. He tries, but, all the mathematical brains went elsewhere in the family. He is a dear chap, but in maths he is an absolute duffer. I, on the other hand, am pretty good. The Hollingdale gift came to me. May I sit down?'

Grace gestured to the chair.

'The problem is, you see, that my Papa and my brothers don't see that it does any good for a girl to study mathematics - not beyond the basics anyway. I fancied university, but I was sent to finishing school in Paris to learn French and deportment, cookery, gracious hostessing, and so on. Paris was entertaining enough, but I should like to pursue the university idea, now that I am over twenty-one and more independent. When I say independent, I mean I am free to make my own choices, but I am short of funds, so if I am to study, I shall need to compete for scholarships. I need to be better than the chaps, in other words.'

Grace could only nod in the face of this onrush of information.

'I was wondering whether you would give me some lessons, but without telling Daniel? I could help Daniel then, between his classes, and motivate him—force him, if necessary—to do his work, and at the same time I could extend my own knowledge.'

'Well...' Grace began.

'No! Please let me make my offer before you decide.' Edith held up her hands. 'I cannot pay a fee—not as such—but I can offer payment in kind, you see.'

'Payment in kind? For maths tuition?'

'Yes. I have a great many practical skills. My father was

in favour of that part of my education, so I can sew well and dance, and cook in both the French and the English manner. Plain food and proper French dinners, I can do them all. I sewed this skirt - look it is adapted for cycling.'

She held aside a panel of the skirt to show it was cleverly divided into culottes. 'I can ride a horse, of course, but also a bicycle - I could teach you that, if you wanted to learn - and I can advise on fashions. The French finishing school was full of nonsense, but they were very keen on us looking our best. I know all the theory, even if I can't be bothered with a lot of it. You know, which gloves to wear to the opera, how to dress for a hunt ball or a morning call on a weekday, that sort of thing.'

Grace could only blink. 'Well, I'm not sure…'

'You have not lived alone for long, I imagine,' Edith looked around at the boxes. 'You may not be a skilful cook yourself. Perhaps you employ a cook?'

Grace laughed at that. 'I employ nobody. The college has lent me a maid, but I will soon need to cook for myself.'

'And are you a cook? Have you the skills?'

'Not really, no.'

'Then I can teach you that. There's nothing to it.' She leapt to her feet again. 'No need to give me an answer immediately. Here is my card. Think my idea over in your own time. I feel sure it will work.'

'Has your brother agreed to this?'

'I haven't mentioned it to him. I would rather he did not know my plan to study just yet. But if I know what he's working on, I can keep his nose to the grindstone, so to speak.'

Grace experienced a vivid mental image of Daniel Hollingdale's rather agreeably freckled nose being pressed to a revolving grindstone. An idea struck her.

'Could we combine your skills?' she asked. 'Could you show me how to cook a few simple dishes, and while doing so, talk to me a little about fashion? Hats in particular? Oh, and did you say you knew how to dance?'

'Hats are easy. I spent quite some time exploring hat shops in Paris.'

'You don't wear a hat now, though, I see.'

'I have a beret somewhere,' Edith said. 'My brother chose me a delightful hat for my birthday. I believe it was with your assistance. He talks rather a lot about you. I keep it for best. Delving into her skirt's deep pockets she produced a little brown beret and twirled it on her finger. 'A beret is the perfect hat for cycling, in my view.' She plonked it onto her head in a single careless movement, and yet the beret ended up elegantly settled among her short curls.

Inexperienced as she was in the world of fashion, this instinctive stylishness impressed Grace.

'You mentioned dancing too, I think. What sort of dancing did you have in mind?'

'Any sort. A waltz, perhaps, to begin with?'

'Easily done. You'll learn in no time.'

'You could come on Monday at ten o'clock, that is well after your brother has left.'

'Thank you. And after a little mathematics, we shall cook an omelette. You keep hens, I see.'

'Yes. They will supply the eggs.'

'Are my bother's lessons going well, if you don't mind my asking? It is really very important for him to pass this examination.'

'He is certainly working hard,' Grace said, carefully.

They were interrupted by the postman knocking on the door. 'Letters for Miss Marshall?' He said. He handed Grace a pile of envelopes.

'A dozen letters! You must be popular,' Biddy said.

Grace cut the letters open and glanced through the first two. 'I am not popular, if these are anything to go by. Not popular at all. I wrote to a number of heads of committees and other officials. They have not taken kindly to my letters,' Grace said, using a table knife to open the rest of the envelopes.

'You are campaigning?'

'Some children in a workhouse. Nobody wants to know.'

'What will you do?'

Grace unfolded two more letters, glanced at them and shook her head. 'I'm at a loss. Keep writing until someone is prompted to act, I suppose,' she said.

Chapter Thirty

There was a new visitor at Professor Toft's tea in Abercrombie House that afternoon. He was introduced as Hugh Roberts, and was a short, fierce Welshman with bushy eyebrows.

'Dr Roberts is from Cardiff University. He is researching - what is it Roberts?'

'Medieval Welsh poetry. They have a number of promising manuscripts in Trinity library,' Roberts said, bowing to Grace.

'How are your lessons with the Hollingdale boy?' asked the Professor.

'We make progress,' Grace said, wondering whether the professor ever did anything but look out of his window.

'I saw a young woman leave earlier. Lively young creature on a bicycle.'

'That is Edith Hollingdale, Daniel's sister.'

'She chaperones him? Very proper. I'm glad to see the proprieties observed at the cottage.'

'Edith is studying mathematics as well.'

'Really? At Girton?'

'She is aiming for a degree, but is only at the preparatory stage at present.'

'Well!' said the Professor. 'Another mathematical young lady. They seem to be multiplying!' This little joke made him cough with laughter so hard that he almost dropped the slice of seedy cake Mrs Mills had handed him. The Welshman looked disapproving.

'I for one am all in favour of the education of young women. I'd fill the universities with them, if I could!' he remarked.

'Women students are free to attend many German universities. Would you call yourself an advocate of women's rights, Dr Roberts?' asked the Count.

'Indeed I would. I am a suffragist and a socialist! I have written at length about the education of women.'

'Good heavens,' said the professor. 'We have radicals in our midst!'

'You do indeed!' Dr Roberts looked around at his hosts challengingly. Mrs Mills handed him a slice of cake with an expression that suggested radical ideas were not to her taste. 'Social reform is cause that is very dear to me. Frightful poverty and exploitation we have endured in Wales. The miners most of all. Nobody could live in my country without seeing the injustice of it.'

'Do you know about the running of workhouses?' Grace asked.

'I do, as it happens. Most are a disgrace. They are characterised by a deliberate lack of generosity to the unfortunates souls obliged to live in them,' he said. 'It often amounts to cruelty.'

'Do they accommodate orphan children?'

'They did once. On the whole, children are moved to special orphan homes or foster parents these days.'

'Everybody says that.'

'Why do you mention children?'

'I have seen documents from a particular local workhouse. There seem to be all sorts of irregularities in the record-keeping. Above all, there is a regular intake of children. Infants. They stay for a while and then move on, but where they go is never very clear.'

'That could be a case of baby farming,' Roberts said. 'I have read of such cases before, in London.'

'*Baby farming*? What is that?'

'The ruthless exploitation of the poor is what it is. There have been several prosecutions.'

'How does one farm babies?' Grace asked him.

Roberts shook his head. 'By taking infants from mothers who cannot support them and trading them to the highest bidder. Given the conditions the poorest women live in, there is no shortage. The children are kept in appalling conditions. Many simply die. It can be highly profitable.'

The rest of the company in Professor Toft's living room had fallen silent. Along with Grace, they could only stare at him, appalled.

'But if the woman who runs this workhouse were doing such a terrible thing, why would she keep records? She would surely just hide them. She writes their names and ages and writes constant letters to the board asking for funds to cover the expense of them.'

'Well, there you have it. She will be paid by the Board for the upkeep of these children, by writing them into the records she gains more money. So she is paid by the parents, the adopters, and the Board. Quite a nice little profit, if you're ruthless enough.'

'But don't the Board notice? Surely they would see that children come and go through the registers. There are inspectors.'

Roberts shook his head. 'Corruption frequently runs through the whole system. The inspectors themselves might be paid a dividend to turn a blind eye.'

'There are three little children there now. They are supposed to go to the National Home in Haverhill.'

'Heaven help them,' he said. 'I can only hope that the National Home is not as grim as the one I saw in Cardiff last year. The place was a death trap. It was rife with disease. Conditions you wouldn't keep a dog in.'

Grace looked at him in horror. 'I thought it would be a safe haven, a place they could escape the workhouse. I thought perhaps the National Home would find them a kind foster home where they could all stay together.'

'Siblings were routinely separated in the home I saw.'

'Their names are Rose, Ivy and Violet,' Grace said.

'Whose names are these?'

'The three little girls in the papers I am typewriting.'

Roberts sighed. 'Endearing names, but I fear that is all they have on their side. Good luck to them.'

'There must be *something* to be done,' she said.

'Well, yes. Find a solution to poverty and despair. Find a solution to injustice, corruption and mismanagement!' Roberts said, 'And when you do, please let the rest of us know, Miss Marshall.'

Chapter Thirty-One

'I am not interrupting, I hope,' Daniel said. He had returned unexpectedly in the late afternoon of Monday and found Grace in the garden with the chickens. She had taken to cleaning their house weekly and was wearing an apron and carrying a bucket. She looked charming, he thought, like the sort of pretty country maiden he had seen modelled in china on people's mantlepieces.

'Not at all,' she said, 'But I need to continue this work, so you can come with me.'

'I hope you don't mind my calling unannounced. I have something for you.'

'Would you mind holding this bucket?' Grace said.

James the handyman was still whitewashing the outside of the cottage walls. He looked the visitor over rather carefully from a distance.

Daniel, who was wearing clothes smart enough for a chapel choir rehearsal, held the bucket carefully at arm's length. He was startled to notice that Grace's presence filled him with unaccountable joy. Seeing her was like drinking champagne. He repressed that foolish thought immediately and said, 'I found something in one of the textbooks.'

'Can you hold a chicken?'

'I beg your pardon?'

'Could you grasp one readily, if I handed it to you?'

'I imagine so,' he said, slightly appalled. His was a city upbringing. He had never held a chicken in his life. He hoped he could rise to the occasion.

'I'm not sure how to catch one. Perhaps if I scatter some food?' Grace said. 'Food works for most things with a chicken.'

She dropped a small handful of grain and the hens rushed over to peck at it. 'It is this white one I need to catch,' she said. The white hen was eager enough for the food, but was also quick to dodge Grace, clucking indignantly and flapping her wings.

'Why do you need to catch her?'

'The professor says I am to clip her wings. She flies away otherwise.'

'Will it hurt her?'

'No. I will only trim her feathers. They have no sensation. It's like a haircut, apparently, but if I cut the right flight feathers she will no longer be able to fly away and eat next door's bedding plants. There have been complaints.'

'Perhaps if we tried a pincer movement. I could come at her from the left, and you from the right,' he suggested.

They did so, but the chicken saw them and sprang away again.

'A remarkable number of proverbial sayings come from the sphere of chickens and chicken keeping, Miss Marshall, had you ever remarked on that?'

'I can't say that I have,' Grace said, lunging unsuccessfully for the bird again.

'Chickens coming home to roost; ruffling someone's feathers; being hen-pecked; a pecking order, there are lots of them.'

'Yes, there are, I suppose. If we drove her into the corner there, she would be trapped. I should be able to catch her then.'

Waving their arms, they shooed the bird towards a corner formed by the two sides of the chicken run fence. The bird squawked angrily when she realised the plot, and tried to fly over the fence but it was too high. Grace grabbed her, and managed to pin her wings to her sides.

'Now, I will hand her to you, and you must hold her on one side between your elbow and your waist, keeping her wings down. Can you do that?'

'I think so,' he said.

They managed to transfer the bird and Daniel held her firmly. Grace stretched one of her wings and, drawing her scissors from her pocket, carefully cut the bird's feathers. The bird mumbled a quiet complaint, but clearly felt no pain. They turned her round and repeated the process on the other side. Daniel played his part rather well, he thought. They had to stand close. Close enough for him to admire the wisps of Grace's hair along her neck and cheek.

'You can set her down now.' Grace told him.

The bird was annoyed, but undamaged. She shook herself thoroughly, then joined the others scratching for the last grains of wheat.

'I haven't done that before,' he said, brushing a stray feather from his jacket.

'Neither have I. I am a novice chicken keeper, but I grow to like them. They have more personality that one might imagine. Miss White here wants freedom to roam.

Most of the others are without wanderlust, but Miss White longs to explore. It gets her into trouble.'

'She is a chicken with ambitions.'

'Yes. A chicken with a mind of her own.'

Grace smiled. Not really at him, just at the thought of the chicken and in his direction.

Daniel thought that he would happily chase several chickens a day, if it won him even such a smile.

'You said you had found something,' she said. He followed her over to the chicken house, where Grace opened the lid of the nest box and collected four eggs from one nest and two from another. She handed him two to carry.

'Yes, I found an envelope addressed to you.' He transferred both eggs to one hand and pulled an envelope out of his coat pocket with the other, handing it to her.

'Oh!' Grace said. She looked shocked. 'This is my father's handwriting.'

He had not expected such a shocked reaction.

'Are you quite well?'

'It is a surprise. I searched and searched after he died, but could find no letter. I was certain there must be one. It was tucked inside the textbook, you say?'

'Yes. I found it this afternoon.'

Grace suddenly pressed the envelope to her heart. 'Oh thank you! I'm so glad. So glad. You see when I couldn't find anything, it felt as if he left without saying goodbye.'

To his shock, there were tears in her eyes. 'I knew he would write to me. I looked everywhere. He must have just tucked it into the nearest book. So like him.' She smiled, then turned her head and brushed away the tears abruptly as she walked ahead.

'I could stay while you read it. It might be upsetting to read it alone,' he said.

'Oh no. That will not be necessary. But thank you for bringing it. And for helping with Miss White.'

'It was nothing,' he said. He stopped and watched her carry the letter across the grass and into the cottage alone, but then remembered he was holding a pair of eggs and wondered what to do with them.

Alice spotted him from the kitchen and opening the window, leaned out so he could hand the eggs to her. 'I found a letter from her father,' he said, helplessly.

'I'll keep an eye on her,' Alice said.

Chapter Thirty-Two

My Dear Grace,

The doctors advise me that now is the time to put my affairs in order. I have set about it, and this letter will follow final additions to my will. Such thoughts have caused me to reflect on the life I have lived, and particularly upon the life I have lived with you, my dear child, so I wanted you to have this letter and read it after I have left you.

I am not, as you know, particularly skilful at expressing sentiment. My language is mathematics. The wonders of all the universe lie there for me, but they are inexpressible except through the beautiful patterns of numbers and formulae. You understand this.

Grace, you have brought me nothing but happiness. When your poor mother died, I had little notion what I should do with the tiny babe she left behind. Nursemaids and Miss Wright kept you away from me most of the time. To begin with, you represented a lack to me—a negative—your presence reminded me of the mother who should be there with us, which was painful. Gradually, though, my little dot of a daughter sought me out. You pursued me into my study and brought me gifts. Sometimes you just wandered in and smiled at me or patted my knee. Soon you were sitting beside me on the sofa; coming for walks; making friends with cleaners and porters. Miss Wright oversaw your education. You seemed to find it all very easy, even if you did wriggle, as she once reported, during the longer poems of Keats.

I look back on it now, my dear, and see a perfectly good education being given to a bright little girl, but I see also your great and regrettable solitude. You never complained. You did have one or two friends to visit, but the greater part by far of your time was spent here in the college with adults and with books. I have given you, I see it now, a solemn and secluded childhood.

When I became Master, we moved into the Master's Lodge and this was even more the case. You were a young lady of twelve years at that time, and when Miss Wright chose to retire, you elected not to have another governess, but to learn from a series of tutors. Mathematics, which you had enjoyed since your earliest days, became your focus. You picked friendly undergraduate tutors at first, but soon we were working together, and you checked my proofs and helped to organise the writing of my papers. So began our collaboration.

This suited me so well that I am guilty of neglecting other aspects of your life, I now see. I did little to encourage the kind of independent social life a young woman should have. We were not anti-social. We attended all manner of college events, you always at my side, but these were not of your choosing. They were formal occasions. Undergraduates might have been present, but they were not the casual dances or tea parties that lead to new friendships and social variety.

I suppose I kept you to myself. You were so good at our work together. It was easier to work with you than with anyone else I had ever known. There was ever a certain competitiveness in working with my colleagues. Using professional proof-readers and checkers took enormous amounts of explanation. But you had the natural instincts of a collaborator. Your mathematical gifts are extensive. By the time you were fifteen or sixteen you had completed most of the undergraduate curriculum and at seventeen I ended up passing on your first tutee. Do you remember poor Richard who took a blow to the head and lost most of his learning capacity at the same time? What a case he was! But long after everyone else had abandoned hope, you sat with him, and encouraged him, you nudged him forward step by painstaking step with the patience nobody else in the faculty would ever have, and the boy doomed to failure was finally able to graduate with a respectable mark.

There could be no looking back after Richard. I could have filled your every waking hour with hopeless cases for tuition, but I refused to have your own work neglected.

Even as I write this, I see that what was a convenience for me meant also that, much to my shame, your own education, instead of being given a chance to develop in its own right, was thwarted and refashioned in the service of mine. I have treated you badly. I have heedlessly assumed that what suited me would also be best for you. This is a grave error for a father to make. I regret it. I hope you will forgive me.

Perhaps there are ways to compensate. I would encourage you, once the will is enacted and you are settled in your life, not to abandon your own mathematical career - it is your calling and your natural gift - I urge you to pursue it in any way possible. The openings for a young woman may be limited here at Cambridge, but there are places to study. London University is one possibility. You could even go abroad. I believe that in France and Germany women are welcomed and free to study mathematics in perfect independence. Your work can contribute to the new developments, particularly in algebra and calculus, that are so exciting. I urge you to pursue this.

Perhaps even now I am attempting to wield undue influence. You should be free to follow any path you choose. The Arts may beckon you. Your dear mother was a gifted pianist and painter. She spoke several languages. You may wish to follow her example. Your judgement, as I have seen it so far in your young life, has always been excellent. I urge you to trust your own heart and be brave enough to follow your instincts. Whatever choice you make, you will have my blessing.

A Match for Miss Marshall

I have had the huge good fortune to live exactly the life I most hoped to live. Something that can be said of very few. As a boy who loved numbers, my dream was to earn my keep by experimenting with mathematics all day long. I could, in those days, hardly imagine that such a life was even possible, yet I found it, and was able to live it comfortably in the beautiful surroundings of a Cambridge college. What good fortune I have had!

Perhaps you want to venture somewhere far away and have an entirely different life. Perhaps you wish to marry and make a family of your own. I hope you will, and that it will bring you happiness. I send fond love to my future grandchildren. My only advice in this area - in which I am ill-equipped to dispense advice, I admit - is not to marry too quickly, and not, if you can help it, to choose an academic as a partner in life purely because the nature of this life and this work is the most familiar to you. There will always be mathematical gentlemen in search of an economical source of proof checkers and editors for their learned papers! Beware!

And speaking of things to beware of, I should also mention the name of Edmund Hillyer. Hillyer has been asking after you for the past two years. I have been as discouraging as a father can be, but he is persistent. You, with your knowledge of my work, would be his ideal future collaborator. Allegations of plagiarism have already harmed his reputation, and I predict he will do further damage to it, through his own naturally dishonest tendencies, before long. I would encourage you to avoid him, my dear, if you can.

Apart from that, Grace, I only wish you to know that the publishers believe the new book will be successful enough to provide for your future. Thank you, my dear Grace, for making the life of your selfish father so happy. If there is an afterlife (I have my doubts, as you know), I shall watch over you from it. What I do not doubt is that all your future actions will bring me the utmost pride and joy, just as your life so far has done, my dear, dear girl.

I know you will be brave, Grace, and have the courage to do the right thing. Be bold in your choices. I have held you back for too long!
I hope you will forgive your fondest and most loving Papa,
Herbert Augustus Marshall
PhD Cantab

Chapter Thirty-Three

The workhouse papers were tidy now. Grace had sorted them, and typed most, using carbon paper to make a second copy as Miss Froment had instructed. The few that were left were extracts from accounts. She had put these off until last because lining up the columns looked so difficult, but now that the college was to take the papers back, she set about the task.

The porter arrived to collect them at six. It was George, the head porter. Grace had known him since she was a child.

'The Bursar's asking for his papers, Miss Marshall. I said I'd collect them on my way home.'

She invited him in. 'Perhaps you would like a cup of tea, George?' she said.

'I'll say no, Miss. Very kind of you, but the Mrs'll have my supper waiting.'

'Did you have to make a big detour to come here?'

'No, it's on my way.'

'The thing is, George, I hoped to finish the typewriting, but I have a few papers left to go.'

'I see,' he said. He looked puzzled. He was standing in the little sitting room, holding his uniform bowler hat in front of him.

'I would be grateful for another few hours, just to finish the job completely. I hate to leave a job half done.'

'I see,' George said again. 'Did they not give you a lamp, Miss Marshall? It seems dark in here already.'

'Oh, yes, there is one. It is in the kitchen.'

'Only one? Only one lamp?'

'I just carry it from room to room. It's perfectly enough. '

The Head Porter shook his head. He clearly did not agree.

'I was wondering,' Grace said, 'if I were to complete this typewriting immediately, would you allow me to bring the papers round to your house later tonight? I need an hour - two at most.'

He shook his head. 'And have you walking the streets alone in the dark, Miss Marshall? I should say not! The Bursar will have gone home by now. It's no matter to him if you keep them overnight. I shall collect them on my way to college in the morning, if that suits you. I shall come by at half past seven.'

'That would be perfect. Thank you, George.'

'And, if you don't say no, I shall bring you another lamp tomorrow evening on my way home. They're bound to have a store of lamps somewhere in the college. I can't see you living with a single lamp, Miss. I won't have it. It's a disgrace. Your father was a good man. He knew all the porters by name. He never forgot us at Christmas. They ought to be ashamed of themselves, leaving you with a single lamp in a dark little place like this.'

Grace's protests that she was entirely happy with her living arrangements at the cottage fell on deaf ears, and George left muttering about the injustice of it all under his breath.

The moment he was gone, she rolled paper and carbon into the typewriter and set about reproducing the most recent pages of the workhouse accounts. It was slow work, but she had it done before midnight, and climbed into her bed exhausted but unable to sleep.

The next day, with the workhouse papers finished and carried back to college with George the porter, Grace found herself at a loose end. She cleaned the chicken house and collected the eggs, then returned to the cottage and sat at her table. The list she had made in her notebook now read:

1. Tuition for New College

2. Hat articles

3. Papa's royalties –where? - see Mr Grant at Purley Press.

Chapter Thirty-Four

Her pile of carbon copies from the workhouse papers before her, Grace's thoughts returned again and again to Violet, Rose and Ivy, and she leafed through the pages, wondering if there was something she could do herself to help them. Who else could she appeal to? There must be someone who could intervene. They were not unloved. Their mother had cared about them, she asked that they stay together, she had written a careful note on a potato sack, weeping over it as she wrote. Dreadful to think of them - the baby sick - waiting silently in a miserable unhealthy place, with a future that might be even worse.

Restless with the frustration of it, Grace put on her hat and coat and set out for town. She could at least call in at Purley Press's offices and make an appointment to see Mr Grant. It wasn't raining for once, although the sky was a uniform sheet of grey. The address was a good walk away, right at the other end of town, but it would be good to stretch her legs. She would take her notebook and note down any new hat styles she spotted, as well as calling at any hat shops that might agree to be mentioned.

This part of her plan worked well. By the time she reached *Purley and Sons, Academic Publishers*, as it said on the doorplate, Grace had arranged to write about two more hat shops: one small, fashionable and expensive; one larger but catering for the more practical lady living a country life.

'Mr Grant is in his office. If you would care to see him, I could ask if he's free,' said the smart young woman at the front desk.

Grace had been expecting to return at a later date, but willingly agreed. Apart from the lively young creature who showed her to the waiting room, the general air of Purley and Sons was solemn and extremely quiet - somewhere between a cathedral and the office of an expensive doctor.

Mr Grant was as small, dapper and grey-bearded as an academic publisher should be, but his general seriousness was off-set a little by friendly blue eyes behind his gold-rimmed spectacles.

'I knew your father well,' he told Grace, welcoming her to his office and gesturing her to a seat. 'It was always a pleasure to see him. We published his work for more than thirty years. A great loss, a great loss. My condolences.'

'He always spoke well of Purley and Sons, Mr Grant.'

'That is good to hear. So, how can I be of assistance?'

'I sent the latest manuscript two weeks ago.'

'Indeed. The *New Introduction to University Mathematics*. A fine volume. We have great hopes for it, Miss Marshall. Great hopes indeed. There is a place in the market - a real demand for such a volume. There is nothing quite like it, you see. Written by someone of your father's reputation, we are highly confident of its success. And the most perfectly presented manuscript. You helped your father with the final edits and proofreading, as usual?'

'I did, yes.'

'He was lucky to have such expert assistance.'

'Thank you,' Grace said. 'It is generally not work that is praised in its own right.'

'Correct! But publishers appreciate that sort of thing. Excellent copy editing is the foundation stone of a fine book, but, like many foundation stones, it often remains hidden.' He nodded, clearly waiting for Grace to raise the main reason of her visit.

'I was wondering whether you ever, whether Purley and Sons ever, that is, whether you ever have any such work available on a freelance basis?'

Mr Horace Grant took a moment to register all the implications of this question. He picked up a fountain pen and turned it slowly in his fingers. 'You seek editing work?'

'Or proofreading,' Grace said.

'For all its importance, it is not well remunerated work, Miss Marshall. We employ regular proofreaders, of course, but for mathematics and other specialised texts we do often have to use freelancers.'

'Perhaps I could be added to your list of such freelancers, if there is such a list,' Grace said.

'Of course.' Mr Grant looked away for a moment. 'This would be a hobby or pastime? Perhaps to help you to remain in touch with the field, now that your father has left us?'

'Well, yes, of course I should like to remain in touch, but I also need to support myself, so less a pastime, more a professional undertaking,' she said.

'Excuse me for asking, Miss Marshall, but is your father's income from his books not available to you? We have eight or nine titles of his in print. They sell well. Obviously they are highly specialised in their nature. The *New Introduction* is a departure for him. It should attract a far larger, more general readership, but the older titles sell widely to universities and institutions of learning all around the world.'

'Do they?' Grace said. 'I have never had any way of knowing.'

'They produce a decent annual income, I can assure you.'

'Everything is in the hands of the lawyers.'

'Ah well, there may be legal complications, I cannot advise about those, but from the point of view of his publisher, your father was receiving a good income from his books. The details of payments etcetera I should have to look into, but there is no reason to suppose the sales or the royalties have fallen off.'

'Where do the royalties go, then?' Grace asked.

'That I will look into. And meanwhile I recommend you speak to the lawyers.'

'I shall,' Grace said. She paused, looking worried, then added, ' There is one more thing, Mr Grant. About the most recent book - the *New Introduction*. I may have contributed more to it than …'

Grant sat back in his chair and held up both hands to stop Grace from saying any more. 'Miss Marshall, I have seen cases in the past once or twice where a collaborator or close family member - a widow, say, or a long-time student or colleague - has, for one reason or another - contributed rather more to a publication that might ordinarily be expected. Illness intervened, perhaps, or something like inescapable enforced absence. If the main author of the work is well-known, and if they are the person contracted to us for the publication, but for these very good reasons a co-author ends up contributing substantially to the work, this can occasionally lead to *complications*. Disputes, even, over the real authorship. Do you follow?'

He was still holding his hands up, but he continued.

'Any sort of dispute will inevitably lead to delay. Publication will have to be postponed. Royalties, however the matter is finally resolved, will not be paid until later - sometimes much later. In cases such as those, Miss Marshall, my general advice would always be to avoid raising any issue that might cause someone like me to be forced to delay a book's release. You understand?'

'It was not a matter of dispute,' Grace said. 'It was just that I …'

'… I shall stop you there again, Miss Marshall, if I may. Let's go ahead on the basis of the contract I had with your Papa, and meanwhile I shall look into the royalties on the existing books and let you know. Can I write to you at New College?'

'No, I am at Abercrombie Cottage, Station Road now.'

He wrote the address down.

'You will keep me in mind for freelance proof editing?' Grace added.

'If you wish, yes.'

Chapter Thirty-Five

A whole day without rain was such a rare treat that spring that most of the population of Cambridge seemed to be out taking the air. The pavements were thronged. Grace, deep in thought over her slightly odd meeting with the publisher, side-stepped a perambulator and then had to jump aside to avoid a group of young cyclists hurtling down Castle Hill with their jackets flapping behind them. In doing so she stumbled into a passer-by. It was Eddie Parks, editor of the Chronicle.

'Miss Marshall! Are you hurt?'

'No. I had forgotten how fast cyclists race down this hill.'

'Never stand in the path of a hungry cyclist!' he said, cheerfully. 'But I'm glad we met. I was hoping to see you. I have had warm responses from the staff to the first of your hat columns. It should go out next Thursday.

A maid pushed a baby by in a large perambulator and a dozen schoolboys in uniform swarmed past carrying books.

'It's difficult to talk here. Shall we divert and walk along the river where there are fewer people?' Parks suggested.

The path along the river was wider, though still popular. They followed the towpath, watching swans dabbling around the reeds and oarsmen carrying their boats in and out of the boathouses opposite.

'Have you made any progress on the workhouse story you mentioned—St Benet's, I think you said it was?' Parks was greeted by several people as they walked along, and touched his hat in polite reply. He was clearly a well-known figure in the city.

'I have more information,' Grace said. 'I examined the accounts books, and they clearly show expenses being claimed for the upkeep of the children. I began looking at the older accounts, but I can see no clear pattern yet, except that there have been similar claims for small groups of children in past years.'

Parks, who was strolling with his hands in his pockets and his hat pushed back on his head in a very ungentlemanlike way, considered this for a step or two. 'They wouldn't be so foolish as to put payments for farmed children through the books. They'd just pocket them.'

'Then how can it be proved? I'm told the whole system may be corrupt,' Grace said, 'from the Board to the Inspectors, as well as Mr and Mrs Lemman. I have written numerous letters, but nobody wants to know.'

'Most of us are guilty of turning a blind eye to what goes on inside the workhouse walls,' Parks said. 'My readers would generally rather read about hats or cricket matches than dark misdeeds among the poor.'

'But if I can show evidence—good evidence—that the children are being traded. *Sold*, even. Surely such overt cruelty would catch your readers' attention?'

'Maybe so,' Parks said, with a shrug. He seemed unconvinced.

'Wouldn't a real journalist be the best person to find what's going on?' Grace asked. 'You employ several at the Chronicle. One of them would know how to locate the necessary information far more effectively than I can.'

'Would you care for an ice?' Parks said.

'I beg your pardon?'

He ambled over to the nearby ice cream seller's cart and bought two ices without waiting for her decision. Returning and handing her a ball of ice cream on a wafer cone, he said, 'I think you yourself will make a better job of the workhouse story. Stick with it. Don't let it distract you from the hats, though. The hats are going to be popular. The Chronicle needs more lady readers.'

'Why do you seek lady readers, in particular?' She had never eaten an ice cream in public before, and was wondering whether to remove her gloves.

Parks licked his ice cream thoughtfully. He was the least fastidious man Grace had ever met, perfectly at ease wandering along eating an ice with his jacket unfastened, ink on his cuffs and his hat on the back of his head.

'Circulation,' he said. 'The Daily News—our main competitor—has upped its figures by several thousand largely by attracting more ladies. They have a whole page for ladies. They even publish *fiction*, if you can believe that. The ladies lap it up. My own wife laps it up.'

'What sort of fiction?' Grace asked.

'Some sort of ghoulish adventure last time I looked. It's supposed to be a *news*paper.' Parks shook his head in disgust.

'You do not sound very convinced by this fiction idea.'

'Frankly, I am not. For one thing, I don't know that most ladies, or readers in general, want fiction in their weekly newspaper at all. If they do, I'm not sure that a Cambridge readership wants *that* kind of fiction.'

'What kind?'

'Sensational. *Mistreated by the Dastardly Earl* - that sort of thing.'

He looked seriously at Grace, who was contemplating the river with a thoughtful expression. She seemed less shocked by this departure from good taste than he might have expected.

'*Mistreated by the Dastardly Earl*,' she repeated slowly, still looking at a pair of ducks bobbing in the wake of the narrow boat.

'I invented that title. But you get a sense, perhaps, of the sort of potboiling nonsense I am talking about?'

'I do. So you plan to include fiction in the Chronicle?'

He looked irritable. 'The owners press me to do so.'

'You would serialise an existing popular novel?'

'Far too expensive. The Daily News paid hundreds of pounds for the rights to the ghastly nonsense they're serialising. *Hundreds!*'

'But it did bring in a large number of readers,' Grace reminded him. 'Perhaps you should consider it.'

'The funds are not there.'

'Could you not commission the stories one at a time, in the same way as you commission other articles? That would be less of an expense.'

'And who would I commission to write this penny-dreadful nonsense?'

'I will do it.' Grace said, still directing her remark to the ducks on the river.

He turned to look at her in astonishment.

'You?'

'I have a confession. I have spent my evenings reading novels of this kind for many years. I have even written my own versions from time to time. I have a small stack of them. It was my way of relaxing after a day of mathematical brainwork when I was working with my father.'

Parks could only laugh. Grace did too.

'That is the last thing on earth I would have imagined,' he said. 'You! The intellectual daughter of the Master of a Cambridge College and your reading consists of lurid shilling shockers?'

'Oh, I read worthy fiction too. The classics of literature are all my good friends, but *The Dark Lady of Highton Hall* and so on are my little indulgence. I find them immensely soothing.'

'*Soothing*? Five people die and two usually go mad in the first three chapters of these things!'

'Yes. And it is most enjoyable!'

'I am shocked to the core, Miss Marshall.'

'Being shocked is good for the health, you know,' she said. 'They say it stimulates the liver.'

'Well, mine is thoroughly stimulated, so let's hope they are right.'

'But, now to business,' Grace said. 'There is a payment for these fictional stories, I take it?'

'There will be, but not a very large one.'

'I know enough of the Chronicle not to expect anything generous, but how much, exactly?'

'About two shillings a week?'

'Make it half a crown. Two and six a week. I have enough episodes already written to supply the Chronicle's readers for several months.'

'You really are very surprising, Miss Marshall. '

'I shall have a marvellous time writing more. Do you want blood? Murder? Ghosts?'

'The more sensational the better, but nothing that would

upset a Cambridge matron over her tea on a Thursday afternoon.'

Grace laughed. 'All three, then! The Cambridge matrons I know are not easily upset. And when do you need the first episode?'

'In a fortnight.'

'Easily done. I only need to find whichever box I packed my collection of hair-raising stories in.'

'Ah, Parks! Just the man!' A gentleman Grace did not recognise approached and began a conversation with Parks which seemed to be something about a meeting taking place on Sunday. Parks listened for a while before excusing himself and taking his leave of Grace, who turned for home still carrying her half-eaten ice cream.

Chapter Thirty-Six

A trio of cyclists rattled past, but one braked suddenly. It was Daniel in rowing shorts and cap.

'Miss Marshall! I thought it was you.'

Grace laughed. 'Is everyone in the city down by the river this afternoon?'

'The rowers are. I am heading back to college. May I join you?'

'Of course,' Grace said. They strolled towards Jesus Green, he pushing his cycle.

'Have you always lived in Cambridge?' he asked.

'Yes. My father was originally from Scotland, but he came south as a young man. He was already teaching at New College when I was born.'

'So all this must be very familiar to you.'

'Yes. I know the city well.'

'And have you travelled?'

'A little. My father had a passion for ancient monuments. I have visited prehistoric monuments and standing stones in all sorts of places in this country, as well as France and Ireland.'

'Standing stones? How strange!'

'They are. Strange and mysterious. And usually remote and isolated. I stayed with my father in some very unusual lodgings on those trips. Barns, hayricks, stables, and all manner of rough and dubious inns.'

'Goodness!' He looked over at Grace with renewed respect. She was smiling at the memory and watching the river.

'A lot of walking, and some very odd dinners, but fascinating all the same. But what about you, Mr Hollingdale? Where is your family from?'

'I'm a Londoner.'

They paused to watch eight young men climb into their boat with their boy cox, an elaborate performance which involved first carrying the boat out of the boathouse over their heads, then swinging it with synchronised movements down onto the river. The cox called instructions in his sharp boy's voice.

'What brought you here to Cambridge?'

'Choir school at first. We have weak chests in my family, so they thought the air would be cleaner here than in London. I've been here ever since. My sister joined me last year for the better air too. There is also a specialist doctor who has been treating her. She adores the hat, by the way.'

They continued along the river. A narrow boat carrying fruit and vegetables from the college farms downriver made its way past, towed by a handsome feather-footed shire horse.

Chapter Thirty-Seven

The pair of swans that had been dabbling around the nearby reeds glided away up the river. Further along, a spaniel leapt joyfully into the water after a stick. Daniel watched them for a moment, then turned serious and asked.

'Are you still concerned about the children in the workhouse?'

'Yes. I have approached everyone I can think of, but nobody seems to be in a position to help. The Matron knows that she is accountable, publicly, to the Board, but nobody on the Board, and none of the other people who visit the workhouse, such as the doctor or the inspectors, seem to ask any difficult questions. Their negligence leaves her free to do as she pleases. They almost do their duty, but they do not take that last little bit of initiative that would make their oversight of the place really thorough. Only a narrow margin of carelessness is needed: a question unasked; a suspicion not followed-up on, and the damage is done. Meanwhile, as I waste time theorising and writing letters, there are three children in the sick bay whose fate is dreadfully uncertain. At best they are to be sent to the National Home in Haverhill, which has a poor reputation; at worst they are to be the subjects of some underhand bargain whereby Mrs Lemman profits and some contact of hers effectively buys a child to use for their own purposes. I have no idea what they might be used for.'

'I have,' Daniel said. 'I asked around.'

She turned to him in surprise.

'People I asked believe the children will be put to work.'

'But the oldest is only four or five. They are babies!'

'Five is not too young to work by the standards of the kind of people who would take them on. The others would be reared in hard conditions until they were a little older. They send them to mines, to mills, to chimney sweeps, they can be farm labourers, far out in the country.'

'There are laws, surely, against all of these things!' Grace said.

'There are, but there are also people willing to break those laws, and skilled at hiding it. Children like these are ripe for exploitation. Orphans in particular. I would not expect you to understand the world such people inhabit, Miss Marshall. You have lived your life among lovely scenes like this, in a wealthy college among educated people. But there exist many people willing to exploit and abuse children - or anyone else - if it helps them to turn a quick penny.

Grace left the towpath and set out across the grass. Daniel followed. She was gesticulating as she walked. 'I have written letters. Dozens of them. I have told my Member of Parliament, the Lord Mayor, The Chairman of the Charitable Board, the Governors of the National Homes, every single member of the Union Workhouse Board as individuals. I have written to the doctor who visits the children, the

Matron, Mrs Lemman herself, the national governor of Workhouse and Poorhouse Boards, the Mother's Union, the Vicar of St Benet's and the Bishop of Ely. I have quite simply written to everyone I can think of who has any interest - even the most remote - in the running of that place, but nobody, not one of them, has committed to do anything!'

Daniel was struggling to keep pace. His hat flew from his head and he had to pick it up and carry it.

'They have all replied,' Grace said, waving her arms 'in varying degrees of condescension, I may say, they have all replied saying that in their view the workhouse, though a regrettable necessity in many ways, is well-run and doing its best to help the deserving poor in the minimal ways the deserving poor are due to be helped according to the legislation and the rules agreed by every board and parish and town council in the land.' She paused, gasping for breath. 'They say they will *look into the matter*. They say they will *raise my concerns at the next meeting*. They thank me for *bringing it to their attention*. But no one *does* anything!'

'What would you have them do?'

She stopped in her tracks. 'Take action! I want someone to walk straight in and take those little girls out of that terrible place. I want someone to give them a proper home. Food. Medicine. Education! Whatever they need to have a decent life. I want someone to stop that Lemman woman from trading in poor children as casually as anyone else would might trade in - oh, I don't know - potatoes or old boots!'

'That is not the way these things work.'

He was shocked to see, as he caught up with her and she turned her face towards him, that there were tears in her eyes.

'I know,' she said. 'Please forgive my profound ignorance. I suppose expecting anything different is another example of my naïveté.'

They stood a moment, both catching their breath.

'Grace, I didn't call you ignorant or naïve.'

'I know. I am enraged by my own helplessness.' She looked away and down at the ground.

'I'm sorry there is so little anyone can do.'

She shook her head. 'It is hardly your fault,' she said. 'You are a musician, a chorister. Your life has been, if anything, even more cloistered and protected from harsh realities than mine.'

She turned and walked away, her small, vigorous figure soon merging into the groups of other walkers enjoying the autumn sun.

He stood watching before turning away himself. He was experiencing an odd, mixed sensation of anxiety and joy surging together. His hand lost its grip on his bicycle and it dropped onto the grass again. He knew, as he bent to pick it up, that this young woman had great importance in his life - it came to him as a jolt of certainty. Something about the children was certain too, but what? He was left to wonder.

Chapter Thirty-Eight

'Thank you for coming. I fear this may be rather a difficult conversation, Miss Marshall,' Horace Grant said the following week. There was still something of the ancient prophet about him with his grey beard. The stained glass design in the top of his office window added to the effect.

As Grace sat she heard a strange sharp cry from out of sight. A cupboard door was ajar in the wood panelling in one corner.

'Please excuse the noise. That is my pet bird, Timmy.' Mr Grant looked a little uncomfortable. 'I can move him, if you find his presence distracting.'

'You keep him in the office?'

'Only occasionally. My wife is away. He likes company.'

'May I see him?'

Looking slightly unwilling, Mr Grant stood and opened the cupboard door more fully, revealing a white cockatoo with a yellow crest in a large metal cage. The bird seemed pleased, bobbing up and down on his perch, turning to look at Grace with his head on one side. The publisher went to close the door again, but then hesitated. 'He will join our conversation a little too often, if I close the door again,' he said. 'Timmy is usually well-behaved, but he forgets himself and can be noisy if he feels excluded.'

'Good boy, Timmy,' the parrot remarked in an off-hand way, standing on one foot to scratch his head with the other.

'You have something to tell me? You were going to ask your accountant about the payment of my father's royalties, I think,' Grace said.

'Yes. I asked you to come because your father wrote to us just before he passed away. I have the letter here.' Grant produced a letter on New College headed paper from his desk drawer. 'He asked to change the arrangements for paying the royalties on his older books. Perhaps he mentioned his plan to you?'

'He said nothing to me.'

'He asked in this letter that the royalties be paid to a third party from that time onwards, by way of holding them in trust while his affairs were settled. It seems he wished to avoid any delay while probate was organised. The aim was that this third party would continue to receive the royalties and would pass them immediately on to you.'

'Nobody has passed any royalties on to me.'

'They have not? You should have received a payment in August.'

'I received no such payment. Who was this third party you refer to?'

Mr Grant was already looking uneasy. 'I would not normally disclose the contents of a private letter. This was a confidential arrangement.'

Grace did not know what to say to that. She could only sit back in her chair and try to take it in. The bird rang a small bell in its cage in the corner, and muttered something under its breath.

'There has, however, been a development recently, that makes me feel I should let you see this letter now,' Grant said. He handed the document across the desk to Grace.

Grace read the letter with an expression that grew more surprised and shocked with each line. 'Dr Hillyer?' she said. 'My father asked that the royalties be paid to Edmund Hillyer?'

'We had no reason to doubt…'

'But this letter is obviously fraudulent,' Grace said. She held it up.

'I must admit, now that I look at it…'

'It is poorly typed, and the signature is nothing like my father's. Look!'

Grace reached into her pocket and produced her father's letter to her. She handed it to Grant, who unfolded it and nodded in confirmation as he compared the real signature to the poor approximation on the typed letter. His face had drained of colour. He ran a hand over his beard. 'There is more, Miss Marshall, I am afraid.'

'He has syphoned off my father's royalties,' Grace looked at Grant across his desk. 'At the same time as attempting to charm me. This letter distinctly implies…'

'It does, it implies that your father had accepted him as your future husband.'

'And it was a formality that the royalties went to my future husband until such time as he became my real husband and took charge of my income permanently.'

'Yes. There is worse to come, Miss Marshall, I am afraid.'

'Worse! What could be worse?'

'He wrote again and asked for the manuscript of the New Introduction.'

Grace leaned towards him, her eyes wide. 'You surely didn't let him have it?'

'It was a normal enough request. He works in the same field. It is perfectly normal for a reviewer to see an advance copy,' Grant said.

'You *did* let him have it!'

Grant now looked as if he wanted to crawl beneath his desk. 'I let him borrow it under strict conditions. We do not need it for typesetting until next month.'

'But there is nothing to prevent him publishing it in his own name!' Grace said. 'He is a fraud and clearly a liar…'

'Liar,' said the cockatoo in shrill tones in the background. 'You are a lying liar!'

Mr Grant put his head in his hands and said miserably. 'The bird. That is one of the words that sets him off. I apologise. There is nothing I can do to stop him.'

'You are a liar, Sir!' said the bird, loudly from his corner. 'A liar and a cheat, I tell you!'

'The bird is perfectly correct. Hillyer *is* a liar and a cheat!' Grace said. 'Timmy is welcome to say so as often as he likes! These, surely, are criminal offences. I shall report Dr Hillyer to the police myself!'

'Liar, liar, liar! Call the police!' Timmy squawked in the background, rocking from foot to foot on his perch and adding a loud whistle at the end.

'Timmy! That is enough!' Grant said. He had his face in his hands. 'I can do nothing to stop him. He will run through his whole repertoire, I'm afraid. He usually ends by challenging someone to a duel.'

'How could you let this happen?' Grace asked.

'I don't know. There was no reason to suspect …'

'But this letter is a travesty. It is the worst attempt at typing a letter that I have ever seen! Nobody could be convinced by this!'

'It was sent to the accounts office ...'

'And nobody thought to question it, or check the signature against another letter?'

Horace Grant could only look helpless.

A long silence stretched between them, interrupted only by the cockatoo tutting under his breath.

'It seems to me, Mr Grant that I have two choices. I can go straight from here to the offices of the Cambridge City Police and report Dr Hillyer for the criminal that he is. It is very tempting to do so because the man is a liar and a deceiver who will clearly stop at nothing. I should very much enjoy seeing him in jail.'

'Filthy liar!' Timmy chimed in.

'That is exactly what he is,' said Grace. 'But, if I know the law, it will be many months before he comes to trial, leaving him at leisure to steal and publish my father's life's work before anyone can prevent it. That is not good enough.'

She paused for breath. Her father's letter was in her lap. Her eyes filled with tears as she read a few lines from it. She blinked them back and straightened her shoulders. 'The other alternative is to devise a way to regain both the royalty payments and, most importantly of all, the manuscript of the New Introduction and rid the academic world of Edmund Hillyer in a different way.'

'I will do anything I can to help,' Grant said. 'Purley and Sons have a two hundred year history of publishing in Cambridge. I should not want that to end in a terrible scandal. But beyond that, Miss Marshall, I am truly appalled that we have allowed this charlatan to deceive us - and steal from you. It goes without saying that I can hardly apologise enough.'

'Apologies are not what I need,' Grace said. 'A plan is what I need.' She paused, looking thoughtfully at the stained glass window. 'Mr Grant, if you had purloined a manuscript, and you wanted to keep it away from its legitimate owners for long enough to profit by it yourself, what would you do with it?'

Grant frowned. 'I? What would I do?'

'Yes. I want to work out what Hillyer will do next.'

'Oh, I see.' He turned his pen in his fingers, considering.

'It will take a long time to copy it,' Grace said. 'Even longer to re-edit it into something he can claim as his own. He can't be certain there is no other copy. So, realistically, he can't publish it as it is.'

'I imagine that is his plan,' Grant said. 'Even the worst kind of plagiarist cannot simply re-publish someone else's work unchanged, it would be too easy to prove what he had done. No, he will need several months to re-work the manuscript and make the material plausibly his own.'

'Liar!' muttered the bird in the background, ringing his bell for emphasis.

'He has a post in Zurich now.'

'Well, if it were me, I should post the whole thing to myself straight away. It is safe in the post and…'

'He has probably already done so!' Grace said, sadly.

'Was there any - legitimacy in his claim that you are his fiancee, Miss Marshall?'

'Absolutely none, I assure you! He has made no proposal of marriage to me.'

'Perhaps he still hopes to do so?'

'He would be mad to try!'

'He needs you to re-edit the manuscript. It would be so

much easier for him, if you could do so. His future would be secure. You would be his helpmate and a truly worthwhile publication would cement his academic reputation.'

'He must know that I would never do that!'

'He perhaps still has hopes of persuading you. It strikes me that Dr Hillyer is not one to give up easily. Nor, from what you have said, is he particularly sensitive to the feelings of others.'

'I should like to see the blighter try it!'

'Could you not play along a little? Win his confidence? So that he takes down his guard and gives you the opportunity to seize the manuscript back?'

'Absolutely not!'

'Only a suggestion.'

'Anything I can do - anything at all - to help. Please, just ask.'

'You are a cowardly liar!' cried the bird in the background. 'Scoundrel! I challenge you to a duel!'

Chapter Thirty-Nine

It was raining again. The buckets were out in the apartment upstairs and neither of the Venables sisters had any customers when Grace took shelter in the hat shop.

'Ah, Grace. I have had a busy week,' Christabel remarked. 'I believe I have your article to thank for that.'

'It brought you more customers?'

'Yes, and I sold two wide-brimmed felts and a beret to them.' Christabel, looking pleased, was adding a froth of lace to a grey toque. Grace felt a small flush of satisfaction in being able to identify the different hats she mentioned.

'The Chronicle has asked that I write about other shops as well. If I write only about Maison Ladoré - why is it so named, by the way?'

'Oh, I inherited the name from the previous owner. She intended it to sound fashionably French, I believe. It wouldn't have been my choice, but I'm used to it now.'

'Anyway, if I only write about your shop, it amounts to advertising it, so I must visit others and write about them too.'

'Will you make overt comparisons? Will you write how very fine my designs are compared to the dreadful puddings and buckets they sell at Pelham's, say?'

'I shall probably not call their hats puddings or buckets. I think it better to avoid direct comparisons. I shall simply mention some of their designs as well.'

'Readers will soon see for themselves,' Christabel said. 'A blind ox could spot the difference between one of mine and something Marcia Pelham inflicted on the Cambridge hat landscape! It's a wonder people don't point to them and burst out laughing in the street. Anyway, you have achieved a column in the Chronicle, which is quite a success.'

'Thank you,' Grace said.

'You do not seem very thrilled, Grace, if I may say so. Is it not the result you wanted?'

'I am pleased, but I have heard this morning something very troubling.'

'About the Chronicle?'

'About my future.'

'Oh dear. Not an unwanted admirer?'

Grace looked around the shop. It smelled of new felt and slightly of perfume. The colours and shapes of the hats were oddly comforting.

'How did you know?'

'It was just a guess.'

'It's much worse than that, though. He is unwanted, but I believe he has stolen what amounts to my inheritance. My future.'

'Stolen it?'

'In the form of my father's latest manuscript. He has forged …'

Christabel held up her hand and took up the tiny handbell she kept on the counter. She rang it three times in quick succession, sending its piercing ring echoing around them. Grace looked on, puzzled.

They heard footsteps on the stairs and Lucia Venables hurried in, summoned by the sound, three rings indicating an emergency. 'Yes?' she said.

'You will want to hear what Grace has to say,' Christabel told her sister.

When Grace had explained all that Hillyer had done, Lucia and Christabel both looked at her, appalled.

'He must be stopped!' Christabel said.

'The scoundrel must be stopped immediately,' Lucia added.

'I shall tell the police, but I fear they will not be fast enough,' Grace told them. 'He will make off back to Switzerland before he can be stopped.'

'Cunning is needed,' said Lucia. 'Are you prepared to use it?'

'I'm prepared for anything that is necessary,' said Grace, 'though personally I would rather just knock the man down and steal the manuscript back.'

'But then he may not return your father's royalties. If you simply let yourself into his room and take the manuscript back, that will solve one problem, but he will have no motive to return the royalties he has already taken. He must be persuaded; seduced, even.'

'*Seduced?*'

'Not in the literal sense, that would be going much too far. I mean that he must be charmed into handing back your money.'

'Charmed? How, exactly?' Grace asked.

'Well,' Lucia said, 'although I would not call myself an expert, I have discussed this with ladies in various situations. The key seems to be the use of flattery. The sort of gentleman we are discussing—the lesser sort—is extraordinarily susceptible to flattery, both of the direct and indirect kind.'

Grace seemed confused by this.

'The direct form is when a lady actively compliments him. She might say he is charming, for example, or allude to his wit or his great intelligence.'

Grace spluttered, as if choking. 'Charm, wit and intelligence are all entirely lacking in this case,' she said. 'Alluding to them in any way would be an outright lie. I should fear being struck down by lightning.'

'I can see that might be a step too far. One way round this obstacle is to use the words 'charm', 'wit', and 'intelligence' in a more general way in conversation. One does not say, 'You are so charming, Dr Hillyer,' one says instead, 'how charming the view from your window is, Dr Hillyer.''

'How does that help?'

'It is as if the word 'charming' were left in the air. The gentleman takes possession of it and applies it to himself.'

Grace looked at Lucia in astonishment. 'You mean I compliment one thing, and he adopts the compliment and applies it to himself?'

'Exactly.'

'That is ludicrous.'

'I've seen it work successfully, ludicrous or not.'

'Well, I never!' Grace said. 'How many times would I need to do this?'

Lucia looked out of the window, pondering, 'it depends on the gentleman, obviously, but many are so ready to snap up a compliment of any sort that only two or three instances are necessary to convince them that a lady is quite helplessly smitten.'

'So, I mention three things that are charming and he will do anything I ask?'

'It is a little more complicated than that.' Lucia said. 'You have a clear aim in mind. You want Dr Hillyer to return the manuscript immediately.'

'Yes. And I want him to hand over the last payment of royalties and give up his claim on all future payments.'

'Good. That is perfectly clear.'

'He should also abandon all hope of marriage - to me, that is.'

'That will probably be the easiest to achieve. He is likely to have other irons in the fire,' Lucia said. 'If I know anything about that kind of gentleman, they usually pursue several ladies at once.'

'Do they?' Grace was astonished to hear this.

'Oh yes. Dr Hillyer clearly has his eye on a marriage that will elevate his prospects considerably. He will almost certainly have identified other ladies that might suit this purpose. If we examined his activities we should probably find him visiting or corresponding with a number of other ladies who might suit his purposes. He has almost certainly designated a well-placed Swiss lady or two already.'

'Good heavens! You make him sound like a circling shark.'

'Less heroic, I think. More like Blossom here eyeing a flock of little birds. If he misses one, he will simply go for the next.'

They both looked over at Blossom who was asleep on the carpet with only an occasional swipe of his tail to show that he was listening.

'Right, so I compliment him indirectly, and that brings down his defences. What next?'

'You make him feel extremely intelligent.'

'Oh dear, I fear what comes next. Do I do this by saying how wise the wardrobe or the teapot is?'

'If you're not going to take this seriously, Grace, I shall not be able to help you.'

'I apologise. It's just that I am so angry with him!'

'I know, and rightly, but keep your aim in mind. So, how can you give his intelligence a chance to shine?'

'I suppose I could ask him to explain something to me. Some method or calculation.'

'Excellent! You ask his help. Could he explain this or that problem you have had difficulty with? You listen attentively. You follow his method; you succeed in solving the equation, or whatever it is, with his help. You thank him. The gratifying compliment to his superior intelligence is never spoken, but it is perfectly clear.'

'Oh dear, that will not be easy.'

'But it will work, Grace, don't you think?'

'Yes. I imagine so. If I can bring myself to do it. It goes against my deepest instincts.'

'I can see that. You must be brave, and remember it is in a good cause.'

'The cause of justice,' Grace said.

'Yes!'

'And the cause of preserving my father's final publication!'

'Indeed!'

'Oh well, I imagine I can even manage to compliment Dr Hillyer's superior intelligence just once in that cause.' She sighed, though, and did not sound altogether convinced.

'There might be one or two other compromises. You might, for example, need to smile at him once or twice. In order to be convincing.' Lucia said this warily, looking at her pen as she spoke.

'Oh good heavens!'

'You could even - although I leave this entirely to your discretion - you could even lay a hand on his arm. Once should be enough.'

'That may be too much. I shall keep that in mind and use it only as a last resort.'

'Excellent! He will do exactly as you ask, it is almost guaranteed.'

'Well, we shall see. I would still prefer just to punch him on the nose.'

'Perhaps later,' Lucia said, with a smile.

Chapter Forty

Miss Froment took one look at the letter and turned pale. She clutched a hand to her chest in her little office under the stairs in New College.

'This is the letter Dr Hillyer sent to the publisher? Oh my! I knew he was doing something strange, but ...'

'You *knew*?' Grace asked.

'Oh dear, dear me. One of the clerks told me that Dr Hillyer kept coming into the office in the evening. The clerk was working late - they were overwhelmed with work, that's why I brought you the workhouse papers, if you remember - anyway, he said that Dr Hillyer kept coming into the office and asking to use one of the typewriters. Several nights in a row, he came in and tried very slowly to type a letter. He refused the offer of help. The clerk thought it an odd thing to do. Hillyer was very secretive about it. He clearly didn't want anyone to see what he was doing.'

'He must have been typing the letter he sent under my father's name to the publisher.'

'I didn't know what he was doing, but then the same

clerk brought me a piece of paper he found screwed up on the floor. It must have fallen out of the wastepaper basket. Look. I kept it.'

Miss Froment went to a shelf and pulled a rumpled piece of paper out from between two accounts ledgers. It was a sheet of New College's headed paper with the Master's Lodge as the address at the top. The first lines read, '*Accounts Office, Purley and Sons, Castle Hill, Cambridge. Dear Sirs, My health being compromised at the current time, I should like to amend the arrangement for payment of my royalties as follows: from hence, all remittances should be directed to the account of Dr Edmund Hillyer at Coutt's Bank, Trinity Street. Dr Hillyer is to administer my affairs whilst I am indisposed through illness. As an esteemed colleague and future son-in-law, I should be obliged if you would treat him as my trustee and confidante in all matters related to my published work.*'

This particular attempted draft of the letter had clearly been rejected because of it's many imperfections. It had every fault a poor piece of typewriting could have, from uneven margins to sloping lines and letters typed with uneven pressure, so that some made a hole in the paper while others were only a pale blur.

'Did you not think to show this to my father, Miss Froment?'

Miss Froment shook her head and looked pained. 'Your father was very ill at that time, Miss Marshall. What was I to say? I assumed at first that he and Dr Hillyer had, indeed, made this arrangement. Why Dr Hillyer should feel the need to type a letter himself, I could not explain. I felt there was something amiss, but really there was no way of knowing what it might be.'

'In order to avoid Purley and Sons seeing the handwriting was not my father's, he thought he would typewrite the letter, but of course he underestimated the difficulty of doing so correctly. On the final version, which was only slightly better than this one, he added a forged signature - a *badly* forged signature - at the end.'

Miss Froment pursed her lips and shook her head. 'I have never liked the man. I knew he was up to something, but it wasn't clear to me exactly what it was. All I could think of was to keep this letter.'

'You did very well. Keep this safe. It is damning evidence.'

'Will you report him? Will the wretched man be arrested?'

'I want first to retrieve my father's manuscript.'

'He has taken it?'

'The publisher let him take it. He will plagiarise it, or even publish the whole thing under his own name, unless he is stopped. The publisher thinks he might post it directly back to Zurich. But we can't be sure. He may still have it. Where is he staying?'

'Here in Guest Room Four. How will you retrieve the manuscript?'

'I shall confront him and demand he returns it.'

Miss Froment looked startled. 'Is that safe? He is very determined. The manuscript means a great deal to him. It must represent all his hopes for a comfortable future career. He might not part with it easily.'

'I shall retrieve it one way or another, that man is a lying swine and he shall not have it! I shall punch the wretch on the nose, if I have to!'

'Good heavens!'

'I apologise if I startle you, Miss Froment, but I am quite determined.'

'I can see that. You have changed a great deal lately,

Grace. You used to be a shy little thing, and here you are, threatening to do violence to a gentleman who is a foot taller and probably twice your weight!'

'Well-deserved violence, only,' Grace said, 'and in a good cause! He shall not have that manuscript! I shall break into his room, if necessary.'

'Or you could simply use the key,' Miss Froment said, 'I keep a full set of spares here.'

Chapter Forty-One

Grace woke in the bedroom of the cottage the next morning with the memory of her father's voice vivid in her ear. What had they been discussing? She must have said that someone had acted too hastily.

'Better than hesitating,' her father had said.

'But surely, all aspects of a situation must be considered before taking a serious step,' Grace had said. Her father had shaken his head.

'No, Grace. That leads to no action at all. Sometimes one must simply decide with whatever evidence is to hand, then act. Some decisions offer no second chance. It is a great mistake to imagine that one can always go back and remedy one's errors. That is not true. Sometimes there is one chance and one chance only.'

All Grace knew, later that afternoon, was that in a sudden twitch of restlessness her feet carried her out of her front door. She found herself striding across town at double speed, so fast were the excitable thoughts tangling about in her head. It was a strange sensation, this scheming;

completely unfamiliar. When was the last time she, Grace Marshall, had acted in any unusual way? Perhaps never. This thought made her footsteps slow at the edge of Parker's Piece. *If I have never taken any sort of risk in my life, is that something to be ashamed of, or is it the very opposite?*

Three boys were kicking a ball around, and it headed her way. Grace picked up her skirt and kicked it back with all her might. It soared over the head of the nearest boy, who looked resentful, but his friend caught it behind and they ran off.

Whatever has come over me? Less than a quarter hour later, she was standing on St Benet's Green, a triangle of open grass, with trees and several benches, and there, plain at one end, was the long perimeter wall of the workhouse.

Without a plan, Grace could only follow the pavement along the wall. There was little to see from the outside, only a high red brick wall with a gate in the middle. Barred windows on either side of the gate seemed blocked on the inside. Grace was too shy to peer and certainly too uncertain to knock. What could she say, after all?

She could only feel foolish and keep walking past the gates where the three little sisters had been left all those weeks before. They probably weren't even inside any more.

Mr Jorrocks' grey mare was too fidgety for a good dray horse, but his steady old gelding was lame again, so he had no choice but to harness her into the cart that morning.

Opinions differed, later, about the exact sequence of events, but most agreed that as the cart swung round the corner of the Green, a beer barrel came loose. It rolled off the cart outside the workhouse wall. The loud crash as it hit the pavement frightened the grey mare, who reared, kicked herself free and rushed off across the Green, trailing her harness. Meanwhile a passer-by, referred to in the Cambridgeshire County Gazette as an *unfortunate lady*, was knocked over by the barrel, before it careened into the wall of the workhouse and, bursting open, leaked frothing best bitter ale all down the street.

Grace, the unfortunate lady concerned, immediately became the centre of a great deal of attention. Witnesses ran from all sides, fearing the worst. A lad was sent to fetch a doctor. Others rang the bell and shouted at the nearest door, that of the workhouse. When it was opened, they carried the victim in, and set her on the sofa in the neat front parlour of the matron's house.

'It's really not so bad,' Grace tried to tell them, 'only a bruise, I think,' but she was pale and bleeding from a cut to the head, so in the hubbub of concern nobody listened to her protests.

Dr Williams, summoned from his dinner by half a dozen neighbours, quickly established the extent of her injuries. He cleaned and bandaged her head wound, and strapped her wrist, which was swelling and painful.

'This may be broken,' he told Grace. 'Too soon to tell. It needs to be strapped and kept lifted and still for at least a week. The shock may still affect you. A blow to the head is not to be underestimated, Miss …?'

'Marshall. Grace.'

'See to it that Miss Marshall is sent home in a cab, Mrs Lemman. Can I leave that to you?'

'You can, Doctor,' Mrs Lemman said. There was a clear tone of irritation between them, even in this brief exchange.

'Well, Miss Marshall, as I said, there is a bruise forming

on the side of your head. Any worsening of symptoms - headache or dizziness - you are to call your own physician. Is that clear? Is anyone expecting you at home? I could send a note.'

'There is nobody expecting me.'

The doctor shook his head at this, but left, along with the rest of the rescuing bystanders. Grace, alone, looked around her. The Matron of the workhouse kept a fastidiously tidy parlour, but its spotless good order was undermined by the bleakness of the view. The window looked over a large bleak courtyard criss-crossed by paths which linked four similar plain buildings. Almost all the windows in the brick facades were shuttered. All Grace could see were the figures of a few women, dressed alike in uniform grey dresses and matching bonnets. A bell rang somewhere and the door of one of the further buildings opened. A group of men, most of them elderly, came out and made their way, tottering and limping in many cases, along a path. They seemed intent, as hungry people do, on the way to a meal. It was a look Grace recognised. She had grown up in a college, and knew the way undergraduates looked on their way to the refectory.

But these gentlemen were not Cambridge undergraduates. They were elderly, sick and stooped. Instead of laughter and good cheer, they demonstrated only grim purpose. They rarely looked up or acknowledged one another, as though the effort of walking was enough to preoccupy them in itself. Even from a distance their clothes were shabby and their cheeks sunken. Grace wondered what food awaited them. Mrs Lemman's house was flooded with the good smell of roasting beef and fresh bread. The Master and Matron of the workhouse clearly dined well, and evidently did not share their kitchen with the inmates.

Grace stood, still feeling a little giddy. She wanted to make the most of her opportunity to see the workhouse for herself, but had no idea how to explore. In the end, she decided a frank request might be the best idea. So when Mrs Lemman bustled back in, she said, 'Mrs Lemman, might I see round the workhouse? I have never set foot in one before, but I have read about them. Would it be a great inconvenience if I asked to be shown around?'

Mrs Lemman had entered the room with a tall thin young woman dressed in the workhouse's grey uniform. The Matron's face showed no enthusiasm for Grace's idea, but the maid bobbed a curtsey and said, 'I can show the visitor round, Mrs Lemman. Your dinner's waiting.'

This made it difficult for Mrs Lemman to refuse, so she said, 'Well, don't take too long about it. This young lady does not want too many details, I'm sure. And the cab will be here for her shortly.'

Chapter Forty-Two

'This way, Miss,' said the maid, as soon as Mrs Lemman had left to return to her dinner.

The maid led Grace out of the Matron's cottage and along the straight central path which divided the walled compound. From there she could see that the workhouse grounds were divided by low hedges into four squares.

'That's the women's house over there. The men's is on the other side. That low one there in the far corner is the workrooms and sheds. The women mostly work at sewing in their own house. The men break stones or bones for the farmers. Or they pick ropes. Sometimes they sort spuds. Depends on what work's going.'

'May I see the women's quarters?'

The maid nodded and led her to the path.

'Are you employed here yourself?' Grace asked.

'I'm the Lemmans' maid-of-all-work now, Miss. I work in the house.' After a brief hesitation, she added, 'I came here on the parish with my poor mother. When she died, Mrs Lemman give me the job. I been here eight years now.'

'And what's your name?'

The maid broke her stride and looked at Grace sideways. 'Jane,' she said, in surprise.

'Jane. And do any children stay here?' Grace tried to sound as if this were a casual question. She did not look at Jane, but smiled vaguely towards the women's house they were approaching.

'Not as a rule, but there are some here just lately,' Jane said.

They had reached the women's house. Jane opened the door and led Grace inside. It was a bare-floored and undecorated hall with four doors leading off it. The first was open and revealed a large workroom with tables and chairs. The table was piled high with old clothing. Women had clearly been at work sorting the rags into piles for mending or for sale. The room was poorly lit and the rags smelt musty.

Jane walked on and threw open the next door, behind which Grace saw a dormitory with iron bedsteads down either side. The beds, with thin mattresses and grey blankets, all looked exactly alike. Each was tidily made, but the air in the long room was sour and unpleasant with an undertone of mould and damp. No bright piece of fabric, cushion or eiderdown seemed permitted to relieve the thorough greyness of everything.

The third door led to a corridor with rooms off either side. 'These are the sick rooms,' Jane said in matter-of-fact tones. 'I won't open the doors, you might catch something nasty.'

'You mentioned there were some children,' Grace said.

'They're on the other corridor. Why? Do you know them or something?' Jane now looked over her shoulder at Grace.

'No. No. I was just curious, I suppose.'

'Funny wee things, they are. They don't speak. Hardly eat. They just look at you. They don't even cry. It's not natural. They might not be right in the head, I think.'

'You've seen them yourself, then?'

'I take care of them sometimes,' Jane said, sounding defensive. 'Mrs Lemman doesn't want anyone mixing with them. They're being moved.'

'Where will they go?'

Jane shrugged. 'A big children's home. She's tried, but nobody will foster them, what with them being strange and three of them together.'

'The National Home is probably a better place for them,' Grace said.

Jane shook her head. 'I was in a place like that once. If I had my way nobody would ever be sent there again. Not ever. Specially not babbies.' This was said with sudden fierceness.

Jane had paused with her hand on the handle of the fourth door. She realised she had spoken out of turn and looked anxiously at Grace. 'Don't tell Mrs Lemman I said so, though, Miss. Please don't.'

'I won't,' Grace said. 'Are they down here?'

Jane looked shocked. 'I'm not supposed to …'

'You can wait here if you just show me which door,' Grace said. 'I'll just look in. I promise not to scare them.'

'Mrs Lemman won't like it.'

Grace was already walking that way. 'In here?'

'It's the last one on the right.'

Grace, aware of the stale air and unpleasant smells of sickness around her, hurried down and softly opened the last door.

The room was dim, with a single shuttered window. An oil lamp burnt in a holder on the wall. In one corner an old woman in a cap was slumped asleep in an armchair. In the corner opposite her, a little girl in grey clothes sat on a mattress on the floor beside the sleeping figures of a baby and another sister. All had shaven heads. As Grace looked in, the oldest of the three girls turned her head and looked her way. For a moment their eyes met, and Grace found herself drawn into the gaze of the child's solemn brown eyes. There was, at first, no hint of reaction. The child's look was neither hostile or friendly. Almost imperceptibly, she leaned closer to her sleeping sisters, gravely, watchfully protective. Then, in a movement that went straight to Grace's heart, she opened a hand and lifted it momentarily. It was no more than a flicker of movement, something instinctive, but it was a small, silent plea.

The old woman groaned in her sleep, and the baby squirmed and threw an arm to one side. The child dropped her hand, her look turning vague and inward again. Grace withdrew, and could only shake her head as she walked back towards Jane.

'Did you want to see the men's section?' The maid asked, as they stepped out of the women's house and back onto the path.

But they both looked up and saw Mrs Lemman across the courtyard standing at her front door, waving. 'The cab's here for the patient,' she called. 'Hurry and take our visitor to the front gate, Jane.' Mrs Lemman disappeared back into her cottage, doubtless eager to return to her dinner.

Chapter Forty-Three

The maid went to move along the path towards the front gate, but Grace suddenly grasped at her sleeve.

'Jane, those children should not be left here, you said so yourself.'

'No, Miss,' Jane said, hesitating.

'I believe I could find them a better place.'

'Please do it, if you can, Miss.'

'Does the old lady ever leave that room?'

Jane's eyes grew wide. 'For her meals. She'll leave in a few minutes and go to the refectory for dinner,' she said. 'I sit with them, as a rule, while she's gone.'

'Can Mrs Lemman see the front gate from wherever she is eating her dinner?'

'No, they eat in the kitchen at the back. But she'll not be long.'

'And the cab is waiting outside the front gate?'

'Yes, that's what she said.'

Grace reached into her purse and pressed a coin from it into the maid's hand, saying, 'Jane, I am going to take these children away. They will not survive here. I think you know that. All I ask is that you look away for ten minutes.'

The maid, she noted, did not look down at the coin. She hurried it into her skirt pocket, then nodded, turned, and led the way back across the hall.

In the sick bay corridor Jane opened a linen cupboard door and nodded to Grace to hide in it. With the pulse pounding loudly in her ears, Grace stepped in and peered through a crack as she waited for the old lady to pass on her way to her dinner. The huddled figure from the children's cell soon shuffled by, and Grace hurried back to the dim little hospital cell. Jane was there. She had wrapped the baby in a thin blanket and put another round the shoulders of the middle child.

Grace bent and spoke as gently as she could to the oldest child.

'It's time now for you to come with me. You shall be safe, I promise.'

The child looked steadily at her, then nodded her head and standing up, pulled her sleepy sister to her feet too. Grace reached down and picked up the baby, tucking her under the flap of her coat. 'Violet, I am called Grace,' she said to the oldest child. 'Please hold my hand and come with me very quickly and quietly. Can you and Rose manage to walk? We shall need to be as quick as we can.'

Violet nodded her head, she held her sister's hand tightly. Little Rose just looked sleepily up at Grace with confusion and fear in her eyes.

'You shall be safe. You shall all be safe, but we must be quick. Come this way.'

With the blood throbbing in her bruised head and her throat dry, Grace led the girls, praying nobody would see them, along the dim passageway, out of the building and across the path to the front gate. She wanted to run, to hurry, but the children could not. The baby's weight pressed painfully on Grace's bandaged wrist. At every step she waited for a shout or the sound of footsteps as someone hurried to interrupt them, but nothing came. For an anxious moment could not see how to open the gate, then noticed a small latched door cut into it. She lifted Rose and Violet one at a time over the threshold, still clutching the baby, stepped through herself and hurried them over to the waiting cab.

'I didn't know there was little'uns coming,' the driver began to say, cheerfully. But the urgency with which Grace bundled the children into the cab stopped his words.

'Please drive. Drive as fast as you can! Abercrombie Lodge, Station Road,' Grace said. As they pulled away, Grace saw the latch on the front gate lifting, but by the time Mrs Lemman was out and looking after them, they were rounding the corner and the horse was gathering speed.

Chapter Forty-Four

Daniel's next lesson was at seven o'clock the next morning. He arrived punctually, and it was Grace who, after a long, sleepless night, found herself in disarray when she heard his knock at the door.

'I hope I am not early.' He was smiling on the doorstep, but noticed her harassed look.

'No,' she said. 'You are punctual, as usual. Come in and sit down.'

At the table he took out his book and produced with a slight flourish a notebook with several pages of answers written out. 'It is a bonny morning, Miss Marshall. A beautiful spring day. The robin is singing, squirrels are leaping on the college lawns.'

Grace was already examining his answers, checking them one by one.

'As I say, the sun is shining its golden light on the college tower and the stained glass windows were...'

'I must release the chickens!' Grace suddenly said, remembering.

'No. Allow me,' he said and left her to continue her marking.

He was back quickly but Grace was finding it difficult to concentrate. 'They are correct, all but number nine, and that, I think, is a simple arithmetical error. Can you see it?'

He could, once she pointed it out. 'I should have spotted that myself,' he said.

'You should. You will need to cultivate the habit of careful checking. It is otherwise too easy for an error to be introduced. Even at this simple level, it is worth double-checking every step of a calculation.'

He nodded, feeling suddenly like a schoolboy caught in his carelessness.

The door opened and Alice came in with a basket over her arm. She was used to seeing them already at work, and simply nodded a greeting and went straight to the kitchen. They heard the sound of the coals being raked over and then a kettle being filled at the pump in the scullery and put on the range to boil.

'Your working here is correct, but long-winded,' Grace remarked. 'I will show you another method that will be useful as you progress to more complex calculations. If you take the number to be divided and put it here, like so…'

She caught him looking at her face. He was smiling. '… do you follow, Mr Hollingdale?'

'Oh, yes,' he said, recovering himself. 'Yes, I follow perfectly.'

'Good. I think you'll find that if you use this method and try number twenty-one now, you will save yourself time, and eliminate one of the stages at which an error can creep in.'

'Thank you,' he said.

She was surprised at the warmth of his words. 'Not at all.'

'If you don't mind my saying, you seem a little out of sorts this morning. I do hope you are quite well,' Daniel remarked.

In the kitchen the kettle whistled. Alice appeared and asked whether she could make them tea.

'Not during the lesson, thank you,' Grace replied. 'It would interrupt our work.'

'Yes, Miss. Sorry, Miss.' Alice said, returning to the kitchen.

Grace had dismissed her automatically. Her father's stern rule had been that refreshments were never offered to students. It was an interruption, and once offered it set a precedent. They would forever be expecting drinks, and that would only lead to interruptions, informality and chatter. A supervision of fifty minutes left no time for such distractions.

They continued their work for a few moments during which Alice could be heard moving about in the kitchen, but then Grace made a decision.

'I shall change my mind!' she declared. 'I should love a cup of tea. May I offer you one, Mr Hollingdale?'

'That would be most welcome,' he said.

'It may not happen every time,' she warned him.

'I would not expect it.'

'It's just that I was a little…delayed this morning, and ran out of time myself.'

'No need to explain,' he said, attempting to conceal a smile.

The tea was brought in cups that matched neither each other nor their odd saucers.

'I was at St Benet's Union workhouse yesterday,' Grace said, sipping her tea. She was looking out of the window.

'You had business there?' he said, raising one eyebrow.

'I had an accident and was carried there.' She pointed to a raised bruise on one side of her forehead. It was the side turned away from him, and he had not seen it. He had not seen the bandage on her wrist either.

Hollingdale found to his surprise that the sight of these injuries brought him an unexpectedly painful jolt of concern. 'How dreadful. You were not seriously hurt, I hope?'

'No. A barrel fell off a cart. Anyway, they carried me …'

'You were *knocked over*?'

'Yes. Anyway, they carried me …'

'You were injured by a barrel? Knocked off your feet in the street! You might have been killed!'

She frowned a little at this interruption. 'I was not, though, obviously. I am here, and almost perfectly well.'

'Excuse me, but I felt concerned.'

'No need for that. I had not been inside a workhouse before. It is a large establishment, this particular one. There are about sixty people resident there. There is a hospital wing for the treatment of the sick.'

'Yes, I believe that is often the case,' he said.

'I saw it. It is not a wholesome place. The air is fusty and, although the matron's house is clean and pleasant, the houses for the residents are cold and well, they are not particularly clean.'

'That is most regrettable,' Hollingdale said. He was looking at the textbook. At problem number twenty-six, which was particularly puzzling.

'Mr Hollingdale, you have some knowledge of law-breaking activity.'

He looked at her in astonishment. 'Law-breaking?'

'You stole the little Venus?'

He bristled at this. 'It was a foolish prank. It was returned almost immediately.'

He looked back at the textbook for several minutes before clearing his throat and saying in a low voice, 'I am not proud of what I did, Miss Marshall. I regretted the impulse almost immediately. It was a dare. I should never have done it.'

'You are the only law-breaker I have ever met.'

'I resent that designation! As I said, it was simply a passing moment of tom-foolery, and…'

'I want your advice, you see. On law-breaking, I mean. I have never done anything illegal, but I find, now, that I have committed a crime of my own.'

Hollingdale looked up at her sharply, his pencil in mid-air.

Chapter Forty-Five

'I have stolen the three children I mentioned out of the workhouse.'

Her student stopped looking at his books and turned to look at Grace in frank astonishment. 'When you say you have *stolen* these children...?'

'I was there. I saw the conditions. I could not bear to leave them.'

'You simply removed them? Nobody prevented it?'

'Nobody saw. It was dinner time. Their nurse - if you can call her that - was distracted. I took advantage of an opportunity.'

'Great heavens! And what did you do with these unfortunate infants? Where did you take them?'

'To a safe place.' She said this rather primly, brushing a speck of dust from her skirt, avoiding his gaze.

'Oh well, that is a great mercy, at least.'

Alice brought more hot water for their tea. The maid seemed a little flustered at what she was overhearing, he thought.

'In your view,' Grace asked, sipping her tea, 'would that be classed as a kidnap? An offence against the law?'

'Well, yes, I should think it would be. Stealing away three children. Yes, I believe that would be classified as an offence.'

'A serious offence, I imagine?'

'Serious enough, I should say.'

Grace coughed a little. She set her cup on the tiny table. 'Serious enough to be sent to prison, do you think?'

'But you were taking the children to a better home, you said?'

'I was. I stole them, all the same.'

'Those would be mitigating circumstances.'

'I might not be sent to jail, then, perhaps?'

'It would depend on your motives, I imagine. If your aim was to save the poor creatures, then you might be given a light sentence. Perhaps only a fine.'

'I am a criminal, Mr Hollingdale,' Grace said. 'But there seemed no alternative. They were wasting away. They have no-one.'

'I'm sorry, Miss Marshall, but I don't follow you.'

'Yesterday I went to the workhouse,' she began, as if teaching an exceptionally slow student his next lesson.

'Yes. I heard that part, but I think it would be better if you began at the beginning. If you wouldn't mind.'

Grace nodded, looking down at her hands, now clasped tightly in her lap.

'I have been typing up the notes about this workhouse. About the Matron, Mrs Lemman. There have been many complaints about the way she runs the place. There is to be an investigation. But they move so slowly. It will not start until a month's time, and even then they will probably drag their feet, and meanwhile these three little girls were there in a dim damp room with a sleeping old lady.'

This came out in a landslide of words that left Hollingdale blinking.

'They were abandoned outside in the street. Left with a note from their poor mother. The note is there among the papers. It is the most heartrending plea I have ever read. It begs someone to look after them and keep them together. She must have been desperate and not able to care for them.'

'Is there no charitable organisation to care for orphans left in this way?' Hollingdale asked her. 'There must be, surely?'

'Perhaps there is, but everyone seems so slow to react. I think Mrs Lemman was planning to sell them.'

'*Sell* them? What would make you suspect that?'

'The accounts. She seems to have done it before.'

'Who in the world *buys* children?'

'I don't know. This whole world of workhouses and orphaned children is new to me, and I know nothing about stealing children. I only know that I saw them there yesterday, and I could not leave them.'

'Are there no authorities you could appeal to?'

'I tried. They are not capable of acting swiftly enough.'

'Surely someone - a doctor, or a magistrate - could intervene?'

'It's all paperwork, you see. There is a doctor, and somewhere there is probably a magistrate, but there is no time to wait. I honestly thought the baby would not survive.'

'Miss Marshall, this is very serious. One cannot steal children!'

'One cannot leave them to the mercy of someone like Mrs Lemman either! I know it is a kind of madness, but there was simply nobody else willing to help. I had to take action. But, of course, I had no idea how to go about it. My life has been so entirely law-abiding. In the end, I must admit, I did no planning of any sort. I was hit in the street outside the workhouse by a barrel. A complete accident. They carried me inside for treatment. The maid showed me round, and I found the three little girls. Their living quarters were so dreadfully grim and dingy. They were the most pitiful sight. I stole them by leading them out of the front gate.'

'You simply walked out with them? Nobody intervened?'

'Didn't you just walk out with the statue?'

Hollingdale blinked at her, astonished. 'As I said, that was hardly the same thing! But, yes, I did just carry it out. And where did you take them?'

'They are upstairs.'

'What? Upstairs? Here?'

'Yes. There was nowhere else.'

'Good heavens!' Hollingdale leaned back in his chair and contemplated his teacher with new eyes. 'I hardly know what to say!'

'You need not say anything. I should not have told you. But, I thought, as a practised law-breaker…'

'I really do not care to be labelled that way, Miss Marshall. You make me sound like the worst kind of life-long criminal. In fact I simply got carried away in a foolish moment. Mine was a prank! Mere youthful high-spirits. A fleeting moment of irresponsibility.'

'Ah yes. We are not the same, then, at all,' Grace said. 'I don't think the outcome of my crime will be fleeting. I think I have done something irretrievable and permanent. But my main worry is not what will happen to me, but what will happen to the three little girls asleep upstairs. They must not be sent to some dreadful prison of a children's home and forgotten. I simply cannot allow it.'

'Well, that is all very admirable, but who will care for them?'

'I haven't finalised arrangements for that, yet.'

'Finalised them? Have you thought this through at all?'

'Well, no, I accept that I shall be improvising for a few days, but I shall find a way. I imagine. I shall find a proper home for them.'

'Do you know a great deal about caring for young children? Do you have a lot of younger cousins and so forth?'

'I have no cousins. I know nothing whatever of how to care for little children. I admit that is something I had not considered very deeply.'

'Can you yourself provide everything three children need?'

'I imagine I can provide a safe haven while a foster home is located,' Grace said.

'And have you the means, the financial means, to support them? I hope you won't mind my asking.'

'Not immediately, but I am learning to use a typewriter, and writing the articles about hats, and there may be other students for tuition.'

'I am no expert, Miss Marshall, but I am fairly certain that a hundred students like me would not cover the cost of keeping three little children.'

'Probably not,' she agreed. 'But Daniel, what else could I do?'

She had used his first name. The sound of it distracted him for a moment.

He looked helplessly out of the window.

'Perhaps you have experience of young children?' Grace asked.

'I have seven younger cousins,' he said, 'so I know a little of them. They are very demanding and hungry all the time, as I recall. And noisy! If there are three little girls upstairs they must be asleep, I hear nothing.'

'They are very quiet. Unnaturally so, I believe. They stare and stare, but even the baby makes no sound. It concerns me, but at least they are calm.'

'I should very much like to meet them,' he said, but added, 'only if it will not alarm them in any way, of course.'

'I have no way of knowing what will alarm them,' she said.

'They will be hungry, I imagine. They will need food.'

Chapter Forty-Six

A knock at the door silenced both of them. They looked at one another in alarm. Grace's eyes wide with horror. The knock, urgent but quiet, was repeated several more times. Grace stood and hurried to the door, signalling Hollingdale to be quiet about the children by putting her fingers to her lips.

On the doorstep, she found the thin figure of Jane, the maid from the workhouse. She was hunched and trembling, her face pale, the gloveless knuckles of her fingers blotched with blue. She could barely speak.

'I ran...' she started to say, but then her knees buckled and she almost fell.

Grace helped her inside and sat her down. She continued to shiver as Hollingdale moved the chair and they set her beside the fire. While the kettle boiled again, Jane could only tremble. She had no coat, only a thin shawl over her workhouse uniform. 'I had nowhere to go. I could not stay. Mrs Lemman...'

Grace ran and fetched a blanket, a tablecloth and the

feather eiderdown cover from her own bed, everything she could think of to cover and warm the trembling young woman. 'Are they here? Are the babbies here?' Jane managed to ask between blue lips.

'They are upstairs, safe, but they have eaten nothing. I'm not sure what I can give them. I have a little milk, and some porridge, would that do, Jane?'

Jane nodded. She was holding a teacup in shaking, white-knuckled hands, but beginning by now to tremble a little less.

'Alice, there are three little girls upstairs. They are my guests for a few days.' Grace said.

Alice looked at her warily, but she had overheard a lot of what was said. 'Could you make them some porridge? And some for Jane, please, if there is enough.'

There was enough porridge, but bowls were in short supply. Alice brought it in the saucepan and put some on a saucer for Jane, who was showing signs of recovery.

'Are you well enough to come upstairs, Jane? They might be glad to see a face they know. As far as I could tell, Violet did not sleep at all last night. She sat and watched over her sisters.'

Jane followed Grace up the twisted staircase. At the top she found the three sisters in an improvised bed on the floor. All three were awake and watching warily. Violet stretched one arm around Rose's shoulders. The other gripped the baby's sleeve tightly.

'You remember me?' Jane said.

Violet looked silently at Jane for a moment. Her eyes

then filled with tears, and she began to shake with silent weeping.

'I believe she fears I will take her back, Miss.' Jane said, helplessly.

'No, no, Jane will not take you back,' Grace said. 'Nobody will take you back, Violet. You are all safe here. I promise.'

But the little girl could not stop her tears. They flowed over her cheeks in torrents. Little Rose, seeing her sister weep, burst into tears herself, but she was less restrained. She howled with her mouth a round pink O. The baby was startled and looked alarmed at this sudden sound, opening her own mouth and joining the outcry, throwing her arms out to either side. Soon the whole attic was filled with wailing and sobs.

Grace looked at Jane in helpless dismay. The three little girls in tears at once was the most desperately saddening sight she had ever seen. But, oddly, Jane seemed perfectly calm.

'They have never cried, Miss. Not in all the time I've seen them. Not once. This is the most normal thing I have seen them do. If we can get them to take a little breakfast, I think that will help.'

It took some doing. Grace, Alice and Daniel were all needed to hold one sobbing child each. Jane held the porridge pan and offered spoons of the mush towards each of them in turn. Little Rose stopped crying first, her eye caught, mid-sob by the porridge. She lunged for the spoon, grabbing it stickily and cramming porridge snatched from it into her mouth with an eager hand. A lot of it went astray, but some, at least, stayed in her mouth, and once tasted, she hurried to reach for more. Her big sister, still shuddering with fading sobs, watched this. She calmed a little, blinking back tears. Rose was on her fourth or fifth handful when Jane offered some to Violet, but the oldest sister only turned her head away and looked at the baby. Baby Ivy, supported on Daniel's arm, now reached both her little hands out hopefully. Jane spooned a little into her open mouth, and, although she looked suspicious at first, the baby chewed and almost immediately opened her mouth again like a little bird, asking for more.

Violet refused to take any porridge until her sisters had been eating for some time. Rose had oats and milk sticking happily in her hair, her clothes and all over her cheeks. Baby Ivy was lying back, beginning to fall into a doze on Daniel's arm, a small beard of oats on her chin. Only then did Violet accept the handle of the spoon and eat a little of what was left from the saucepan. She never took her eyes from her sisters.

Cleaning the porridge from the three little girls when they had finished eating was a job in itself. It was while Jane was applying the damp cloth to their faces that they heard Rose say, in a matter-of-fact way. 'Wet.'

She certainly was. And so was the baby. Another job presented itself. But since all three girls had taken a little food, and Rose had even spoken, that first breakfast was generally agreed to be a triumph.

Chapter Forty-Seven

'I must leave,' Hollingdale said, as the cleaning was underway. 'There is a service in chapel.'

The mathematics lesson had been forgotten in the flurry of Jane's arrival, the children and porridge.

'I do apologise. I owe you a lesson. Shall we say tomorrow morning at the same time?' Grace said.

He was backing away. 'You might be rather pre-occupied for the next few days,' he said. Jane had taken baby Ivy from him and offered him a cloth to sponge some of the porridge from his sleeve.

'We will be organised enough for a lesson, though.'

'No, I don't think… I mean it probably is not a good idea to assume …' He looked around him at the flurry of activity caused by the children… 'to assume that we can continue our classes. Not for the time being.'

'Will you work from the book on your own?' Grace was surprised. He looked anxious to leave. 'I will look over any exercises you complete, if you bring them.'

'It would be better if I managed alone, perhaps. While

you organise...all this.' He gestured in a general way around the room towards the children and the maids. 'Mathematics is clearly not your priority at present.'

After he left, Alice saw Grace's look of surprise. 'He is not used to little ones, I suppose, Miss,' she said. 'College gentlemen are not accustomed to them, generally. The baby only wet his trousers a little. I sponged them and they will dry on the cycle ride. He has nothing to worry about.'

'If you need a place for these children, you should ask Miss Goggins at The Dales, Miss,' Alice said later. 'I know her from Church. She is a strange lady, but she is kind to children. The Dales is a charity school. She takes all sorts. Orphans and so on, they live there.'

'Of all ages?'

'I think so. It's near where I live. Everybody round our way knows it. It isn't the tidiest of places but the children seem well cared for.'

'How can you be sure?' Grace asked.

'They play all day in the garden and make a lot of noise about it. They give concerts and sing. We see them in Church. They are not always the best behaved children, or the smartest in their clothes, but they are always cheerful.'

'I shall need to visit this Miss Goggins,' Grace said.

'You need to tread carefully,' Alice told her. 'She is a strange lady. Kind to children, but fierce to anyone she does not take to.'

Chapter Forty-Eight

Number six Harrington Road had once been a grand townhouse. Double fronted with ample bay windows, a full basement and four floors, it had belonged to the Makepeace family for fifty years, but when Henry Makepeace consolidated his fortune in patent medicines, he moved out to the country and left the house to a group of Cambridge charities working for the relief of the poor.

Run ever since on a tight budget, the house had long ago been stripped of its stylish furnishings. What was left were the bare bones of its neo-gothic architecture - arched doors, steep stairs, and an annual list of repairs that made the trustees frown and shake their heads over the accounts.

Nobody designing a school would have chosen anything like The Dales, as number six had been named by the Makepeace family. The attic bedrooms were small and chilly in the winter, and the basement kitchen was dim and prone to damp, but a certain residual elegance remained in the high ceilings with their elaborate mouldings of plaster fruit and flowers. There was a long walled garden with a lawn, trees for climbing and a swing, and the ballroom which had been added at the back made a generous schoolroom.

So, if the Trustees remarked, on their visits, how lucky the children and Miss Goggins were to be so royally accommodated, they did so while sidestepping holes in the floorboards and damp patches in the plaster.

Grace was climbing the front doorsteps by nine o'clock. She pulled the long bell-pull, which had a handle in the shape of a dragon's head and waited on the doorstep, listening to the sounds from within. These were principally running footsteps on stairs - it sounded like a small but indecisive army running up, and then back down, but there were also incoherent shouts and scufflings and finally a gong rang out. Grace pulled the dragon's head again. Very far in the distance she could hear that it sounded a bell. This time she heard a scrambling behind the door almost immediately and it was opened by a boy of about eight years old wearing a paper crown decorated with bright splurges of paint representing the Crown Jewels.

'Hello,' he said. 'Today is my birthday.'

'Many happy returns of the day,' Grace said, not knowing how else to respond.

The boy grinned, but was then distracted by something inside the house and turned as if he would run away, so she added. 'I was hoping to see the lady who runs the school. Miss Goggins?'

'She is in the school room. Come with me. I'll take you,' the boy said. He began to lead her through the house, but then remembered his manners and added, 'if you please, Miss.'

There then followed a series of steps up and steps down and dog-leg corridor bends until they arrived at a large room, lit by a roof lantern with stained glass, in which a number of children of differing sizes - Grace found them difficult to count, they were so very mobile - were running about. There were desks and books. It was clearly a classroom, though it was nothing like the sort of classroom Grace had previously seen. She looked about, and spotted a lady at the far end, who, with her back turned, was writing on a blackboard.

'Miss Goggins?' Grace enquired.

The lady turned, revealing that she had been writing, '*Ancient Egypt. Queen Cleopatra*,' on the board.

'Do you know very much about Ancient Egypt?' Miss Goggins asked, as if she knew Grace well, and had been expecting her to visit.

'I? No, I am not a specialist in that era,' Grace told her.

'I wonder now whether it is a suitable subject at all for my infant class. I chose it some time ago, but the more I read about the goings-on in the Egypt of the pyramids, the more unsuitable it seems to be. They married their own siblings for one thing. But the hieroglyphs are fascinating, I always think. Don't you? We shall just have to concentrate on the pyramids and the hieroglyphs. The girls are already building a pyramid in the garden. It's more difficult than you think. What can I do for you?'

Grace had no idea how to talk to this lady, but it was clear at least that directness was in order. 'I came across some children. Three little girls.' Miss Goggins stopped writing and turned round, directing her full attention to her visitor despite the children running about in the background. 'In the workhouse at St Benet's. I was taken there - carried inside - after an accident.' She pointed to the bump on her head. 'And I took the opportunity to look round. There were three little girls in the hospital wing. In a dark, damp room with an old lady watching them. They had been there for many weeks. Their living conditions were dreadful. It was cold. Their health was in danger. I was told you might be able to help.'

'Perhaps, before we go any further, you had better tell me your name.' Miss Goggins turned, brushing chalk dust from her hands onto her apron.

'Grace Marshall.'

'Is the dreadful Iris Lemman still in charge there, Grace?' Miss Goggins asked.

'Yes. I was taken into her house after the accident.'

'Wretched woman! They should have rid themselves of her long ago. I would not trust Iris Lemman to look after a bent penny, never mind three little girls. Iris Lemman is only interested in her own pocket. She's been lining it for years. She has no business keeping children at the workhouse, and she knows it.'

'I wasn't sure what to do.'

'Whose are these children?'

'Nobody knows. They were left on the street, outside the door.'

Miss Goggins sighed and shook her head. 'Abandoned at the workhouse door! It was common enough when I was young, but I thought we had made progress since those days. Poor little dots!'

'Is there no magistrate or doctor who could take action against Mrs Lemman? It looked, from the papers I have read, as if she made a habit of taking in children, but there was no record of where they eventually went.'

'No Magistrate will act against the Workhouse Union Committee. They will want to do things according to the letter of the law, and that takes too long. The nearest doctor would be Williams. I know him well enough. He is a mild as milk and will not stand up to Mrs Lemman. She will overrule him. And she will refuse to pay his fees if he says anything against her. She has them all under her thumb. Has done for years.'

Miss Goggins shook her head. The room around them had gradually resolved into quiet. The children had settled at their desks, and all were reading or drawing, except the boy in the crown who had opened the front door. He was lying on his back on the floor with his arms and legs spread wide. 'It is Rufus's birthday,' Miss Goggins said, by way of explaining this.

She turned and rested her chalk behind one ear before announcing to the children, 'Continue with your work, class. I must leave you for a few minutes,' and leading Grace out of the schoolroom and by a side door, into the garden.

It was a bright day. Miss Goggins led them along a path to a garden bench, and indicated that Grace should sit beside her.

'There have been questions raised about Mrs Lemman for several years. I have written many times to the authorities, but they took no action,' said Miss Goggins.

'I tried that too, without result,' Grace said.

'Tell me exactly what you saw. I am particularly interested in the children, their manner and appearance.'

Grace described the three little girls, how the oldest one leaned protectively over her sleeping sisters, their silence, the hand that had been raised.

'I took it to be an appeal for help,' Grace said, 'but perhaps I am sentimental.'

'You do not seem sentimental to me,' Miss Goggins said. 'What else could the poor creature do to entreat you? She may not have the power of speech. Or she may not dare to speak. I have seen both in children who were badly treated in their infancy. I have known hidden children who lived so secretly that they were not permitted to make any sort of noise. They were trained to be silent because a landlord or a member of the family could not know of their existence. They are dosed up, sometimes, with sleeping medicine.' She sighed and added, 'It usually comes down to poverty.'

'Miss Goggins, I have asked some people I know about the National Children's Home at Haverhill...'

'... and they told you it was a grim, cold and insanitary place, where children suffer ill health in large numbers?'

'Yes, that is exactly what they said.'

'I know it. I visited on several occasions and, well, I agree with that opinion completely. I would not send a child there for any reason on earth.'

'What is to be done?'

Miss Goggins looked across the garden towards the tall conifers along one side. A pair of plump pigeons flew in and ambled companionably across the lawn. 'If I had my way, I should march to the front door of that workhouse this instant and demand that Mrs Lemman hand those poor children over immediately.'

'That is what I did,' Grace said. 'Well, no, I am not as bold as you. I was carried in after my accident, and I walked out with the children when nobody was looking.'

Miss Goggins looked at Grace with renewed respect. 'Well, bravo!' she said, 'Good for you!'

'But I have no idea what to do with them next. I was wondering whether you might be able to take them into your school.'

'Sadly, Miss Marshall, I am at the mercy of the Board that runs this place. Their quarterly inspection takes place this week. I am strictly restricted in the number of children I am permitted to take here. Twelve is my limit, and twelve is the number I have at present, and all in groups of siblings. Groups that would otherwise be separated and are hard to find a foster home for. In most places they are split up and sent to different homes without a second thought, but I've always found that keeping them together leads to more steadiness and far happier young people.'

Grace watched the pigeons for a moment, disappointed.

Chapter Forty-Nine

'My problem is that the Board that runs this place are constantly looking for an excuse to move us on,' Miss Goggins continued. 'Any infringement on my part, and they would give me my marching orders. Heaven only knows what would become of the children, if that happened. This house represents the only steadiness they have known. Our future here has never been secure. The Board was given the use of this house many years ago, but now they are convinced that the charity would benefit from a sale. It is a valuable property on the open market, you see.'

'Where would you go? Where would the children go, if you had to leave here?'

'Where indeed? I have no answer. My only hope is to oblige the Board by following their rules and keep them at bay until the youngest I now have—that would be Evie, she is three—is old enough to move on to an apprenticeship or some sort of employment. We have achieved this with twenty-three children who have lived here in the past twelve years. We know it can work. Ten more years, and Evie and her brothers and sisters will be grown. That is my ambition.'

'What can I do with the three little girls?' Grace asked.

'What is your situation in life, Miss Marshall, if I may ask?'

Grace was surprised by the question, but willing enough to answer. 'I have recently moved into a small cottage belonging to New College. My father was the Master, before he died.'

'My condolences. Is the cottage self-contained?'

'Yes. It is in need of a few repairs, but it is quite separate from Abercrombie House next door.'

'Would there be room for the three bairns there?'

'There is only one small bedroom in the loft upstairs.'

'Warm and dry, at least?'

'Yes.'

'Perhaps they could stay with you, at first?' Miss Goggins was smiling. 'You could find them some medical assistance, and so forth. Their health could be restored, and decisions about their future could be taken in a calm and measured way.'

'But I know so very little about children,' Grace said.

'You have domestic help?'

'The college lent me a temporary maid. And the Lemman's maid has arrived. She has run away.'

'Iris Lemman will not like that! Are they both kindly? Good-natured? Capable?'

'Alice is. Jane seems to be.'

'Well, that should be enough to get you started.'

'My means are very limited at present,' she said, 'My future income is uncertain.'

'Oh, don't worry about that,' Miss Goggins said. 'A way can always be found. I've never had any money but more than twenty children have been raised and educated here somehow. You risk prosecution, obviously. For kidnap, or some such nonsensical charge. Mrs Lemman and the authorities who run the Union House will not take kindly to what you have done. I have incurred their wrath before, and it was not pleasant. They are litigious and self-righteous, and, in my experience, they do not hesitate to spend charitable donations on legal fees. Your helping these infants might lead to the police being called, and a criminal record. You should prepare yourself.'

'I am willing to risk that. I have good evidence of malpractice at St Benet's and the Chronicle will publish my article about it.'

'Excellent! It's high time somebody stopped Mrs Lemman. Is she selling them? I suspected as much!'

'The accounts show that she takes money from the Board for their keep and then another larger payment before they disappear from the records.'

'She probably is selling them then. Wretch! She will stop at nothing!'

Grace thought of something. 'Is there a Mr Lemman?'

Miss Goggins smiled at the question. 'Nobody really knows. He is reputed to help her run the place, but has not been seen for years. Some say she ate him, but that's probably an exaggeration.'

Grace glanced in alarm at Miss Goggins, who was looking inscrutably into the distance. She still had a piece of chalk behind one ear. She stood abruptly. 'I must get back to Cleopatra in the classroom. What do you teach?'

'Mathematics.'

'Mathematics!' Miss Goggins was already striding back across the grass, but stopped mid-step. 'Do you have any spare time? Could you give the children here some lessons?

We have been without a mathematics teacher for several months. A fee is available. Only a small one, but you could bring the orphaned children with you.'

'My teaching has all been at undergraduate level,' Grace said.

'Then you should find teaching these young people very easy indeed,' said Miss Goggins, throwing open the door to the school room. 'Simple arithmetic! A little geometry and algebra! What could be easier? Keep the lessons practical. You'll find them very amenable, as long as you give them something practical to do. Come next week. I shall send a few things for the three you have at home. Call again any time, if you need help. Back to Cleopatra!'

Grace spent the rest of the day with Alice devising ways of accommodating three small children and Jane in the tiny cottage. The baby was allotted an empty drawer, and her two sisters were given an improved blanket bed under the eaves in Grace's bedroom. Alice, who had little sisters, asked James to make a gate to fasten across the steep flight of stairs, so that the baby should not tumble down. Grace had not thought of this possibility. Some time in the afternoon Rufus, from The Dales, still wearing his paper crown, arrived with a parcel which turned out to be children's clothing.

'You're to have these for the babbies,' he explained, 'Miss Goggins sent them.'

'Thank you, Rufus. I hope you are enjoying your birthday,' Grace said.

'Yes, I am. I can do whatever I like on my birthday. Miss Goggins allows it.'

'Like lying on the floor?'

'Yes, I did that at first. Then I climbed the big tree and

did some singing. Then I ate some toffee. Then I came here.'

Alice appeared from the kitchen with a plate of jam tarts. She was not sure what the new arrivals would need to eat the next day, but was reckoning on jam tarts suiting most occasions. They certainly suited Rufus.

Chapter Fifty

Leaving the chapel deep in thought, Daniel was intercepted by Dr Hillyer. 'Ah, Hollingdale,' the older man said, falling into step as Daniel hurried along the path towards the Porter's Lodge, 'a brief word, if I may?'

Daniel kept walking. He disliked Hillyer's manner as much as he disliked being accosted.

'You still take lessons with Miss Marshall?' Hillyer asked.

'I do. She is kind enough to tutor me for…'

'Yes,' Hillyer interrupted. 'A punitive summer school. I know the arrangement. The point is—well, the point is that these lessons are no longer suitable. I should like them to cease.'

'Is that any business of yours?' Daniel asked.

Hillyer's legs were shorter. His face was turning red and he was trotting to keep up. He bristled at this question. 'It is every business of mine. Miss Marshall and I are engaged to be married. She will be far too preoccupied with arrangements for our nuptials and our removal to Zurich for any more teaching.'

Daniel stopped walking and turned to Hillyer, astonished.

'She has not mentioned our plans to you, I see,' Hillyer was clearly gratified. 'Grace is a very private person, as is wise and proper for a young woman alone in the world and in mourning.'

Daniel almost smiled at this. His last meeting with Grace had seen her anything but 'alone in the world'. The cottage had been crowded with three little children and a newly-arrived maid, as well as Alice and James. He decided to keep this to himself and looked away. Could Grace really have decided to marry this man? Did she love this oaf? It made no sense.

'I hope I have made my wishes clear, Mr Hollingdale.'

Daniel shook his head. 'Perfectly clear, yes,' he said. 'The tuition was ending anyway, as it happens.' He hurried away, leaving Hillyer to catch his breath before walking with an air of considerable self-satisfaction back towards his rooms.

In the Porter's Lodge, George was sorting mail into pigeonholes. 'Rather a special one there for you, Mr Hollingdale,' he said, nodding towards the H row. Not knowing what he meant, Daniel picked a large, thick envelope out and examined it. It was made of the highest quality paper and addressed to *D. Hollingdale Esq. New College, Cambridge*, in elaborately ornamented copperplate handwriting of the sort Daniel had only seen before on scrolls and certificates.

George was nodding conspiratorially. 'From the royal household, sir, unless I'm much mistaken.'

'Why would someone from the royal household write to me?'

'It has the look of an invitation about it to me, sir,' George remarked. 'You'll be going up in the world!'

Daniel opened the envelope with the paper knife George kept handy and read the letter. 'Well!' he said, finally. 'Believe it or not, George, the Master of the Queen's Music appears to be asking me to compose a piece of music for the Diamond Jubilee!'

George, rising to the occasion, stood to attention and saluted Daniel. 'Please allow me to be the first to congratulate you, sir.'

'Thank you, George. And now I must go and ask someone who knows what this really means.'

Chapter Fifty-One

Biddy was in bed. Even her lips looked pale. Her brother dreaded the return of her terrible cough.

'How was your lesson?' she asked, as Daniel brought in her tea. 'Did you send my apologies?'

'I did. It was all very odd at the cottage this morning,' he told her.

'But you did go for the lesson?'

'I went, but almost no lesson occurred.' He moved his sister's pillow so that she could sit more upright. She looked at him, curious. Biddy's eyes seemed larger and brighter when she was feverish, her brother thought.

'Is something troubling you, Daniel?' she asked suddenly.

He looked serious, but said nothing for several minutes, then sighed and ran his hand through his hair. 'In all honesty, Biddy, I could not say.'

'But nothing so dreadful, surely?' she was smiling, hoping to cheer him.

'Grace has taken children from the workhouse. Just

stolen them away. And brought them to the cottage. Three little girls. One is only a baby. They were hungry. We fed them porridge.'

She blinked at him, astonished.

'It is madness!' Daniel continued. 'She has no funds to support them. If you saw them, Biddy. Such shadowy things, so pale and sorrowful. Their heads are shaven. Children with nothing. No family. Nothing.'

'When did she do this?'

'Yesterday. She just carried them out and brought them home with her.'

'That is extraordinary! I knew she was worried about some little children. She mentioned them once. Good for her!'

He shook his head. 'You say that, but the consequences will be serious and long-lasting. I will not go back, Biddy.'

'Why not? You did not care for them? You did not like the children?'

'It is not that.'

'What then?'

'I can't say. I had to leave. I said I would not go for another lesson. She is bound to be pre-occupied.' Biddy watched her brother frown and chew his thumb nail. She had rarely seen him look so grim.

'But why not go on with your lessons? She can spare an hour, surely?'

He stood and began pacing back and forth in front of the window. 'It all seemed so trivial, suddenly. So futile. Mathematics as a punishment. I am a spoiled wastrel. A fool. And those helpless innocents face life with nothing—*nothing*—while I drift about Cambridge, playing the piano and singing holy music in the chapel.'

He sat on the side of the bed, looking away. His shoulders were hunched.

'Daniel, what is this?'

'I held the youngest one, the baby. Ivy is her name. I held Ivy on my knee. She is thin, Biddy. There is nothing of her. She has none of the warm flesh a little one should have. Her cheeks are not round. She is gaunt. Her eyes look too big in her face. She was not glowing and clean, the way we would think of infants. But she wants life. She saw that food and she grabbed it! I felt the great force of determination in her.' He shook his head as he remembered. 'That little creature has probably never had a day of comfort or ease in her whole life, but she wants life. The middle child is the same, but the oldest one, Violet, has almost had the spirit taken from her. She is their protector. She is four years old, perhaps. But she watches and watches over her sisters. She trusts nobody. Nobody has ever earned her trust. It is almost too much, Biddy. Almost too much to bear.'

'But Miss Marshall has taken steps that could save them.'

'Yes. It is truly admirable. What courage! Foolish courage, but impressive. I fear for the consequences for her. She risks prosecution.'

'Is that what makes you fearful?'

He hung his head. 'No. I just feel that I cannot be trusted, Biddy. Responsibility is always too much for me. I am not reliable. I have always lived for myself. For music, and for—well, for the pleasures and light-heartedness of life.'

'For art. You have a genuine talent - a gift. You have always worked hard at your music.'

'That makes it all sound too noble by far. I can sing. I play the piano and the organ. I write music. What does any of that mean when there are people even in the same city so poor that they have to abandon their children because they cannot feed them? I have none of the qualities needed to help these little girls. Someone like me would only let them down. I fail people. I would only fail them. Fail Grace. Break everybody's heart. I cannot do that. Far better to step aside now. They have been failed too often already.'

A long coughing fit seized Biddy. It left her breathless, lying back on her pillows. He leaned over and touched her forehead.

'You have not failed *me*, Daniel,' Biddy said. 'You have given up your life in college to live here with me and help me recover. They had to grant you special permission. The Daniel you describe is long gone already, can't you see that?' The coughing spasm returned. She lay back, exhausted, on her pillows.

Daniel poured her a glass of water. 'Grace is engaged to be married,' he said. 'Her fiancé accosted me in college to tell me.'

'Who is he?'

'Hillyer is his name. A mathematician who worked with her father.'

'Unpleasant?' Biddy asked.

'Deeply.' He put the back of his hand to her forehead. 'I am fetching Dr Sallett immediately,' he said. 'No arguments.'

His sister gasped for breath in the empty room as the door closed behind him.

Chapter Fifty-Two

'She is feverish,' Sallett said, coming downstairs from Biddy's room. He was carrying his black bag, and set in on the table. 'I have given her some medicine to help. Your sister needs country air and rest.'

'Will the breathlessness return?'

'I don't think so. I believe this is just a slight set-back. She does too much too quickly, despite my warnings.'

'She has taken up mathematics, did she tell you?'

Sallett smiled. 'She did. It makes her happy. I see no harm in intellectual stimulation, but she should stay indoors and warm.'

'My sister is not easy to control.'

'Her independence is one of the qualities I most admire,' said the doctor.

'You do admire her, then?'

'I am very much hoping that Edith will consent to marry me, Daniel. Your father has given his permission.'

'Already?'

'I went to London last week to see him,' the doctor said.

'He was not, I admit, over-enthusiastic—my practice is still small—but he agreed after I had argued my case. I hope you will be able to accept me as a brother-in-law.'

'I will, with great pleasure!' They shook hands warmly. 'Edith worries that her poor health might be a burden to you.'

'Nothing about Edith could be a burden, Daniel. I hope to convince her of that as soon as she is a little stronger.' He smiled and picked up his bag.

'Would you mind visiting three small children I have become acquainted with this morning?' Daniel asked. 'They are guests of someone I know, and they are not in the best of health.'

'A contagion? A disease of childhood?'

'No. They are thin and have been uncared-for.'

Sallet looked curious, but asked no more. 'Of course I am happy to see them, if you give me the address.' Daniel wrote the address on the back of one of his own cards.

'Send the bills to me, if you would, but don't mention that I sent you.'

'I can't just arrive unannounced.'

'You could say someone from New College asked you to call in.'

'Very well. Are you quite well yourself? You look a little weary.'

'May I ask you something - something personal?'

'I don't see why not. We shall soon be brothers-in-law, I hope.'

'Do the daily responsibilities of your work not wear you down? People always depending on you to restore their health and the health of their dear ones? Do your spirits not fail you sometimes? How do you sleep at night?'

John Sallett, taken by surprised by the earnestness of

this, paused and put a hand to his chin. 'I am from a family of doctors, remember. I've watched my father and brothers at work. If we thought of ourselves as constantly responsible for people's lives, it would be too much for any of us to bear. Either that or we would be corrupted by our God-like powers! No, real doctoring teaches humility, first of all. We can only do so much. Be kind. Bring comfort. A pill here; a procedure there. We can only do what we can: be kindly; be understanding.'

He took his watch from his waistcoat pocket and glanced at it. 'Oh, and be on time. I shall call in to see the children this afternoon.'

After the doctor had left, Daniel stood for a long time watching the rain out of the window. Then he took the royal invitation from his pocket and read it again.

Chapter Fifty-Three

In twelve years of meritorious service, with a medal to prove it, Sergeant Gladwell had never dealt with a charge of kidnap before. He approached the cottage with a certain wariness, knowing only that his suspect had, in a daring raid, allegedly carried off three children the week before. He approached it also in the full knowledge that Mrs Iris Lemman, the complainant, was one of the most disagreeable members of the public he had ever encountered. Running a workhouse did not tend to make a person sweet-natured or generous, he imagined. In Iris Lemman's case, he suspected it might not make her honest either.

He was seen by the neighbours to remove his helmet before knocking on the front door. He did this out of good manners, but also because the doorway was far too low to admit all six feet three inches of him, even without it. A thin maid in grey answered his knock and promptly fainted away at his feet, so he was obliged to set the helmet on the floor and pick her up instead. As an entrance, it was a lot more dramatic than Sergeant Gladwell might have chosen.

Once the swooning maid had been revived, she burst into tears and hid her face in her apron, sobbing. Another, healthier-looking maid went to make tea and the suspect, Miss Grace Marshall, brought him a stool to sit on, there being very little furniture. There was a wooden armchair, but that was filled with three little children. Two, wrapped in blankets, were asleep, and a third, tucked in beside them, watched him with the piercing intensity of an owl.

'I'm sure you know why I'm here today, Miss Marshall,' the Sergeant began. 'A complaint has been made that you abducted three young persons from the St Benet's workhouse last week. These three young persons, presumably.'

'You can arrest me. I will come immediately,' the lady in question told him. 'But the children are safe and well cared-for here. Please let them stay in the warm.'

The maid in grey sobbed even more loudly into her apron. The other maid ran from the room and returned with a young man in a white decorator's overall. The small room felt crowded.

'No immediate arrest is necessary, Miss Marshall. But I shall need your account of events. I must ask you to accompany me to the police station.'

The Sergeant stood. He had no intention of laying hands on anyone. He meant only to indicate that it was now time to go. But all hell broke loose. Jane's sobs became wails. The two maids rushed and stood guard on either side of Miss Marshall. The painter in white ran out of the door and the child who had been watching so acutely squirmed down from her armchair, ran over and solemnly kicked his ankle. She wore no shoes, so it hardly amounted to a blow, but when he put his hand down to fend her off, she seized it and bit it with all her might. He called out in shock, this woke the baby who started to cry and the middle child joined in.

This was the chaotic scene as the Count, who had seen the police officer arrive from Toft's third floor apartment, and was breathless from hurrying down the stairs, threw open the front door several minutes later. 'I command you to wait, sir, wait!' he declared, his German accent coming to the fore. 'You shall not take her before you have spoken with the Professor!' And he placed himself with outstretched arms across the front door to form a burly barrier.

The Sergeant shook his bitten hand. It now bore a small set of toothmarks on one side. He held his tiny attacker, still kicking and biting with all her might, at bay with the other arm. 'Who, sir, are you?'

'I am Count Heinrich Von Robst. I am the neighbour. You will wait here. My colleague from New College, Professor Toft, is on his way. He cannot walk fast. He is not a young man.'

The child took advantage of the police officer's distraction to bite his other hand before Miss Marshall saw what she was doing and led her away. Attempts were also made to comfort the smaller girls, but without success. Their sobbing continued to rend the air.

At this point an elderly gentleman appeared in the doorway on the arm of an aproned housekeeper on one side and the young decorator on the other. The Count stood aside to allow them to enter. The professor took a moment to catch his breath after the exertion of hurrying, but eventually he leaned forward and peered at the Sergeant, then slowly lifted his walking cane and pointed it at him. 'Gladwell, isn't it? They made you a sergeant, I see. I shall need to talk to you immediately. A great error is being made here. A reputation-damaging error. The Chief Constable, as you know, is a close friend. He would be most upset to hear of this. You enter New College property uninvited. You frighten ladies! You cause innocent children to weep pitifully! What do you mean by it? You should know better!'

An unexpected silence fell. All eyes in the cottage looked curiously at the policeman, who drew himself up to his full height, his head an inch from the low ceiling and was about to speak when he was interrupted by Grace.

'I shall go with you to the police station, Sergeant. Let's get this over with. Please take care of the children, Jane and Alice. Do you need to put me in chains?'

'Chains will not be necessary,' said Gladwell. He looked offended.

'Help shall be sent, Grace. Have no fear,' said the Professor, as they passed him.

The Deputy Chief Inspector read the statement an hour later.

'I have already been sent three notes about this case, Gladwell. A Professor of Law, a solicitor and a barrister, all up in arms and threatening us with Acts of Parliament, Habeus Corpus, and Lord knows what else. Miss Marshall has friends in high places.'

'I had a taste of that at the arrest, sir. And as for Mrs Lemman.'

'Indeed. But we cannot allow people to stroll in to workhouses and orphanages and such like and simply carry children off when it takes their fancy. Where would that end?'

'St Benet's workhouse is a grim place, sir. I went there.'

'She needs to prove that in court. Have her released on her own recognisance. There is room on the court list next week. Let's get it over with.'

'My own recognisance?' Grace asked.

'It means you sign a document to say that you will attend the court next Tuesday. If you do not attend you will be fined £100.' Gladwell said.

'I do not have £100.'

'Then you had better attend the court.'

Chapter Fifty-Four

Hillyer was waiting outside the police station. She heard his voice as she descended the steps and felt a pulse of anger.

'Grace!' He hurried over. 'They told me you had been brought here. I was about to come in and remonstrate with them. What do they mean by...'

'It is nothing for you to concern yourself with,' Grace said.

'But of course it is! I am.. you and I are...well, we are connected, Grace.'

Grace stopped walking and looked directly at him. 'We need to discuss that matter, among others. It has been an upsetting morning. Would you mind accompanying me to your rooms, and offering me refreshment, Dr Hillyer?'

He blinked at her in surprise, but then looked rather pleased.

'Naturally,' he said.

The sky that afternoon was like a sheet of steel with steady rain oozing out of it. The guest rooms at New College overlooked the old court and looked towards the river. Despite this promising view they were unwelcoming, Grace thought. The air in Hillyer's set of rooms was chilly, and the light, on such a grey day, was dim, especially in the corners. He filled a kettle from a tap on the landing and set it over the fire.

'Dr Hillyer…'

'Grace, I really think you could address me by my first name. We are old friends by now, surely? Do call me Edmund.'

She decided to ignore that. 'I believe you have borrowed the manuscript of my father's latest book from the publisher,' she said.

'Why, yes,' he said, carefully spooning tea leaves into a teapot. 'I am one of the reviewers.'

'I should like you to return it.'

'I have yet to read it in any detail. May I ask why you want it returned?' He looked at her calmly, stirring the teapot.

'I would feel happier if it were in the publisher's care.'

'They need it next month, but not before.'

'I believe you will steal ideas from it.'

He laughed. 'Grace, I think you misunderstand how the world of academic publishing works, my dear. It is normal for a reviewer to work from a manuscript. It is expected, even. Colleagues review each other's work prior to publication in order to offer informed reviews.'

'Why have you forged a letter asking that my father's royalties be paid to you?'

He laid out a pair of cups and saucers out with great care, placing a teaspoon at the same angle in each saucer, before looking up and smiling at her. 'It was really only a way of securing the money on your behalf. Avoiding delays with probate and so on.'

'You do not deny the forgery, I notice.'

'You are being absurd. You are overwrought, Grace. It is the distress of this police matter, I imagine. Here, drink your tea. I have added a little brandy. We can settle all this easily.'

'You have kept my father's royalties.'

'Don't be foolish. You do not know what you are saying.'

'Well, where is the money? I do not have it. I have, in fact, almost no funds at all at present.'

'That must be inconvenient, but we can soon resolve all that.'

'Dr Hillyer…'

'*Edmund*, I insist.' He came to her and placed her tea on the side table, leaning across her to do so. His shoulder was close. As he straightened his back he turned, his face hovered, close to hers. 'We have no cause to disagree, Grace,' he said it breathlessly. 'None at all. We are old, old friends …' and with no warning he brushed his cheek against hers.

All Grace's instincts told her to push the thieving oaf aside and run for the door, but instead she picked up her teacup and frowned into it, trying to recall Lucia Venables' advice. The tea smelt strongly of brandy. She inhaled the fumes, hoping they would give her courage, but they only made her wince. She did, however, remember that flattery was recommended.

'These are charming rooms,' she said.

'Not particularly,' he replied. 'The guest rooms on the other side of the court are sunnier.'

'Your rooms in Zurich are very grand, I imagine,' Grace said, changing tack.

'They are nothing special. I plan to move shortly.'

Grace sighed into her teacup. Flattery was more difficult than she thought.

Hillyer straightened up and walked back across the room to collect his own cup.

'Now,' he said, with his back turned, 'about your shortage of money. I can easily help you with that difficulty. Allow me to write a cheque. It's what your father would have wanted. How much do you need?'

Grace felt a such a stab of rage at his casual mention of her father that her muscles clenched, making her teacup rattle in its saucer. She took a deep breath and attempted a smile.

Hillyer carried his cup over and sat unnecessarily close to her on the sofa. 'Your father and I had an agreement, Grace. He assumed that we would marry. He approved it. He wished it. He thought it the best possible future for you. And as to the money, I am merely managing our finances as straightforwardly as possible. You clearly have little understanding of how such matters are arranged.'

He was sitting so close that she could feel the warmth of his leg through her skirt. He pressed closer. 'I think you know how much I admire you, Grace. I have felt for many years that our future lay together.'

He leaned across and ran a finger along her cheek before lifting her hand and kissing it lingeringly. 'All is easily arranged, my dear, if you will agree to be my wife.'

Grace pressed herself back into the sofa.

'I am prepared to overlook the events of the last week or two,' Hillyer continued, setting his cup on a side table. 'A young woman alone is easily misled. You were exposed to the dubious influence of Hollingdale, for one. And that old fool, Toft. In my absence you clearly developed some sort of mania or obsession regarding orphans in the workhouse. I put it down to grief. That grim little cottage is highly unsuitable accommodation. It all contributed to your hysterical behaviour.'

He leaned closer, the sour smell of brandy on his breath.

'Many gentlemen in my position—the position of having a fiancée who has been arrested for a serious crime—many gentlemen would take the easy way out and abandon that fiancée for fear of future recurrences of such a mania. Who knows what else someone who kidnaps orphans might be capable of doing? But I am not so easily swayed. I am loyal. I shall stand by you, Grace, as a loyal husband should.'

Grace's teacup was clutched to her chest, a small china defence against Hillyer's looming person. Looking desperately over his shoulder, she caught sight of a familiar envelope on a table in a shadowy corner. The manuscript!

'I shall never marry you,' Grace said. 'I am about to report you to the police for the crimes of fraud and forgery. I am fairly certain that you have presented my father's work as your own in the past. I shall gather evidence and prove it. How will the Mathematical Society react to that? No gold medals for you, I rather think! No professorship for Dr Hillyer the plagiarist!'

He tried to laugh that off, but the smile froze on his face. His eyes were cold. 'Nobody will believe you,' he said. 'Nobody in their right mind would take your word over mine. Frankly, I fear for your sanity after this absurd business with the workhouse children. It's time you saw sense, Grace. Your Papa indulged you. He encouraged you in the idea that you had some real understanding of mathematics, but you have no such thing. You are fit only to make a real mathematician's work look pretty and polished on the page. You are useful for tidying a manuscript but the real significance of this work is well beyond you. There is no depth to your understanding. You are just the meddling daughter of a man with his best work well behind him. I was willing to give you a helping hand, but ...'

Grace threw the remains of her tea, and the cup and saucer, in his face. She leapt to her feet, bounded to the corner, picked up the manuscript and threw open the door. Hillyer was roaring and flapping his hands to fan reddening skin as she ran outside, along the cloister, through the porter's lodge and out into the street.

At Purley Press Mr Grant's eyes shone with relief behind his silvery spectacles when, still breathless, Grace handed the manuscript back.

'Everything is there and unchanged, as far as I can tell,' Grace said.

Grant leafed through the pages quickly.

'I need hardly tell you how much I regret allowing this manuscript out of the building, Miss Marshall. I have spoken to the police personally about the forged letter. Matters are in hand to recover your lost royalties from the fraudster—I cannot bring myself even to mention the name—and meanwhile we are happy to pay what is owing directly to you. If you wouldn't mind waiting here, I will fetch the cheque.'

Timmy the cockatoo rang his bell in the corner as soon as his owner had left the room. Grace went over to his cage.

'Hello, Timmy,' she said, unsure how to start a conversation with a bird.

Timmy bobbed up and down on his perch and then raised his yellow crest. 'Lovely day, sir,' he remarked. 'Fancy a ginger biscuit?'

'You were right about Dr Hillyer, Timmy,' Grace said.

Chapter Fifty-Five

'You knew Sergeant Gladwell?' Grace asked Professor Toft later.

'Pure luck. I have not taught police recruits for many years, but Gladwell is old enough to have been in one of my classes.'

They were in the professor's sitting room, overlooking the cottage. Two floors below the two maids had brought the children out into the sunshine. Grace and the professor could see them from the window. The baby was sitting on a rug. Rose was picking daisies and Violet was watching the hens.

'What did you teach them?'

'The law, of course. I did it for years. Six weeks of introductory law for the new recruits. Some of them are now quite senior. Even poor Gladwell is a sergeant. You gave him a statement?'

'Yes. I am to appear before the magistrate next week.'

'You did remove those children from the workhouse, I assume, Grace?' the Professor asked.

'I did. Nobody else was willing to act. I apologise for the disruption.'

'No apology is necessary, I shall dine out on this story for months to come! Nothing so exciting has happened at Abercrombie House for a long time.'

'It has brought you trouble, nonetheless. I can't even tell whether I will be able to make things better for the children. I fear they may simply be taken back to the workhouse.'

'I doubt that. You have acted bravely. Your father would be proud, Grace.'

'I hope so,' Grace said. 'But I have no way of knowing what will happen next.'

'Dr Hillyer has been putting it about that you and he are to be married. It was mentioned to me by three separate people when I was at college yesterday.'

'He is entirely mistaken,' Grace said.

'I must say I am very relieved to hear that. You know he stands accused of plagiarising a colleague's work in Zurich?'

'I did not know, but it doesn't surprise me.'

'He seems extremely confident that he will be offered a teaching post here, replacing your father, and that you will marry.'

'He is deluded on both counts,' Grace said. She was watching the children out of the window.

'I hear young Hollingdale has turned over a new leaf,' the professor continued. 'They say a piece of music he has written has been selected for the Diamond Jubilee. A great, great honour. They're all very pleased in the chapel. The music department are positively falling over themselves to claim the credit. Nobody ever doubted his genius, apparently! Of course, it brings esteem to the College. They're all inclined to forgive and forget his earlier misbehaviour. It was ever thus. An undergraduate can wreak havoc for years on end at the college, but the moment he distinguishes himself in the outside world, his sins are immediately forgiven. He can do no wrong now. His stock is high here in Abercrombie House too, he mended Mrs Mills' favourite teapot, did I tell you?'

'He was here? I have not seen him.'

'I imagine he thought it would not be proper to visit you, as Dr Hillyer's fiancée.'

'I thought he was avoiding the children.'

'Anyway, Mrs Mills dropped her blue teapot and it smashed into several pieces, but young Hollingdale somehow reconstructed the thing. It must have been many hours' painstaking labour. An odd young man, but a formidable talent.'

Grace was still looking out of the window.

'I meant to ask you something about the chickens, Professor. I almost forgot. I found one of them sitting on some eggs. She stares at me fiercely and tries to peck my hand if I reach for them.'

'Broody,' said the professor.

'What shall I do?'

'Throw her off the eggs and take them,' he said. 'Or, if you want her to rear some chicks, you could let her alone. There is a small coop under the far trees. You could put her in there with her eggs. She'll do the rest.'

'Chicks!' Grace said. 'I should like there to be chicks.'

Chapter Fifty-Six

'Hollingdale, there you are.' The Director of Music caught Daniel up as he left the chapel after evensong. 'I wanted a word.'

Hollingdale looked at him warily.

'I have good news. Rather exciting news, as a matter of fact. There is a post.'

'A post?'

'Teaching. You asked me to keep my eyes open for a teaching position.'

'Ah, yes. A school, is it?'

'No, as a matter of fact it is not a school.'

'A private household? A college?'

'The Royal College of Music.'

'A post is available there?'

'Yes. An old friend is retiring. He mentioned the vacancy. One day a week, but the possibility of more. You'd have to catch the train, of course. It would enable you to study composition while you're there. Mendelssohn, Chopin, Liszt, they have all visited the Royal Academy.'

'Why do you mention it to me?'

'Why? You are the finest musician we have. Your work has caught the attention of royalty! Why not?'

'I have never taught, though.'

'You can learn to teach. You really should apply.'

'I stand no chance, surely? What with the theft, and so on. I haven't even been allowed to graduate. I still have to pass an examination in mathematics.'

'Nonsense, that was all a storm in a teacup. It's practically forgotten already. I'll write you a reference.'

'Why? I have been such a trial to you.'

'Agreed. But your music has never wavered.'

'Hundreds will apply, no doubt.'

'Write today,' said the Director of Music. 'Perhaps you can head them off.'

'I shall not be able to sing here on that day of the week.'

'We'll manage. All choristers move on at some point, Hollingdale. Except the dullest ones who become Directors of Music, as I did.'

The letter of application hastily written and sent, Daniel put his head round Biddy's bedroom door. She was reading.

'I have just applied for a post at the Royal Academy,' he said.

'Wonderful!'

'It would be, but all I can do now is to wait. It could be a career, Biddy. A proper musical career.'

'You were always going to have one, Daniel. Nobody else doubted it.'

He shook his head at that.

'You do not look like someone who has just heard exciting news, I must say.'

'It's Grace.'

'You're worried that she's in trouble?'

'I have left her to deal with everything alone. I think I might love her, Biddy.'

'That has been obvious for some time,' she said, smiling.

'Has it?'

'You are happy when you are about to see her, and miserable when you have just left. No special powers were needed to work it out.'

He sighed. 'I am predictable as well as lovelorn,' he said.

'I didn't mean that. I only mean you are plainly in the grip of something, but at the moment it doesn't seem to be making you happy.'

'She has a fiancé.'

'Has she told you that herself?'

'No. Nothing has been said.'

'Then how do you know for sure? Does she know your feelings for her?'

'No. Why should she even entertain a duffer like me?'

'A duffer who might soon be teaching at the Royal Academy? A duffer whose compositions are gaining in popularity? A duffer whose music might be played at the Diamond Jubilee? You must tell her your feelings. She may reject you, but you must tell her, Daniel. You'll regret it, if you don't. Besides, she needs to hear before she makes the wrong decision.' Biddy sat up and wrapped her arms around her knees. 'I've been thinking about the orphanage children Grace rescued,' she said. 'They are not necessarily orphans are they? She told you they were left at the gates of the workhouse. Perhaps it was a parent who left them.'

'No parent would do so, surely?'

'If they were desperate enough?'

'So they might be found?'

'It's just a thought,' Biddy said.

Chapter Fifty-Seven

An hour later Daniel was outside the workhouse. Like Grace he looked at the long brick wall and the tall wooden gates and imagined the children left there at night. He also pictured a beer barrel flying off a cart and knocking Grace to the ground, and shuddered. At four in the afternoon there was little movement on the triangular green opposite, but a couple of men made their way into the White Horse. The public house was a hundred yards from the workhouse doors. It was a quiet place at four in the afternoon, he was greeted only by a nod from two silent drinkers and a murmur of hushed conversation from one of the other rooms. The landlord put aside the newspaper he had been reading behind the bar and asked him what he would care to drink.

Daniel ordered a glass of porter and it was delivered, dark and creamy-headed.

'Would anyone here know anything about the workhouse?' Daniel asked, after a sip of the treacly beer.

'Depends what you want to know,' said the landlord.

'Some children—three little girls—they were left outside a few months ago,' Daniel said.

The landlord blew on the glass he was polishing behind the bar. 'They held a public hearing about it. Right here in the bar. That was a strange one. We've had inquests here before, but never inquiries into children left on the pavement at night. Breaks your heart to think of it.' He rubbed the glass and put it on a shelf before taking up the next one.

'Were you here at the time?' Daniel asked.

'Yes. I saw it. The Magistrate called witnesses. There was only two: one was a Frenchman. The other was Jeb Wallis. They was the only two that said they saw the sacks - well, they thought it was sacks - took off the cart and left by the workhouse doors. Jeb Wallis was drunk at the time, the magistrate didn't much care for that. And the Frenchman just saw what he saw, asked no questions, and kept on going. It wasn't much of an inquiry, really. Mr Lemman might be able to tell you more.'

'Mr Lemman?'

'Used to be the master of the workhouse, before he took sick. His wife runs it now. He's not quite right since his illness, but he talks sense some of the time. He's over there. You can ask him. He likes a chat.'

A small, grey-haired man sat alone at the far end of the bar, looking into his glass.

'And where would I find Jeb Wallis? Is he a local man?'

'He's here every day by five, regular as clockwork. Likes his ale, does Jeb.'

Daniel took his glass over to Mr Lemman and joined him at the end of the bar. 'You know the workhouse, Mr Lemman?' he asked.

'I know it? I ran it for years. I still live there, but the Missus runs it now.'

'Does she keep children there?'

'No, no. Children aren't allowed. It's not a good place for them. The air isn't good.'

'So Mrs Lemman doesn't allow them in?'

'Only a few times. When nobody wanted them.'

'There were a few children, then?'

'I never saw them but there were a few stayed for a while, I think. My wife found them a place. Somebody to adopt them.'

'That was kind,' Daniel said.

'Kind?' Mr Lemman looked up at him suddenly, as if trying to work something out. 'Iris?' He laughed a wheezy laugh that turned into a cough. 'There's not many would say that of her.'

'I mean to say it was kind of her to find homes for those poor children.'

'Oh no, she did that for the money,' the old man said.

At this point, the door opened and a man in a carpenter's apron sauntered in, greeted the whole pub and was welcomed with a ready pint of ale. 'Gentleman over there was asking after you, Jeb,' said the landlord. 'Something to do with those children left outside the workhouse.'

'Was he now?' The carpenter strolled over and joined Daniel and Mr Lemman. 'You were looking for me, sir?'

'Yes, you are Jeb Wallis? You spoke at the public inquiry held here?'

'About the little children? Yes, that's me, Jeb Wallis, carpenter. And you are?'

'Daniel Hollingdale.'

'And what work do you do, Daniel?' There was a challenge in this.

Daniel hesitated, but then answered, 'I am a musician.'

'Oh! A musician? Play the piano, do you?'

'Yes. I just wanted to ask you some questions about …'

'Give us a tune, young man, and I'll be glad answer your questions.' He nodded towards the piano against a wall in a shadowy corner of the bar. Even from a distance, Daniel could see it was an instrument that had lived a hard life. He looked doubtful. The carpenter shrugged and took a long pull of his ale. 'Or maybe we're not good enough to hear your kind of music?'

Daniel walked over to the piano and threw open the lid. It had, at least, the full complement of keys, though several had lost their ivory veneer. He played a chord or two to test it, and found it dreadfully stiff and out of tune, but capable of something approximating music.

All pianists of any standard are used to being called upon to 'give us a tune'. Daniel, like most others, had a small repertoire of crowd-pleasing ballads and roistering patriotic songs. Since his musical education had taken place entirely in college chapels, he had many hymns and Christmas carols by heart as well, but on this occasion in the White Horse, he plumped for a sea shanty, which he sang loudly enough, he hoped, to drown out a few of the piano's weaknesses.

In Amsterdam there lived a maid,
Mark well what I do say!
In Amsterdam there lived a maid,
And she was mistress of her trade.
I'll go no more a ro-o-oving with you fair maid!

On hearing the introduction and first line everyone in the pub looked up. They were all smiling by the second line. By the time they had heard that the Amsterdam lady was mistress of her trade, they were all tapping their feet or clapping along, and by the chorus most of them joined in. It was as if every one of them had opened their curtains that morning and wished only for a sea shanty they could join in with.

There was no chance of playing only one song, of course. By the time the neighbours and wives of the men in the pub had been fetched to hear the performer, and a few drinks had been bought, it was two hours before Daniel could leave. But when he did, he knew not only who the carter was who had carried the children that night, but who was with him: a poor young woman, from way out in the Fen.

The carter lived down a muddy lane by the river. Jeb Wallis took him there, humming sea shanties all the way. They found the man smoking his pipe on a bench in the yard.

'You know that night you dropped them sacks that turned out to be children at the workhouse, Bob?'

'Why?'

'This gentleman wants to know.'

'Why does he want to know?'

'His friend is taking care of the three little 'uns. They're after finding the mother.'

'What d'you want with her?' said the man, between puffs on his clay pipe. 'She only done what she thought was the right thing. She was weeping and moaning all the way. I thought she should die of it, she wept so hard, or take a fit, maybe. Howled all the way home, the poor wretch. I shouldn't want to get the poor girl in trouble with the law. She's seen enough miseries.'

'If we can find her, she might be reunited with the children,' Daniel said.

The old carter looked sceptical. 'She couldn't afford to

keep 'em. She had no money for food. Her man died. They lost their cottage.'

'Where was she from?' Jeb Wallis asked him.

'Miles away out in the fens near Cottenham. There's workhouses nearer. I told her that. There's one in Cottenham itself, but she wouldn't have it. She wanted them left at a big one in the city that would have a place in it for sick people. That's why she made me bring them to St Benet's.'

'Tell him her name, Bob, it's for the best.'

The old man puffed again on his pipe. He looked Daniel up and down and finally said, 'Harkness is her name. She works in the dairy at Widdey Fen Farm.'

Chapter Fifty-Eight

The stipendiary magistrate looking down on the court from the bench was a lean dark-haired gentleman of military bearing. His manner was brisk.

'You are charged with the kidnap of three children from St Benet's Workhouse on Broad Street, Miss Marshall. How do you plead?'

'I am guilty,' Grace said.

'What are the facts, please, Sergeant Gladwell.'

'I was called to St Benet's where Mrs Lemman, the matron, complained that this young woman had carried off three children.'

'How did you come to be there, Miss Marshall?' The magistrate asked.

'I was carried into the workhouse because I had an accident outside.'

'Ah yes. Hit by a barrel? That's what it says here,' the Magistrate looked at his papers. 'You were injured?'

'My head was bleeding and my wrist was damaged. They called a doctor.'

'So, you were carried inside, he treated you and …'

'I asked to look round the workhouse, never having seen one before. A maid called Jane showed me.'

'And you found these children?'

'I came across them, yes.'

'And what were the conditions you found them in?'

'They were in the hospital wing in a cold damp room that was poorly lit. They were on a mattress on the floor being cared for by an old lady.'

'But they were being cared for?'

'They were silent and thin. They looked grey and miserable. Someone had shaved their heads.'

'You are an expert in the health of children, Miss Marshall?'

'No. I can't say that I am.'

'How, then, did you assess their health so thoroughly at a glance?'

'It was not a medical assessment. I could only guess at their health, but to the inexpert eye they appeared oppressed and the conditions unhealthy.'

'So you decided to take them with you.'

'I did.'

'What provision had you made for the care of these children after you left with them?'

'At that time I had made no real provision.'

'So you were taking them away from poor conditions, as you saw it, into unknown conditions with you?'

'I knew I could offer them a warmer drier place. I knew I could be kind to them.'

'Miss Marshall you knew no such thing. You decided quite high-handedly that you could provide something better for these children—based on no practical experience—and you carried them off with very little thought.'

Grace had no answer.

'What did you plan as their future?'

'I thought of trying to restore their health and finding them some sort of education when they were old enough.'

'This is all very vague. You may have had good intentions, but you cannot commit a crime like kidnap on the basis of a vague idea of doing some good in the future. Besides, we have only your word for it that your intentions towards these children *were* good.'

'I thought the baby would die if she was left in the workhouse.'

'Again, you say this on the basis of very little knowledge of the health of infants or children. Mrs Lemman has told us they were in good health, well fed and well looked after. Mrs Lemman is highly experienced in the care of indigent people of all ages. She planned to find them each a foster family that would take them in.'

'She planned to see if she could get money for them!' Grace said.

'What evidence have you of that?'

'The account books of the workhouse. They plainly show that she claims money for the support of children when they are brought in. She presses for extra money for special food and milk, and then, as soon as the children are well enough, she makes note of a lump sum in profit as they leave.'

'Do you have these account books?'

'New College has them. I have carbon copies.'

The Magistrate wrote something down. 'Carbon copies may not be admissible as evidence,' he told the court. 'I shall need a legal opinion from the Clerk of the Court. Meanwhile, Miss Marshall, since you plead guilty and kidnap is a serious offence, too serious to be dealt with here,

I shall remand you to appear in the Crown Court in three weeks' time. Is there any objection to bail?'

The Magistrate was moving on to the next case when a court usher hurried in and spoke to the Clerk of the Court who in turn went to the bench and spoke quietly to the Magistrate, who nodded. 'Very well. Bring her in,' he said.

A pale young woman in a threadbare coat was led into the court. She looked anxiously about her.

'You must swear to tell the truth,' said the Clerk. He held the Bible up to her and she repeated the words he said in a low voice.

'Your name?' asked the Magistrate.

'Eliza Harkness.'

'Speak up Mrs Harkness, please. You are not in any trouble.'

She nodded, her knuckles white as she clutched the rim of the witness box.

'Tell us about your children, Mrs Harkness.'

'I left them at the workhouse, Sir. I couldn't keep them, so I took them there on the cart. They have a hospital there. I thought they should be cared for.'

'You could not care for them yourself?'

The young woman's thin shoulders were shaking, her voice could barely be heard. 'My husband was killed in an accident soon after the baby was born. He laboured for Farmer Bulling. I had to leave the tied cottage and find other work. I thought I could keep my girls with me. I wanted to, but I had no savings. I couldn't work and care for them. I could barely feed them. I couldn't see a future. Someone told me about Mrs Lemman at the workhouse in Cambridge. That she would take children in and care for them. I borrowed money and paid her to take them in.'

'You paid Mrs Lemman a fee?'

'Yes, sir. I paid her nearly six pounds. I had to sell my wedding ring and all my furniture and I am in debt since. But I did it because she said she could find them a kind home with a good family. All of my girls together in a nice house. They would be well-fed and people would be glad to have them. They weren't welcome on the farm where I work. I had to hide them. They had to stay locked in and quiet. It wasn't right. I thought a nice family—one like I've seen in church on a Sunday—might take them and they could play in the sunshine and wear nice clothes.'

She dissolved into tears and was not able to speak for several minutes. The court fell silent. Even the Magistrate seemed unwilling to interrupt. 'After I left them, I knew it was a mistake. She didn't care about them. She took the money, but that was all she cared about. People started to tell me stories about St Benet's. Nobody had a good word to say about Mrs Lemman. But it was too late then. She had my babies, and she could do what she liked with them.'

She stood silent, her head hanging down, without even the spirit to weep any more.

The magistrate looked down at his notes, turning his pen in his fingers. 'Miss Marshall, these children should be re-united with their mother. Do you agree?'

'I do, absolutely.'

'Can you arrange this?'

'She can come to the cottage with me immediately.'

'Then let that be the case. You will still have to face the charge of kidnap.'

'Yes, sir.'

'But the mitigating circumstances suggest that can be dealt with quickly. Sergeant Gladwell, I leave you to investigate these allegations against Mrs Lemman.'

The Sergeant nodded.

'Good. You are bailed as a formality, Miss Marshall, but you are free to leave the court. I suggest you take this unfortunate witness to her offspring.'

The magistrate drew himself up and ended by addressing the whole court. 'A case like this is an indictment against us all. That we should have, here in this city, a place where the poorest children can be neglected and mistreated is, in my opinion, a disgraceful stain on the reputation of our city.'

The court reporters both quoted these words in the detailed newspaper reports of proceedings they published in the next few days. Both also named the workhouse at the centre of the allegations and Mrs Lemman.

Daniel was waiting outside the court. Mrs Harkness hurried to him. 'Please, where are they, Sir? Where are my girls?'

'They are staying with this lady,' he led the still trembling mother over to Grace.

'Please, Miss, are they living and well?' Eliza asked.

'They are well, Mrs Harkness, quite well. Come, I will lead the way.'

But Eliza Harkness had no strength left. Her legs could not carry her. Daniel and Grace took an arm each and bore her along. She asked after the children at every step, and at every step Grace reassured her. Yes, they were well. Yes, they were eating and drinking. Yes, they were calm. They slept at night. The baby was well, and beginning to crawl.

Chapter Fifty-Nine

At the cottage, they found the three little girls playing with Jane and Alice on a rug in the sun-warmed garden. Daniel and Grace stood back as Eliza stumbled across the grass towards them. From a distance they saw Violet catch sight of her mother, and stand, holding up her arms, and Mrs Harkness fall to her knees, and sweep the little figure into a long embrace that soon included the other two.

'Was it you who found her?' Grace asked.

'Yes.'

'How, Daniel? How did you do it?' She turned to look at him and felt a rush of joy at the sight of him standing beside her in the dappled sunlight under the trees.

'I played the piano and sang a few sea shanties in the pub near the workhouse,' Daniel said.

Grace could only laugh. She took his hand and held it with both of hers. 'Thank you, Daniel. Thank you on behalf of those three children and their poor mother. Thank you, thank you for finding her. Nobody else thought to look.'

'What will become of them now?' he asked.

Grace laughed again. 'We've come this far. We'll get by. I imagine Mrs Harkness has nowhere to go, so she'll have to stay in the cottage too. Perhaps she can have my room. Mrs Mills will perhaps allow me to stay in a room in Abercrombie house for a few days. We'll manage.'

'I would like you to marry me, Grace,' he said, holding her hands now with both of his.

'This may not be the best moment to ask,' Grace said. 'There is rather a lot to do, and perhaps we're being carried away by the powerful emotions we're witnessing.'

'I am not carried away,' he said. 'Look. I am as cool as a cucumber.'

'I'm not sure that coolness is the hallmark of the most earnest suitors. I was hoping for a little ...*warmth* in mine,' Grace remarked, looking up at his face.

'Oh, I can provide warmth too,' he said, 'I assure you.'

She looked away for a moment and squeezed his hands. 'Will you teach me to dance, Daniel?'

'My dear, you will be the finest dancer Cambridge has ever seen when I have finished with you. Will you teach me mathematics?'

'Absolutely not! But I will teach your sister. I intend to get her into Girton College.'

Laughing, he wrapped his arms around her and kissed her there under the trees with the blackbird singing across the garden. Nobody noticed except Professor Toft, who smiled down at them all from his window and wondered who to tell first.

Chapter Sixty

The shriek was sudden and loud enough to send both the ladies in the basement kitchen rushing up the stairs in alarm. When Lucia and Miss Peach reached the top floor, they found Christabel clutching her bosom and pointing a trembling finger at the window.

'A face!' she gasped. 'I just looked up and saw...'

'Morning ladies!' A head and shoulders rose up again outside the attic window. The owner grinned and raised his pork-pie hat. He was a dark-haired, muscular young man with bright blue eyes and a nonchalance about him that belied his position balanced at the top of a thirty-foot ladder. 'You are well, I hope, Miss Peach? Forgive me if I frightened anyone. I did not know you had tenants up here in your crow's nest.'

'Oh Gabriel, it's you!' cried Miss Peach, hastening to open the window. 'I am perfectly well, thank you. And how is your father?'

'He's well, thank you, but visiting family. I thought I'd take a look myself.'

'You are very kind, Gabriel.'

'Can't have you ladies getting wet now, can we, Miss Peach? But there's no need to worry. It was the lead had lifted a little in one place. I fixed it down. You'll be dry from now on.' With a grin, the face bobbed out of view. They could hear him singing in a fine baritone as he clambered down.

When that I was and a little tiny boy,
 With hey, ho, the wind and the rain,
A foolish thing was but a toy,
 For the rain it raineth every day.

'Who is this builder who sings Shakespeare songs on high ladders?' Christabel asked.

Miss Peach's eyes twinkled behind her little spectacles. 'That is Gabriel Murphy, dear. I know his father very well. The whole family has a literary bent.'

When the rain did rain later, Lucia and Christabel were dry in their apartment. No buckets were needed. They ate supper blissfully free of the drips and splashes they had grown used to.

'So much for not being able to manage the stairs,' Lucia said. 'She was up three flights like a greyhound.'

Christabel looked at her plate. 'Two sausages each? Are we celebrating?'

'We are! I have three new clients.'

'Since yesterday?'

'Yes! Three in one day. It is a record.'

'And what has caused this sudden torrent?' Christabel asked.

'Miss Froment of New College. She is so delighted with Grace Marshall's engagement that she has told everyone it was the Moth Agency's doing. She has a wide acquaintance, many of them single and seeking companionship.'

'I do hope the Wrong Suitor is not among them. He was a bounder!'

Lucia speared a piece of sausage fiercely. 'Hillyer has fled to Switzerland. He may not last long there, either. Academic mathematics is a small world and ruthless towards cheats, according to Miss Froment.'

'I hope he is cast out into the mathematical wilderness and forced to sell cheese with holes in it for the rest of his days,' said her sister, chewing. 'I, meanwhile, have sold three more hats thanks to Miss Marshall's column in the Chronicle. She recommended fruit decorations this summer, and fruit is now what all the ladies want. Cherries, to be precise. I ran out. Mrs Palmer had to have a tiny apple, but she seemed content.'

'It is good of you to come and tell me, Sergeant Gladwell,' said Professor Toft. It was autumn now, and the sergeant was visiting the top floor at Abercrombie House. Mrs Mills had already handed him tea and a generous slice of her cherry and almond sponge. Mrs Mills approved of policemen.

'I wasn't sorry to see that one taken down to the cells, I can tell you, sir,' the sergeant said. 'That Lemman woman is a nasty piece of work. The jury agreed.'

'You used Miss Marshall's evidence, then?'

'Indeed we did. It was essential to the case. And her article in the newspaper about the children. It all helped.

Our evidence was well presented, sir. You would have approved.'

'I'm sure I would, Gladwell. You have told Miss Marshall?'

'She was not at home, sir. I put a note through her door.'

'She is at the school, I imagine. She teaches the ragamuffins at The Dales mathematics these days.'

'And the three little ones?' Gladwell asked.

'With their Mama,' said the professor. 'I must say I rather miss seeing them in the garden.'

Chapter Sixty-One

The wedding, which took place in New College chapel in the early spring of the following year, was outstanding for its music, as you might expect. There was a wedding anthem, newly composed by the groom, and an exceptional organ sonata performed by one of his scholars. The choral singing was particularly splendid as the choristers all knew the happy couple and wished them well. The occasion was notable also for the many children in the congregation. A crowd from The Dales, scrubbed and polished, thrummed with excited whispers, giggles and squirms. They did well, generally, but as George, the Head Porter, remarked to the Missus, it was like expecting a box of frogs to sit still.

Of the five bridesmaids, Violet, taller now, and with her hair in ringlets, was first down the aisle behind the bride. Jane followed, leading Rose by a chubby hand, while Alice carried baby Ivy, now with round pink cheeks and a tangle of curls escaping her lacy bonnet.

Mrs Harkness sat in a pew with Miss Goggins, her new

employer, on one side, and Miss Froment on the other. It would be difficult to say which of the three wept the most.

The bride and groom slipped away during the wedding feast in the dining hall to visit the little marble Venus, where she stood, shy as ever, on the landing outside the Waverley Room.

Next in The Moth Agency Romances

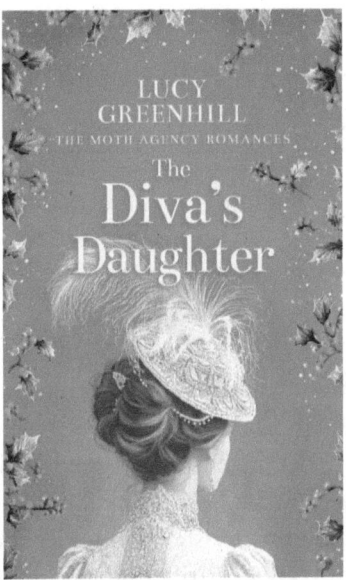

vinci-books.com/divasdaughter

One chance meeting. Two lives forever changed.

Cambridge, 1895. Virginia Bailey manages the whirlwind tours of her famous opera-singer mother. Constantly travelling, she longs for a true home, not expecting to find it on the frozen River Cam. When a clumsy fall on the ice introduces her to Charlie Meadows, a talented but guarded photographer's assistant, sparks fly. But her mother's demanding career pulls Virginia towards London, and she's forced to make a choice.

Turn the page for a free preview…

The Diva's Daughter: Chapter One

CAMBRIDGE, ENGLAND, 1895

No lady wants to buy hats in a frigid atmosphere, so on cold December days Christabel felt torn between warming the shop enough to detain customers, and saving money on coals. When she saw the lady in furs outside, she did not at first move the little brazier she kept under the counter. The lady seemed in a great hurry, and to Christabel's experienced eye, she was rather too grand to be drawn into a shop as small as Maison Ladoré.

A light snow was falling, and the sky looked heavy and white enough to threaten more, but the glamorous lady striding by was sumptuously wrapped in furs. She glanced in passing at the window of the little hat shop and immediately pulled up short. Approaching, she peered in for only a moment before throwing the door open and stepping inside.

'My, my!' she said, in a sonorous southern American accent. 'What delights have we here?' Brushing a little snow from her shoulders, she stood in the middle of the shop and looked about her, taking in the display with an educated eye. 'You are the proprietress?'

'I am. Christabel Venables at your service.'

The lady stepped forward and tested the fabric of the nearest hat with a finger she had just released from a fur-lined glove. 'You buy these adorable creations in?'

'I make them to my own designs, Madam.'

The lady smiled, and looked at Christabel differently. 'I thought so! I have an eye for an original. Fine work, Miss Venables, fine work! I never could resist a lovely hat! What can you show me today?'

'For travelling?' Christabel asked, discreetly moving the brazier so that it would bring its warmth to the shop.

'For winter parties. I have so many invitations: musical soirées, balls, dinners. I really don't know how I am to fit them all in. When one performs for the public, one is often invited here and there, you know. I am Rosanna Bailey, you may have seen me on the posters? I am performing at the New Theatre for a few days.'

'Delighted to meet you, Miss Bailey,' Christabel said.

The lady removed her large Cossack-style fur hat, revealing a crown of golden amber hair and sat herself, smiling in anticipation, in front of the mirror. She was, Christabel thought, a little over forty years old, comfortable, confident, elegant and well aware of her own powers. A great deal can be learnt about a lady by watching her reaction to her own face in a mirror. Rosanna Bailey settled her hair in a swift gesture, smiled, and gave her reflection the tiniest wink of encouragement.

The great sensation of the day that was Rosanna Bailey pointed to a feathery headdress. 'Don't tell me you have that little beauty in a silvery pink? You will tempt me beyond resistance!'

'In pink and in a dusty violet.'

'Oh my word, too divine! Who could say no? It really is just the most darling thing. Could the feather be a little longer? Something to make a real impression? You couldn't add the tiniest sparkle to it somewhere? Just for the Christmas season?'

'A sequin or two among the feathers?'

'The smallest, lightest dusting of gold?"

'Yes. Easily done.'

Christabel rarely worked with a customer eager to enjoy the more dramatic and showy decorations millinery had to offer. Her usual Cambridge customers tended to restraint, even in hats for celebratory occasions. Miss Bailey knew no such inhibitions. Bright colours, sequined nets, ostrich feathers and frothy lace - she warmly embraced them all. Within forty minutes she had ordered three different party headdresses, a winter felt and a jaunty trilby, its practical country sobriety playfully offset by a fan of peacock feather tips on one side.

'My sister will be so sorry to have missed you, Miss Bailey, she heard you rehearsing and was captivated enough to stand outside in the snow to listen. She has hardly stopped talking about it since.'

'Is that so? Why did she stand in the snow? She did not take cold, I hope?'

'She was just passing the side door at the New Theatre when she heard music. An hour later she was still there, half frozen, but delighted. She had never heard an operatic concert before. She had to look at the poster to see what the music was, and to learn your name. She has hardly stopped talking about it, or you, since.'

'Why, bless her heart. Does your sister work with you here in your delightful shop?'

Miss Bailey gestured towards one last feathery party headdress, a playful arrangement of peacock feathers on a sequined headband. Christabel brought it over for her to try. 'No, my sister runs an introduction agency, the Moth Agency, from her office upstairs.'

Rosanna Bailey looked puzzled. 'She runs an agency for collectors of moths?'

'M.O.T.H. It stands for Matters of the Heart.'

'Ah, she is a sort of matchmaker? She performs introductions? Perhaps I should consult her about my daughter, Virginia. I should like my child to marry a titled Englishman, one with a grand, turreted house and a large country estate. And perhaps a castle. Is this something your sister could arrange? Virginia shows no signs of arranging it for herself, I regret to say!'

Both laughed at these playful remarks as Miss Bailey studied the feathery headdress in the mirror, turning to left and right so that the plumes pranced in the air above her.

'Titled gentlemen with large estates are in rather short supply, I believe,' Christabel said. 'Of course, there are many at the University, but they rarely find their way onto Lucia's books, and I believe their families can be rather stern about their choice of bride.'

'Such a shame! I should so enjoy having some blue blood and a castle in the family. Or a grange, whatever a grange is, I always think it sounds thrillingly poetic and appealing. English aristocrats adore an American heiress! Virginia will inherit my little singing fortune one day. Not too soon, I hope. I'm fixin' to enlarge it a great deal further before I pass it on!'

Rosanna gave her reflection one last look, nodded, lifted the delicate headdress off, and handed it to Christabel to be wrapped along with the others. Christabel was busy with the boxes and wrapping paper when Lucia came into the shop and froze with astonishment at the sight of Rosanna Bailey at the mirror.

'I was just telling Miss Bailey that you were captivated by the rehearsal you overheard the other day,' Christabel said, enjoying her sister's shocked surprise.

Lucia had to overcome a brief struggle to speak, but finally said, 'I was! Miss Bailey, your singing was wonderful, so very wonderful.'

'You stood in the cold to listen?' asked Miss Bailey.

'I couldn't move! I was transfixed!'

'Will you attend a performance?'

'Well, no, we …' Lucia said.

'… we have probably left it too late to find a ticket now,' Christabel put in. She did not want their inability to pay for a theatre ticket to be revealed.

'Ah, yes. All sold out long ago,' said Miss Bailey. 'Sadly, I gave my last complimentary tickets up yesterday for a charity raffle prize. Such a shame! But you are only missing a little concert evening. The real thing, the true operatic performance, is a grand opera. You have seen Aida, perhaps? Or La Bohème?'

'Alas no.' Lucia shook her head, embarrassed.

'The outstanding performance of the decade, of course, will be Ernesto Coraldo's season at Covent Garden. It is just starting and will never be repeated. They say he is thinking of retirement. His voice is, well, I would say it is the finest in the world. Exquisite!'

'You have heard him perform?' Lucia asked.

'Many times,' Rosanna said. 'He is unequalled. Once – oh, a long time ago now – but once upon a time I even hoped I might sing with him myself. I have sung with some very fine tenors, but never Coraldo, and now I guess it's too late. I have no reason to complain. I have had a rich and rewarding career. It was just a little dream. But, Miss Venables, I recommend you do everything in your powers to get to Covent Garden and hear him for yourself while you can. You will never forget it.'

And having left instructions that her new hats would soon be collected, the celebrated Miss Bailey settled her account in full, returned the Cossack hat to her head and the fur-lined gloves to her hands, and ventured back out into the snow.

The Diva's Daughter: Chapter Two

An orchestra was playing a jaunty chorus somewhere in the distance.

'How about Wednesday?' Virginia asked. She was tucked into a corner of her mother's dressing room at the New Theatre, perching on a stool, hunched over an open diary. The light on the make-up mirror was strong, but everywhere else was dim. Rosanna, sitting in front of the mirror, was preoccupied by her own reflection, painting pale stage make-up onto her forehead and cheeks and rubbing it in with her finger tips.

'I agreed to go to a luncheon reception on Wednesday at one of the colleges,' she said.

'You have a two o'clock matinée. Is there time?'

'Just a brief appearance. They sent a young man to beg very sweetly. It's a fundraising occasion, for a charity. I forget which one.'

Virginia frowned over the diary and wrote something into it. Her mother reached for a different pot and began dabbing rouge onto her cheeks.

'How can we fit in a visit to Ely, if you keep accepting engagements? We are only here a few days.'

'Oh, *Ely*,' Rosanna said, exasperated, rolling her eyes at the mirror.

'You did promise, Mama,' Virginia said.

'I know, I know. And you shall meet your grandmother. But I have to be seen, you know, spread the word; build the reputation. Especially at this time of year. That reminds me, Ginny, I am nearly out of photographs to sign. I need some new ones. A town like Cambridge should surely have a good photographer somewhere.'

'Good photographers are booked up well in advance, but I can look, I guess.'

'Say it's for me! Use your charm, honey. Find a skilled one,' her mother said with a sigh. 'I'm not getting any younger. I need props and costumes and clever lighting to hide my wrinkles! Coraldo always wears a hat in his portraits these days, have you noticed?' She pointed to a signed image of the world-renowned tenor she had propped beneath the mirror. The celebrated tenor was, indeed, clutching a large tricorn hat to his chest. 'He's losing his hair, poor darlin'. Age comes to us all!'

Rosanna leaned back to examine her face in the mirror, turning her head from side to side. 'Are you so very eager to meet your Ely Grandmama? You don't remember her, surely? You were a babe in arms the last time.'

'I don't remember her. That is the very reason I should like to make her acquaintance again, Mama. My father was fond of her, I suppose.'

'Well, yes, but he left this country for the United States at barely sixteen and never returned.'

'His death must have been a great loss to her.'

The distant orchestra broke off the cheery overture they had been playing.

'It was a great loss to us all, dear.' Rosanna's hand, holding a rouge stick, stopped in mid air for a moment as she briefly adopted a mournful look. 'But it was all more than twenty years ago.'

A quiet knock was heard and the elderly doorkeeper pottered in. 'Good afternoon, ladies. Your post, Miss Bailey.'

'Good afternoon, Fred. You are keeping warm and well today, I hope?'

'Very well, Miss Bailey, thank you for asking. Very snug in my little corner.' He handed a pile of envelopes to Rosanna, offered them both a small salute, and backed out.

Virginia closed the diary and stood. 'I'll go now and make sure the rehearsal pianist is there.'

'You have the Paris Pin, honey?'

'Yes, of course.' Virginia patted the pocket of her skirt. 'I always have it.'

'I know I can depend on you. I hardly know why, but my nerves are a little on edge today. They send scouts from the great opera houses, you know, to provincial theatres like this one. And the tenor and conductor are both new to me. They seem just fine, but I like to have the pin for good luck.'

'I know, Mama. I have it safe.'

'The blue gown, we agreed?'

'Yes, the blue. It's ready, but still at the hotel. I'll fetch it over now …'

'Miss Bailey to rehearsal, please.' The call came from outside the door.

' …and while you rehearse, I'll see if I can find a photographer.'

The Diva's Daughter: Chapter Three

The Van Heusen family, fresh from their annual Christmas portrait, were leaving Meadows and Nephew as Virginia approached the photographic studio on King's Parade. Since there were eight energetic children and a nanny, as well as Dr and Mrs Van Heusen, this process took some time. When Virginia stepped into the shop, she was surprised at how confined a space the front office was. A tall wooden counter and a single armchair almost filled it. Framed portrait photographs covered every wall and stood in tiers in the shop window.

All along one side, large groups of college students and teachers posed in mortar boards and gowns for matriculation and graduation photographs, their names in delicately hand-lettered lists along the bottom of the frame. The other walls displayed different group portraits. Officers of the Cambridge Constabulary, chests out, stood to attention with their boots and buttons polished and the brass chains of their helmets under their chins. Sportsmen posed wearing blazers and college caps. Some sat in ranks, others favoured more of a tableau, with oars or cricket bats held up, or moustachioed young gentlemen lying on the ground along the front, propped on a casual elbow. Cups, medals and trophies were brandished with pride.

On the other wall, the frames held row upon row of distinguished visitors. Academics, politicians, holders of municipal positions, all looked out with varying degrees of self-satisfaction. They favoured large beards. There were few ladies, and those there were looked irritable, Virginia thought, as though life among the bearded colleagues had robbed them of all patience. On the far side, though, ladies abounded, and these were far more cheerful; these were the visiting show people. Dramatic actresses in costume were posed as if in mid-performance, gesturing in the full flow of their art. The music hall artistes, on the other hand, were all cheeky grins and winks, often in costumes revealing a great deal of their legs.

Virginia, at home among the theatricals, was smiling at their determined sauciness, when she was shocked to notice for the first time that a pair of boots was protruding at one end of the wooden counter. She was not alone. Apparently someone – a man, to judge from the boots – had been lying there the whole time. 'OH!' she said, and jumped back.

Her cry galvanised the owner of the boots, who sprang up so quickly that his face popped up from behind the counter like a stage trick. It was Charles Meadows in his shirtsleeves. He was holding a dustpan and brush. 'Forgive me, please!' he said. 'I did not hear anyone come in. I thought I was alone.'

'I thought *I* was alone!' Virginia said, indignant. 'What were you doing behind there? Did you drop something?'

'No. It was more a case of chasing something. A mouse, to be precise.'

Virginia stepped back and looked wary.

'Nothing to fear. Only one,' he said. 'And very small.'

'That is not particularly reassuring.' They looked at each other over the counter. Virginia thought that Charles looked extremely cheerful, for someone whose shop had mice. He was smiling from ear to ear.

'Do you not have mice in America?' he asked.

'America?'

'You are American?'

'Well, yes. I expect they do, but I have not lived there since I was three years old. They certainly have them in Paris and most of the opera houses I've visited in Europe. They get into trunks and chew costumes. They're very fond of sequins. We live in fear of the creatures. But to business. My mother needs some new portrait photographs. She is appearing at the New Theatre: Rosanna Bailey.'

At this moment the door behind the counter flew open revealing a large older gentleman, formally dressed in a waistcoated suit with a red silk tie. 'Did I hear the name of Rosanna Bailey mentioned?' he cried.

'You did. She is my mother.'

'Rosanna Bailey the great opera singer?' boomed the large gentleman. 'And she wishes to have her portrait taken here?'

'If possible, yes,' Virginia said. 'But she is pressed for time, unfortunately.'

'Of course she is! Why, everyone in Cambridge is competing to invite her, meet her, speak to her, *admire* the great Rosanna Bailey!'

'Well, yes,' Virginia said, 'and she has performances to give. As well as rehearsals and luncheons and so on.'

'Naturally she has! Charles, we must shuffle appointments. This is a great honour. The opportunity must not be missed. Miss Rosanna Bailey, here, at Meadows and Nephew!' The thought of it made the gentleman thrust out his chest and beam with pride.

'We could manage something tomorrow afternoon. Could she come at four?' Charles said.

'And you have props, and so on?' Virginia asked. 'My mother will bring costumes, but she would like to try one or two backgrounds.'

'We have all the backdrops anyone could ever need, my dear lady, I assure you of that with every confidence. We are famous for our backdrops and our props. The pyramids of Egypt! The rolling ocean! The snowy peaks of the Alps! The surface of the very moon itself! All are here, ready and waiting. Are they not, Charles? I am Tertius Meadows, by the way; proprietor and chief photographer. This is Charles, my nephew and most talented assistant.'

'How do you do,' Virginia said. Tertius Meadows stepped round the counter and bowed over her hand in formal greeting. 'I should return then at four tomorrow, with my mother?'

'Exactly so!' Tertius Meadows declared.

'I do hope you are able to remedy your other problem,' Virginia said to Charles, as she left.

Tertius stepped forward to hold the door to the street open and with an elaborate gesture of his hand, bowed low as she passed.

The Diva's Daughter: Chapter Four

In Virginia's world, it was eccentric to be an early riser. Opera people work late, socialise afterwards, and are rarely seen before noon. Virginia was by nature a lark, and as they toured the great opera houses of the world, she often left her mother asleep, slipped out of the hotel and strolled the streets of the latest city, discovering the place by watching its people begin their day.

She had a system for her morning walks. She turned left or right out of the hotel door on alternate days and let her feet take her anywhere they fancied. She carried no maps, but she did keep the name and address of the hotel in her pocket, having once, in a German city, left without that information and been unable to ask for help when she lost her bearings. Having changed hotels four times in the previous two weeks, she couldn't for the life of her recall whether she needed to find the King's Hotel in Castle Street or the Castle Hotel in King's Street. It turned out to be the Prince's Hotel in West Street, and luckily she recognised it without having to admit her confusion to anyone.

So, with the address of the University Arms Hotel in her coat pocket, and well wrapped in overcoat, scarf, hat and gloves, Virginia headed out into early morning Cambridge the following day. It was freezing cold and noticeably quiet. A newsagent was setting out his papers nearby, and two bakers, near neighbours in the same street, were already lit and displaying loaves, but generally the city was deserted. Scholars, she thought, perhaps favoured the same hours as opera people.

Following a lane between ancient college walls, Virginia found herself over the river on a slippery hump-backed footbridge. It was still only barely light. Her breath hung in the air around her, and a mist was over the college gardens on either side, but she could see the river completely frozen beneath. And then she saw the skaters. A pair of young men, laughing, appeared under the next bridge along and shot, with their blades hissing on the ice beneath them, under the bridge where Virginia was standing. They were moving so fast! They leaned forward and held their arms behind their backs, pushing with one blade then the other in a smooth rhythm, leaning into the curves of the river until they disappeared from sight. She could still hear the hiss of the blades in the distance long after they were gone.

Virginia had never seen ice skaters before, except in pictures. The grace and speed of their movement was astonishing. Looking in the direction they had come from, she saw another pair, and others behind them. They seemed to come from one place, so she walked a little further and then followed the path under the trees to where the road crossed the river. There were more voices now, and more sounds of skating. At a place where the frozen river broadened into a wide turning place for barges, there were jetties for deliveries to the colleges nearby. A group of young men were sitting on the jetties, strapping blades to their boots, ready to skate. Virginia leaned on the bridge's parapet and watched, intrigued.

Skating might have remained a fascinating spectator sport forever, had not a small group of young women, all carrying skating blades of their own, then appeared at the other end of the bridge. Ignoring the men - and being ignored in return - they scrambled down onto the ice and tied their blades on, before setting off, arm in arm in slow circles around the frozen pond. Some were anxious, clinging to their friends as they wobbled along, but two or three were smooth, confident skaters, swiftly gaining speed, gliding in wide effortless arcs, then turning the blades to cut into the surface for a sudden halt.

'Why not come down to the ice and give it a try?' A voice spoke to her, and she turned to see a smiling young woman of her own age carrying two pairs of ice blades. 'It's cold standing here. You'll be much warmer if you skate.'

'I don't know how,' Virginia said.

'It's easy enough. Come and see how you get on.' The stranger held out one of the pairs of skates and walked on to the place where the other skaters scrambled down onto the ice. 'I'm May Fielding, by the way,' she said, over her shoulder.

'Do you always carry spare skating blades?' Virginia asked.

'Of course,' May said. 'I am Captain of the Skating Society.'

It was too good a chance to miss. Virginia followed and soon found herself sitting on a jetty as May, with practiced skill, showed her how to fasten the blades onto her boots. Then it was out onto the surface.

Although the air above was clear, a thick mist on either

side of the river had the effect of enclosing the icy surface and muffling sounds. All Virginia could hear were the quiet voices of the skaters and the vigorous hiss and scrape of the long blades travelling across the surface. It was easier than she thought it would be to stand. May took her arm and towed her. 'The ice and the skates do all the work,' she said. 'Lean from side to side, press one foot then the other.'

'I'm afraid of falling!' Virginia said.

'Everyone falls now and then, it's part of learning,' May told her. 'Someone will help you up. People are friendly on the ice.'

'We won't fall through? It won't crack beneath us?' Virginia asked, voicing a worry that had nagged her even as she watched from the bridge.

May laughed. 'No, it's a foot or more thick. They measure it every day up by Queen's College. There's no sign of a thaw, so we're safe on here for a long time yet.' She let go and took off in a wide circle of her own, stepping one blade over the other to gain speed, then called as she pointed towards the bridge they had come from, 'I'm going up this way so that I can get up some speed. You can follow, or stay here on the pond and practice for a while. Take your time. Have fun!'

Virginia nodded and watched in admiration as May skated away, leaning from side to side as her blades swept the surface beneath the swaying fabric of her skirt. She made it look easy.

Moving timidly at first, Virginia watched the other skaters and imitated their movements. A few were as uncertain as she was, but there were expert skaters, men and women, too. They swooped and turned, and some of them even spun and leapt across the surface. There was an occasional fall, but the early morning skaters just scrambled up, laughing, and sailed off to try again. Encouraged, Virginia followed May upriver, under the arches of the bridge to the place where the river straightened, running between the ancient brick walls of the colleges on one side and their gardens on the other. She could see several bridges ahead, and the mist was clearing as the winter sun, in a clear blue sky, shone, glittering on the frozen surface. Breathing the crisp, cold air, Virginia set herself the challenge of skating to the bridge she could see in the distance.

She felt warm. The sun was on her face. It was intoxicating. She barely noticed the young man on the ice beside the bridge, holding a camera.

Once she had achieved her goal and was heading back towards the pond, Virginia tried moving a little faster, imitating a few skaters who seemed to be practicing for a race. They crouched forward, with their hands held behind their back, kicking one skate behind them and then the other with their blades swishing to a rhythm. It looked effortless! Virginia's novice attempt was not so smooth. It began well enough, but a few paces in, and gathering speed, a blade became entangled in her fluttering skirt and she lost her footing and tumbled in an untidy heap on the ice.

She was relieved, when she sat up and quickly checked to see how many limbs she had broken, that nobody else was on that stretch of the river at that moment. At least her clumsiness was unobserved. And since, apparently, the only damage sustained was to the hem of her overskirt, which was slightly ripped, and her hat, which had flown off and was growing damp on the ice a few feet away, she decided the best plan was to get up and skate more slowly back. This, however, was not as easy as she had hoped. All sorts of difficulties intruded between sitting on the ice and standing. There was nothing to hold on to. Attempts to go from kneeling to upright on her skates resulted several times in a graceless scurrying of blades, followed by a thump. After three unsuccessful attempts, she stopped and knelt to catch her breath.

A pair of blades appeared in her line of vision, darting over and stopping skilfully. 'No harm done, I hope,' said a male voice. 'I'll help you up, if you give me your hand.'

Grab your copy…
vinci-books.com/divasdaughter

Afterword

Three sisters under the age of five really were recorded as living in one of the Cambridge workhouses at the end of the nineteenth century. I wondered how they got there and what became of them, and they wove themselves into this story. I couldn't resist giving them the happy ending they probably did not get in real life.

The note that Grace finds in the workhouse papers takes much of its wording from a real note that was left with some foundling infants.

Fran Smith (writing as Lucy Greenhill)

Cambridge
June 2024

P.S. I think the nicely eccentric Miss Goggins might have to have a book of her own, don't you?

About the Author

Lucy Greenhill loves to write stories whose starting point is a real incident or place and can often be found searching archives and libraries.

The inspiration for *An Utterly Unsuitable Lady* was the notorious case in the 1860s of a rich man who fooled an innocent young woman into a fraudulent marriage before abandoning her without a penny. Could a happy life be salvaged from such wreckage?

The Moth Agency Romances introduce Lucia and Christabel Venables, an independently-minded pair of sisters living in Victorian Cambridge. Christabel runs a hat shop and Lucia is proprietor of the agency which introduces ladies and gentlemen pursuing romance and generally looks into Matters Of The Heart. There are plenty more Moth Agency Romances to come.

Lucy also writes Edwardian mysteries under the pen name of Fran Smith. She lives with her husband, dog and chickens on the edge of the fens near Cambridge, England.

www.ingramcontent.com/pod-product-compliance
Ingram Content Group UK Ltd.
Pitfield, Milton Keynes, MK11 3LW, UK
UKHW040251230426
470297UK00004B/86